CW00726292

STRANGERS

STRANGERS

Aliens looking for a country of their own

Phil Hinsley

authorHOUSE®

AuthorHouse™ UK Ltd.
1663 Liberty Drive
Bloomington, IN 47403 USA
www.authorhouse.co.uk
Phone: 0800.197.4150

Published by AuthorHouse   01/13/2014

ISBN: 978-1-4918-9033-2 (sc)
ISBN: 978-1-4918-9034-9 (e)

To Anne who has discovered
The pleasure of
Vanilla Strawberry ice cream

They admitted that they were aliens and strangers on earth.

Hebrews

So justice is driven back, and righteousness stands at a distance; truth has stumbled in the streets, honesty cannot enter. Truth is nowhere to be found, and whoever shuns evil becomes a prey.

Isaiah

Introduction

This is a beautiful world of incredible diversity where people find inspiration from what they see, hear and feel. There is the joy of children, the bond within a family, the love between a man and a woman and the pleasure which is shared around the world when good friends eat together. Our thoughts are creatively turned into music, art, and writing. We invest our time and heart in building loving relationships and make sacrifices for those we love. Events of celebration are planned and festivals held, along with a thousand other ways of expressing our feelings as individuals or groups in response to our desire to make something good and lasting.

The apostle Paul emphasised in his short letter to Titus that we should devote ourselves to doing good, as many people from all faiths, and none, are doing.

But never far away is the reality of unfulfilled dreams and frustrated ambitions. Of hopes dashed and plans ruined. For each open hand of friendship there is the closed fist of anger. Lovers are torn apart, illness unexpectedly strikes and disasters happen indiscriminately. The shadows of war are drawn deep and wide and anxiety and fear soak into millions of hearts. Finding clean water and something to eat is for many the most important thing they can do, often done in the grimmest of conditions.

The Bible for many is a collection of unrelated colourful stories that have no relevance to our busy and demanding lives. What can be taken as moral and ethical values from the Bible are held in respect by the atheist as well as the believer, but accounts of what individuals did or didn't do thousands of years ago are regarded as fiction, folk tales and legends better left to the historians and those who have a particular interest in the dusty annals of the past.

The Bible is a finished book but the stories it contains still continue to be acted out, now with different backgrounds, new technologies and in different languages. What happened long ago has shaped our cultures and traditions, but more importantly, decisions people made then are the same decisions we individually have to make today, and what happened to the individuals and tribes then gives us a preview of what lies ahead of us. It is our choice, just as it was theirs. And whoever we are that choice cannot be avoided. That the Bible speaks today is not just a neat saying for Christians, because what the Bible really says does apply to every person who has ever lived and our response to its uncompromising message will decide our destiny.

I speak for no group, fellowship or denomination but identify myself with all those who eagerly wait for the return of Christ and the renewal of all things.

CONTENTS

1

Strangers in the World

'Strangers on a train' was a film made by Alfred Hitchcock and Frank Sinatra sang 'Strangers in the night.' "Don't be a stranger" is often said to encourage someone to keep in touch while the stranger is a person who is unknown to us.

Not only is it that people can be strangers to each other but many situations and experiences can be unfamiliar and distant to us. Winston Churchill wrote about his love of books in an essay entitled 'Hobbies' in his book 'Thoughts and Adventures'. He posed an imagined question of a person saying 'What shall I do with all my books? And he laid out his answer; 'Read them, but if you cannot read them, at any rate handle them and, as it were, fondle them. Peer into them. Let them fall open where they will. Read on from the first sentence that arrests the eye. Then turn to another. Make a voyage of discovery, taking soundings of uncharted seas. Set them on your shelves with your own hands. Arrange them on your own plan, so that if you do not know what is in them, you at least know where they are. If they cannot be your friends, let them at any rate be your acquaintances. If they cannot enter the circle of your life, do not deny them at least a nod of recognition.'

Groucho Marx said, "Outside of a dog, a book is man's best friend. Inside of a dog, it's too dark to read."

It was taken for granted in earlier times that every home had a Bible. It might have been on a shelf or on a table, close to hand and valued. In some homes it was never read, it just sat there like a distant relative whose presence was acknowledged but never consulted. For others it was picked up on a Sunday morning and taken to church as a visible sign to show the other members of the congregation that you had one, and if you were really pious it might be a larger edition than others had, and to really appear as a student of the Bible various types of markers would be seen protruding from the top of this hallowed book.

The Bible is considered by some as such a holy book that it is given its own special place and kissed and caressed as an object of deep devotion. For others it is shaken, slapped and held aloft as a visual reminder that what the speaker is saying comes from this unique book. When Jesus shared with his disciples the uncomfortable news that their future will very likely involve being thrown out of the synagogue and being killed by people who think they are serving God he said the reason for this violent rejection was that these people who proclaimed that they were serving God and who had access to the word of God neither actually knew God or Jesus.

History provides us with a long list of Christians being put to death for just having a Bible in their own language. Others were killed for putting the Scriptures into contemporary language and so making it more accessible to those who could before only listen to it being read, often by people who knew very little of the book themselves, not forgetting the printers, book sellers and the many who financed and helped get these banned books into the hands of those who were hungry to read it for themselves. Reading the wrong book was an extremely costly pursuit.

On 21 November 1526, Cardinal Campeggio wrote from Rome to Cardinal Wolsey on the burning of books by Luther and Tyndale saying how pleased he was to hear of the burning of 'the sacred codex of the bible, perverted in the vernacular tongue, and brought into the realm by perfidious followers of the abominable Lutheran sect; than which assuredly no holocaust could be more pleasing to Almighty God.'

Sir Thomas More called Tyndale 'a hellhound in the kennel of the devil; discharging a filthy foam of blasphemies out of his brutish beastly mouth.' More had those he saw as heretics taken to his family home in Chelsea where they were whipped and interrogated before being sent to the tower of London from where they were taken to be burnt at Smithfield, London's meat market. By far the majority of those killed for their biblical views was because they held theological positions that the established church, both Catholic and Protestant, found intolerable and they did their best to extinguish all dissent in the cause of maintaining unity which was often a unity of ignorance and which was in line with what the state wanted—people who believed what they were told. Control was everything. To disagree made you both a heretic and a traitor. The state and the church worked together in a way that hardly demonstrated the Christian way.

The paradox is that some those who are considered by many as the great figures in Christian history were willing, with the aid of the state, to use force and the ultimate penalty in bringing people round to their orthodox doctrinal position. Would it be legitimate to say that these leading personalities neither really knew God or Jesus when their actions displayed such a different spirit than that of Jesus and his apostles?

On 7 December 1530 the imperial authorities in Antwerp had warned that from then on no one was to write, print or cause to be written or printed any new book on any subject whatsoever, without first obtaining letters of licence. The penalty was to be 'pilloried, and marked besides with a red-hot iron,' or to have an eye put out or a hand cut off at the discretion of the judge, who was to see that sentence be 'executed without delay or mercy.'

Those who were brave enough to speak out or write on what they saw as incorrect and misleading faced a very uncertain and dangerous future, just as Jesus said would happen to his followers. This attitude of hostility has not changed although in the so-called civilised countries people are not being judicially put to death; instead of physical sanctions those who stand for the established beliefs are reduced to calling those they disagree with as heretics, no longer can they call them traitors, and in many cases they do not acknowledge these strangers to the established faith as even real Christians. This mutual animosity is seen to work both ways with all sides criticising each other for their theological beliefs.

What the world presents to an alien visitor is a deeply divided world of different faiths that have at various times attempted to impose their beliefs on an ever increasing number of people. Within these world faiths there are divisions that have set one group against another leading to countless thousands of men, women and children being put to death. The visitor to this world would see differing factions within each grouping who would have little to do with those who they consider as having moved away from basic foundational teachings.

This strange visitor might consider speaking against all those who demonstrate by their intolerant attitudes and actions that they do not truly represent the God they speak of. But if this visitor did say how wrong and misguided all these fellowships, groups and movements are he would face the hostility of all and they would combine their forces to get rid of him. To tell someone that what they sincerely believe and teach is wrong would in most cases be an invitation for them to defend their position and resist in one form or another.

Being human we want to hear that we and our group are standing for the truth while it's the others who have got it wrong, because if the others are right as well then why don't they all come together in unity?

Each group, large or small, have their distinctive teachings which are particular to them, and set them apart from others. Within their group they will support each other and pray for the success of their missionary endeavours but will remain silent about what the church down the road is doing. There are churches that come together for joint worship and evangelistic projects where genuine friendships are made and maintained because they see what they have in common is more important than what they differ on. On the surface it could look as though unity has been achieved but those differences that divide them are real and would not be given up easily as they represent for them the true teaching as opposed to a false teaching that the other group might just as tightly hold on to.

Our visitor would stand alone, a stranger to these well established and in most cases respected denominations. Ears would be closed to his warnings because he would not be numbered as one of them. He would be rejected as someone who could damage their individual position of respect and authority, or at least put it at risk. Life is hard enough without an outsider exposing how many things they have misunderstood and to question who actually they were following might well bring a violent response.

Yet a few would find the stranger's words made sense and brought to light as false what had been thought of as proven and accepted for so long. The visitor had correctly identified what was wrong and pinpointed the unfairness and injustices within the various religious groups and their self-righteous pronouncements concerning their claim to know God.

Individuals within each group recognise that Christians are scattered throughout the denominational spectrum. Although their traditions and doctrines vary they share the same heart and mind and their ears are open to what God says to them, even the uncomfortable things, through the Scriptures. But a great deal of misdirection and misinformation had occurred long before their or any particular fellowship was ever formed. The background to how and when that misdirection happened is only researched in regard to other fellowships, but rarely is a critical analysis focussed on their own fellowship. While one group could easily highlight the misinformation that another group holds it is very unlikely that they can identify the same within their own group.

It is part of our human condition that it is easier to see the shortcomings in another than to see our own. The old saying that when we point an accusing finger at others there are three pointing back to us is true and there is a strongly built wall of mental and emotional defence against any perceived criticism of one's own group while it's open season on those easy targets such as groups that are very different from themselves. What they would never acknowledge is that everyone without exception has been lied to and has been mislead on some important and foundational teachings. The counterfeiting of Christianity began at its birth, but they couldn't see it.

The stranger's voice is rejected so that we can continue in the old and trusted way; our comfort isn't disturbed, our beloved teachers can't be wrong—it's the others that need to change, not us, this is the expected response. It has always been that way.

The stranger was not surprised because he had seen it all before, many times. The divisions, the pride, the hostility and the self-righteousness were all part of this world. He knew it would come to this, he knew that from the beginning.

He was there at the beginning.

He had taught others to be strangers.

2

In the Land of Ur

The land between two rivers came to be known as Mesopotamia, a rich and fertile land that spread from Israel, north through Syria and down into Iraq. The rivers were the Euphrates and the Tigris and following the long course of the Euphrates fabulous and rich cities were built where luxuries and gardens of paradise could be found. Terah and his sons Abram, Nahor and Haran, who died in Ur, were descendents of Shem the son of Noah. Abram's wife was Sarai and Nahor's wife was Milcah; she was the daughter of Haran. Ur at that time was a city with a high standard of living and well-appointed houses for those who could afford it. This was the land of the Sumerians; the land then was known as Sumer and later referred to in the Bible as Shinar, which in turn became to be known as Babylonia. The main temple in Ur was dedicated to the moon-god Nanna, who was also worshipped in the city of Haran bearing the same name as one of Terah's three sons.

In 1950 BC the Elamites, other descendants of Shem, from east of the Tigris, destroyed Ur. Some time before, perhaps 60-70 years, Abram, as he was then called, heard God who began speaking to him. He was told to leave his country and his people and go to a land that would be shown to him. He was being asked to leave everything he was familiar with and become a stranger in a land he didn't know about. Yet there was something about how he was told that convinced him that leaving was the right thing to do.

Although Abram heard God speak it was his father Terah who led them out from Ur, but when they came to Haran, about 700 miles north-west of Ur, they settled there even though their destination was Canaan; Canaan was the son of Ham, another of Noah's sons. The people who lived in that land then were called Canaanites. This small group from Ur had to travel north-west following the Euphrates and the well cultivated and populated route staying within the Fertile Crescent which avoided the Syrian Desert. They would pass Babel which in their language meant '*the gate of God*' where some time earlier a united force of people all speaking the same language proposed to build a city of bricks and a tower that would reach into the sky and that their city would become famous having thousands of people living within its walls, no longer would they be scattered and divided. The Bible records that God stopped this project (perhaps so that they would be compelled to spread over the whole earth) by confusing their language so that they could not understand each other. That brought an end to their building and they went off in different directions. Babel in the Hebrew language sounds like '*confused.*'

They had settled in Haran and it was while they were there that Terah died at 145 years old. It was time to continue their journey as their destination was still a long way off. Abram trusted in the promise God had given him that he would become a great nation looked after by God and through him all the people on earth will be blessed, so at the age of 75 he and his wife and Lot his nephew set out from Haran towards Canaan which was south-west from where they were.

Another great distance was covered in reaching Shechem, in the land of the Canaanites. A particularly renowned tree was there that appears to have served as a location marker and as a place to meet. Again God said to him that his descendants would be given this land and Abram built an altar as a type of divine marker to signify his response to God's promise. He then journeyed further south until he reached the hills east of Bethel and there he pitched his tent, in the heart of the land God promised to his children. This promise which Abram believed was also of great concern to both of them because they didn't have any children and his wife Saria was not yet pregnant.

Abram then moves into the south of the country when serious food shortages led him to move down into Egypt where conditions were better.

Here we see that he was just as human as anyone else in lying to stay alive. He may have fallen for the lie that the Egyptians would kill a man to get his wife so when he got there he presented his wife, who was very good looking, even though she was about sixty-five at the time, as his sister. Considering the life span in those days her age was more like being in her late thirties. This wasn't a good plan because now the Egyptian officials took it that Saria was unmarried and could legitimately be taken before Pharaoh as a potential wife which is exactly what happened.

Abram was treated very well for, as they saw it, bringing Pharaoh this very welcome gift and for that he received many substantial gifts including livestock and servants but he still didn't speak up about his deceit which was rather late or too late to do because she was already in Pharaoh's palace. Abram probably felt in his anguish that he was in too deep to back out now and could do nothing to rescue his wife from the arms of Pharaoh.

In the mess of his own failings and hopelessness God altered the situation by inflicting serious health problems on Pharaoh and his household. Abram got an urgent summons to appear before Pharaoh and was told how mistaken he was to deceive them over the marital status of his wife and that they had to leave Egypt immediately.

Many years later Abraham, as he then was named, made exactly the same misjudgement with another ruler, a Philistine king named Abimelech (or as biblical experts tell us, a Canaanite, as this period of time was prior to the arrival of the Philistines into Canaan). Saria had by now become Sarah and again she was presented as his sister and the same thing happened with the king taking Sarah to his palace, but one night, how many nights later we're not told, God spoke to the king in a dream and told him that he is as good as dead because of taking Sarah as she is a married woman. Fearful of what will happen he pleads with God his innocence and both Abraham and Sarah's duplicity, for his part, he says, his conscience is clear.

Abimelech's encounter with God in his dream continued with God reassuring him that he knew of his clear conscience in this matter and Abimelech learned that God had not allowed him to touch Sarah, God had protected the king from sinning against him. He was told to return Abraham's wife to him and that Abraham will pray for him, but God warned the king that if he didn't return her he and all his family and those close to him would die.

Early the next morning the king confronted Abraham as to his reason for brining potential disaster on him and his realm and he wanted to know the facts. Abraham told the king that he believed that this was a godless community and he expected to be killed if they knew that Sarah was his wife. He even suggested that the fault was God's for causing him to wander from his homeland, and he attempted to explain that Sarah was his half-sister so there was an element of truth in what he told the king, but this was just a cover for his cowardice in not fully trusting God.

Abimelech then loaded Abraham with the same sort of gifts that years before Pharaoh had given him and said "My land is before you; live wherever you like." He had also given a stack of money to Abraham to cover any offence caused and he told Sarah that she shouldn't feel guilty at all. What happened next tells us that this episode must have gone on for some time as when Abraham prayed for Abimelech 'God healed Abimelech, his wife and his slave girls so they could have children again, for the Lord had closed up every womb in Abimelech's household because of Abraham's wife Sarah.' How God kept Abimelech from touching Sarah we are not told and why did Abimelech need healing? We are not told; were the women close to giving birth and how many of them were pregnant? Again, we are not told. But we are told that Abraham messed up by trying to solve problems apart from God and yet God was faithful to the one he called to be a stranger in a new country. Abraham's failings didn't deter God from his promise to him.

After leaving Egypt they entered the Negev and by this time both Abram and Lot had grown rich in livestock. When they reached the area between Bethel and Ai, which was north of Salem, arguments broke out between Abram's and Lot's herdsmen because that part of the land couldn't support their combined numbers.

"We're brothers," Abram said to Lot, "let's not argue over the land—you choose where you want to go, if you go to the west I'll go east and if you go east I'll go west."

Lot saw that the whole plain of the Jordan was good well-watered land, so he chose to go east and he took his men and livestock and lived among the cities of the plain and pitched his tent near Sodom whose inhabitants were known to God as completely evil.

When Lot had parted from Abram the Lord said to him, "Take a good look all around you. All the land you see I will give you and your descendents—I'll make them like the dust of the earth, there'll be so many. Walk over this land because I'm giving it to you."

Abram, who also was rich in gold and silver, moved his tents and went to live near the great trees of Mamre at Hebron, south of Salem, where he built an altar to the Lord.

At the same time war was breaking out between the rulers of small city states in that area concerning unpaid tribute bills. The kings of Sodom and Gomorrah were in the middle of this dispute.

As a result, nine kings, four against five, turned the fertile plain of the Jordan into a battle field and Lot was taken captive along with many others. Lot had pitched his tents near Sodom, an area which was well populated. When Abram was told what had happened, he with the assistance of some Amorite friends and his own force of 318 trained men went in pursuit of those holding his nephew.

They were in the north of the country when they caught up with them. During the night Abram divided his force and made his attack. This surprise assault succeeded in making them attempt an escape north and they were finally beaten at Hobah, north of Damascus. Abram recovered all the captives and their goods, including Lot.

When Abram returned after defeating the four kings the king of Sodom came out to meet him in the Valley of Shaveh, known as the King's Valley. Then Melchizedek king of Salem, later known as Jerusalem, brought out bread and wine. He was the priest of the Most High God, and he blessed Abram, saying, "Abram has been blessed by God Most High, Creator of heaven and earth. And praise to God Most High, who delivered your enemies into your hand." Then Abram gave him a tenth of everything. The king of Sodom wanted his people back but told Abram he could keep all the goods for himself. Abram turned down the offer saying, "I'll accept nothing belonging to you so that you will never be able to say 'I made Abram rich.'

'Jesus has become a high priest forever, in the order of Melchizedek.' So writes the author of Hebrews, a letter written to encourage Christians not to give up, and this letter goes on to speak more of this exceptional individual, 'This Melchizedek was king of Salem and priest of God Most High. Abraham gave him a tenth of everything. First, his name means

"King of righteousness"; then also, "King of Salem" means "King of peace". Without father or mother, without genealogy, without beginning of days or end of life, like the Son of God he remains a priest forever.

'Just think how great he was: Even Abraham gave him a tenth of the plunder! Now the law requires the descendants of Levi who become priests to collect a tenth from the people—that is, their brothers, even though their brothers are descended from Abraham.

'This man, however, didn't trace his descent from Levi, yet he collected a tenth from Abraham and blessed him who had the promises.' David, in one of his psalms, wrote, 'The Lord has sworn and will not change his mind: "You are a priest forever, in the order of Melchizedek." Because of this oath, Jesus has become the guarantee of a better covenant, so he is able to save those who come to God through him, because he is always lives to intercede for them.'

After this God spoke to Abram in a vision at night, "Don't be afraid, Abram. I'm your shield; your reward shall be very great."

"O Sovereign Lord, what can you give me since I remain childless and the one who will inherit my estate is Eliezer of Damascus, my chief servant. You have given me no children; so a servant in my household will be my heir."

"This man won't be your heir, but a son coming from your own body will be your heir."

He took him outside and said, "Look up at the sky and count the stars—if indeed you can count them. So shall your descendents be."

Abram believed the Lord, and he credited it to him as righteousness.

The apostle Paul poses an important question to those of his Roman readers who believed that they were justified before God by observing the law, 'Under what circumstances was this righteousness credited to him (Abraham)? Was it after he was circumcised, or before? It was not after, but before! And he received the sign of circumcision, a seal of the righteousness that he had by faith *while he was still uncircumcised!*

'So then, he is the father of all who believe but haven't been circumcised, in order that righteousness might be credited to them. And he is also the father of the circumcised who not only are circumcised but who also walk in the footsteps of the faith that our father Abraham had before he was circumcised.

'It was not through law that Abraham and his descendants received the promise that he would be heir of the world, but through the righteousness that comes from faith.' Paul had written to the Galatians that, 'in Christ Jesus neither circumcision nor uncircumcision has any value. The only thing that counts is faith expressing itself through love.'

For the contemporary Christian circumcision is no longer the contentious issue it was back then, but the issue of what a Christian is to do in regard to a rule or belief to gain justification before God still is, and doctrinal differences has separated millions of Christians who say that they have faith in Christ and express that faith through love which, as we've just read, is the only thing that counts.

Christians are separated by the day on which they worship, with claim and counter-claim going back and forth. There is nothing in Scripture that makes Sunday mandatory on Christians and the Sabbath, which is at the heart of the old covenant, and which the letter of Hebrews tells us is now obsolete, creating a new relationship with God that is by faith rather than law. Paul wrote that no-one is made righteous by the law—even though the law is holy, righteous and good it's powerless to justify us because it's only by faith that we can be justified. The law was added until the One to whom the promise referred to had come, and yet the legalistic mindset that says a certain day is mandatory is still very much with us today.

Many Christians are taught that the most important and fundamental biblical teaching is the Trinity, which if a person rejects, they're considered as not a genuine Christian, even though that particular teaching only became binding on Christians long after the ink on the last page of the Bible was dry. It is faith expressing itself through love that is the only thing that counts, yet professing Christians have killed each other over differences in theology such as the teaching of God in three persons as well as other teachings. Intolerance over differences has left a deep stain in Christian history.

Sarai thought she had the solution to the problem of them having no children—surrogacy. It had been years since they had received the promise of a child and nothing had happened, perhaps they were meant to show some initiative and play their part in making this promise happen. Sarai had an Egyptian servant and suggested to Abram that perhaps they could build a family through her and Abram saw the logic in it and slept with the servant whose name was Hagar, and bingo! She conceived.

In the city of Ur, Abram's home town, archaeologists had found 16 graves where kings were buried containing the remains of the king's servants lain out in neat lines. These men and women had walked into the burial chambers and drank some type of poison without any violence being done to them. If servants were expected to accompany their masters into the afterlife then bearing their master's children would seem a reasonable command.

It wasn't long before things began to go wrong. Hagar's attitude towards Sarai turned bitter and Sarai shared her distress with Abram blaming him for the sour relationship between her and Hagar; "You're responsible for the wrong I'm suffering. I put my servant in your arms, and now she's pregnant—she despises me! May the Lord judge who's right between you and me." Abram responded by saying that Hagar is her servant, deal with her as you see fit. Sarai then mistreated Hagar to the point that she ran away. Hagar was on the road for Shur which would take her back to Egypt; it was near a spring in the desert. Her life under Sarai had become unbearable, and then, out of nowhere someone began speaking to her.

"Hagar, servant of Saria," the angel said, "where have you come from? And where are you going?"

"I'm running away from my mistress Saria," she replied.

"Go back to your mistress," the stranger said, "submit to her and I will so increase your descendents that they will be too many to number." And then he said to her:

"You're pregnant and you're going to have a boy, call the boy Ishmael, it means *God hears*, and he's going to be a wild and aggressive man who will live by conflict with all his brothers."

Hagar, deeply moved by what she was told named the place *well of the Living One who sees me*. Hagar returned to Abram and Sarai and gave birth to Ishmael. Abram was 86 years old at this time.

The boy Ishmael was now 13 and Abram 99 when the Lord (*Adonai*) appeared to him, "I am God Almighty (*El-Shaddai*), walk before me and be blameless," he said to him, and Abram heard again the promise of becoming a father of many nations and that the whole area of Canaan where Abram was living as an alien would be given to him and his descendents. It was at this time that his name was changed from Abram (*exalted father*) to Abraham (*father of many*). It was also at that time that God commanded that all males when they are 8 days old are to be circumcised, this was to be an everlasting covenant, but for Abraham and Ishmael, and every male in Abraham's household, it was to be done on that very day. No details are given as to who performed the procedure or how they felt about it, just that it was done.

God also said to Abraham, "As for Sarai your wife, you're no longer to call her by that name; her name will be Sarah (*princess*). I'll bless her and give you a son by her. I'll bless her so that she'll be the mother of nations; kings and prophets will come from her."

This was too much for Abraham who couldn't help himself from laughing while thinking to himself, 'I'm a hundred years old and Sarah is ninety, how's this going to happen?' So Abraham said to God "Can't Ishmael receive your blessing?"

"Yes" God replied, but your wife is going to have a son, and you will give him the name Isaac (*he laughs*). As for Ishmael I will bless him and make him into a great nation; he'll be the father of twelve rulers but my covenant will be with Isaac. By this time next year Sarah will give birth."

Shortly after this Abraham was sitting at the entrance to his tent at midday, this was near the great trees of Mamre at Hebron, where he had built an altar to the Lord, when he saw three men standing close by. He hurried over to them and gave a low bow.

"If you would be pleased to allow me to bring some water so you can wash your feet and rest by this tree, and let me get you something to eat before you leave."

"That's good, thank you, we'll stay," the strangers said.

Abraham rushed into the tent and asked Sarah to quickly bake some bread, he then sprinted to his herd and picked a calf and told his servant to prepare it, next he brought some curds and milk to go with the food. All this preparation must have taken a while to get ready but at last the visitors sat and ate as he stood near them under a tree.

"Where's your wife Sarah?" they asked.

"She's in the tent," he answered. Then one of the visitors said, "I'll return about this time next year and your wife will have a son."

Just inside the entrance of the tent Sarah listened to what was said and inwardly laughed at the thought of them in their old age having the pleasure of their own child.

"Why did Sarah laugh at the thought of having a baby at her age? Is anything too hard for the Lord? As I said, I will return same time next year and Sarah will have a son."

Taken back by this incredibly ability of the visitor to know what she was thinking she said, "I didn't laugh."

"Yes, you did laugh." The stranger said. They then made ready to leave and as they headed for Sodom Abraham walked part of the way with them. The one identified as the Lord said "I'm not going to hide from you what I intend to do. You are going to become a great and powerful nation · and all nations will be blessed through you. I have chosen you knowing that you will direct your children and your servants to keep my way by doing what is right and just. I will bring about what I've promised you."

The subject moved to the situation in Sodom and Gomorrah which required immediate action. The Lord was going to personally investigate how corrupt it really was. As two of the men continued towards Sodom the one who Abraham addressed as Lord waited and listened to Abraham as he reasoned with him over what was right and just; the visitor knew that Abraham's concern was over his nephew and his family who were living in Sodom.

"Will you destroy both the good and the bad?" Abraham asked, and he added, "What if there are fifty good people in the city? Will you still destroy the city even with all those good people in it? I know the ruler of the whole world will do what is right."

"If I find fifty good people in that city I will not destroy it." Abraham now felt he could pursue this reasoning over just how low a number of good people living in Sodom would be needed to save the city from destruction.

"What if that number is less than fifty say, forty five? Would you still destroy the city over five people?"

"If there's forty-five good people there it won't be destroyed."

"What if there are only forty in the city?"

"If there's forty I won't do it."

"Would thirty be enough to save the city?"

"I won't do it if the number is thirty."

"What if there are only twenty good people there?"

"If there's twenty, the city won't be destroyed." Abraham had one last request banking on the hope that this number would be enough to cover Lot's family. "What if there were only ten there?"

"If there's ten, the city won't be destroyed." The visitor then left, and reassured, Abraham went back to his tent.

It was evening when two of the visitors who had been with Abraham arrived at Sodom. Lot was sitting at the entrance to the city where he possibly had some responsibility when he saw them and he rose and bowed to them. "Please come to my house, you can freshen up and stay the night and then leave early tomorrow morning."

"Thank you, but no, we're going to spend the night in the main square." The men answered. Lot insisted that they didn't remain outside but came with him to his home, so they agreed and Lot prepared some unleavened bread for them. Later, when they were about to get to their beds they heard an uproar outside the house. There were raised voices and banging on the walls and door of this detached house. "Bring these strangers out" the voices demanded. Lot knew that they intended to gang-rape the two visitors and they were surrounded by increasing numbers of crazed men of all ages.

Lot opened the door he stepped outside and quickly closed it behind him. "No, my friends" Lot pleaded, "don't do this, I've two daughters who have never slept with a man, take them and do what you want to them but don't touch these visitors because they're under my protection." This horrific offer from Lot showed an utter disregard for his daughters' safety, but what amounted to a criminal trade-off had no effect on the mob and they began to direct their aggression against Lot who was backed up by the yelling crowd against the door. They promised to do worse to him if he didn't get out of the way and reminded him of his alien status and that he had no right to be a judge over them. They were set to break the door down when the door was suddenly opened from the inside and Lot was pulled back into the house by the two visitors who promptly shut the door. Then all those outside were exposed to a great bright piercing light that took away their sight.

"Do you have any relatives here or in another part of the city?" They were not asking out of general interest in Lot's family background as Lot needed to know that it was a matter of extreme urgency for him to contact his family members if he wanted them to survive. Lot had to find them and convince them that their city was going to be obliterated very soon. He quickly contacted his future sons-in-law and urged them to leave town before it's too late and they thought he was joking or had drunk something that had played tricks on his mind.

Lot returned to his home at near sunrise when he was told that they had to leave now or they too would be engulfed along with all the others. There was hesitation on his part as he could hardly take in what was about to happen but too much time had been wasted, Lot, his wife and their two daughters were physically taken safely out of the city and told to run for their lives and not to stop anywhere on the plain where these cities were. "Get to the mountains or you won't survive what's coming! And don't look back," they ordered him. There was a further hesitation as Lot appealed to the men that he couldn't make it to the mountains in time, could he not, he asked stay in a small town that's close by and near enough to run to? "We agree, you can go there, that small town will be safe, but get there as quick as you can because I cannot do anything until you reach it."

It was midday by the time they reached the small town called Zoar. At that moment the entire land, the vegetation, people and cities erupted in an explosion of devastating fire, Lot's wife, who was reluctant to leave her home, looked back and in that instant she died; a pillar of salt remained where she had been standing. The year was 1975 B.C.

A little over 2,000 years later the apostle Peter wrote that the cities of Sodom and Gomorrah were burnt to ashes to provide an example of what is going to happen to the ungodly. While many maintain that the ungodly will suffer eternally in fire, Peter and others recorded in Scripture teach that what is thrown into that furnace is burnt to ashes and ceases to exist.

As the sun rose the next morning Abraham went to the place where he had spoken to the Lord and looked down towards the cities of the plain and saw thickly dark oily smoke rising. The whole area was a blackened devastation and all life had been extinguished. Its darkness rose high and filled the sky.

Lot changed his mind about staying in Zoar and out of fear he and his daughters moved into a cave. The girls realised that if they stayed there their future prospects were bleak and without children their family line would come to an end. The elder daughter came up with a plan that seemed to them their only recourse. They would get their father drunk, as they weren't short of wine, and over the course of two nights they would sleep with him in the hope that he would impregnate them both. It worked, and for some unexplained reason he wasn't aware of what he was doing.

The older daughter had a son who was named Moab who, in time, came to occupy the land east of the Dead Sea and the younger daughter named her son Ben-Ammi who became the father of the Ammonites, who came to occupy a small kingdom northeast of the Dead Sea.

3

The Promise

Sarah became pregnant just as she and Abraham were promised. Abraham was a hundred years old and Sarah ten years younger. The child's name was Isaac and when he was eight days old he was circumcised. Now Sarah had something to laugh about, before her laughter was from disbelief, now it was from joy that she at her great age should be able to have a son.

At a great feast celebrating Isaac moving on to solid foods Sarah noticed that Hagar's son, Ishmael, who was by then a teenager, was ridiculing Isaac and her resentment towards Hagar hardened. Sarah immediately insisted to Abraham that Hagar and her boy must leave so as to remove any possibility that Ishmael would someday share in the inheritance with Isaac. Abraham was deeply saddened because Ishmael was his boy and he loved him, but God said to him "Don't be distressed about Hagar and Ishmael, follow what Sarah tells you because it's through Isaac that the blessings are going to come and Ishmael is going to be a nation as well because he's your son."

Abraham put some supplies together early the following morning for Hagar and Ishmael. After he gave the water and food to Hagar they went into the desert of Beersheba which was on her way south towards Egypt. It wasn't long before the water ran out and it looked as if where they were was the place where they would die. Hagar couldn't bear to watch her boy die so she moved some distance away from him. He was crying but she couldn't help him and then a voice came to her saying "What's the matter Hagar? Don't be afraid; God has heard the cries of the boy as he lies there. Get him up on his feet because I'm going to make him into a great nation."

She turned and saw water where she hadn't expected any. She rushed to fill the empty skin pouch and revived the boy. God watched over the boy as he grew and he became an archer. His mother arranged his marriage to an Egyptian while in the Wilderness of Paran.

Some years later Abraham heard his name being called and he recognised the voice as coming from God. "Take your only son Isaac, who you love, and go to the region of Moriah" (the place where eventually Solomon would build the Temple of God). The voice then told Abraham something that shocked him to his core; "On one of the mountains that I'll show you, you are to sacrifice Isaac and burn his body as an offering to me."

Abraham, understanding what God had asked him to do, yet not understanding the reason behind it still obeyed. To have waited so long for a son, and now having to kill that very son, on whom so much depended, was a command greater than any other command before or since, and never asked of a human again. Two writers of the New Testament give us an insight into Abraham's attitude and the frame of his mind. One wrote of Abraham's response to the promise of having a son in his old age and the other refers to why he was willing to go through with the sacrifice of Isaac. If we read them together then we will be able to see why Abraham is called *the father of the faithful*:

'Against all hope, Abraham in hope believed and so became the father of many nations, just as it had been said to him, "so shall your offspring be." Without weakening in his faith, he faced the fact that his body was as good as dead—since he was about a hundred years old—and that Sarah's womb was also dead. Yet he did not waver through unbelief regarding the promise of God, but was strengthened in his faith and gave glory to God, being fully persuaded that God had power to do what he had promised. That is why "it was credited to him as righteousness." 'By faith Abraham, when God tested him, offered Isaac as a sacrifice. He who had received the promises was about to sacrifice his one and only son, even though God had said to him, "It is through Isaac that your offspring will be reckoned." Abraham reasoned that God could raise the dead, and figuratively speaking, he did receive Isaac back from death.'

On the third day of travelling Abraham reached the spot where God told him to sacrifice Isaac. He had two servants with him and Isaac and he said to them, "Stay here with the donkey while Isaac and I go over there to worship and then we'll come back to you."

Abraham carried the fire and the knife while Isaac carried the wood on his back. As they went along Isaac asked his father where the lamb for the burnt offering is. "God himself will provide the lamb for the burnt offering, my son." The two of them continued towards the place of sacrifice. When they got there Abraham collected some large stones and made an altar on which he arranged the wood. He then tied his son and laid him on top of the wood. He took his knife and was about to kill Isaac when he heard that same voice calling his name, "Here I am," he answered, "Don't hurt the boy. I now know that you fear God, because you were prepared to give your only son to me." Abraham looked up and saw a ram caught in a dense group of bushes by its horns. He took this ram and sacrificed it as a substitute burnt offering instead of his son. The laws given centuries later through Moses taught that the spilt blood of the sacrifices were a substitute and atonement that brought reconciliation between man and God. And on that mountain God provided what was needed.

The angel spoke to Abraham a second time saying, "I swear by myself, says the Lord, that because you have done this and not held back your son, your only son. I will bless you and make your descendents as numerous as the stars in the sky and as the sand on the seashore. Your descendents will take possession of the cities of their enemies, and through your offspring all nations on earth will be blessed, because you have obeyed me."

I once asked a pastor, "What is the best commentary on the book of Hebrews?" and he told me "Hebrews is the best commentary on Hebrews, just as Romans is the best commentary on Romans." This made good sense to me. Paul, in writing to the Galatians, was better qualified to produce a commentary on the account of the promises given to Abraham than anyone else. This is what he wrote: 'Brothers, let me take an example from everyday life. Just as no-one can set aside or add to a human covenant that has been duly established, so it is in this case.

'The promises were spoken to Abraham and to his seed. The Scripture doesn't say 'and to seeds,' meaning many people, but 'and to your seed,' meaning one person, who is Christ. What I mean is this: The law, introduced 430 years later, doesn't set aside the covenant previously established by God and thus do away with the promise. For if the inheritance depends on the law, then it no longer depends on a promise; but God in his grace gave it to Abraham through a promise.'

Years earlier Abraham was told that his descendents would be strangers in a country not their own, and that they will be enslaved and ill-treated for four hundred years. But God would punish the nation that they served as slaves and afterwards they will come out with great

25

possessions. This would come about after Abraham had died, which happened when he was 175 years old. Sarah had lived till she was 127 years old and died in Hebron. Isaac and Ishmael came together to bury their father in the cave of Machpelah, which Abraham had bought from Ephron, a Hittite, for about ten pounds of silver. So that field, the cave and all the trees that were within the borders of the field was legally his and this small area was the only piece of land he owned in the whole country.

Abraham described himself as an alien and a stranger among the people of that land and that designation was going to be true for all of God's people, who were to be strangers and aliens in a hostile world that is under the control of the being that the apostle John called 'the evil one.'

When the apostle Paul wrote to the Galatians he was astonished that having been called to be free they were being taught, and accepting, that the Old Testament requirements contained in the law was still binding on them. As a way of illustrating their freedom and their release from the law of the old covenant he used the account of Abraham and his two sons; Paul wrote, 'Tell me, you who want to be under the law, are you not aware of what the law says? For it is written that Abraham had two sons, one by the slave woman and the other by the free woman. His son by the slave woman was born in the ordinary way; but the son of the free woman was born as the result of a promise.

'These things may be taken figuratively, for the women represent two covenants. One covenant is from Mount Sinai and bears children who are to be slaves: this is Hagar. Now Hagar stands for Mount Sinai in Arabia and corresponds to the present city of Jerusalem, because she is in slavery with her children. But the Jerusalem that is above is free, and she is our mother. For it is written: "Be glad, O barren woman, who bears no children; break forth and cry aloud, you who have no labour pains;

because more are the children of the desolate woman than of her who has a husband."

'Now you, brothers, like Isaac, are children of promise. At that time the son born in the ordinary way persecuted the son born by the power of the Spirit. It is the same now. But what does the Scripture say? "Get rid of the slave woman and her son, for the slave woman's son will never share in the inheritance with the free woman's son." Therefore, brothers, we are not children of the slave woman, but of the free woman.'

'Consider Abraham,' Paul wrote, 'he believed God and it was credited to him as righteousness, so understand that those who believe are children of Abraham.' The faith that people from all races have been given brings them all together as children of Abraham and like him they look forward to the city whose architect and builder is God.

God chose from among all the people living in Ur Abraham. It wasn't Abraham that chose God; he worshipped other gods at that time. All God's people are chosen and selected by him and it's not initiated from them. Jesus told his disciples, "You didn't choose me, but I chose you." David wrote, 'The Lord looks down from heaven on the sons of men to see if there are any who understand, any who seek God, all have turned aside, they have together become corrupt; there is no-one who does good, not even one.' It was the same for Israel; God chose them not because of their goodness, because they didn't have any but because of his love and his faithfulness to his promise.

4

Outsiders

At the age of forty Moses had to leave what was familiar to him and go to another country where he needed to adapt to a different society separated from Amram and Jochebed, his parents, and his brother Aaron and sister Miriam. He now lived in the land of Midian which was east of the Sea of Reeds. This land was inhabited by the descendents of Midian, one of the six children of Abraham's second wife, Keturah. They were sent east, away from Isaac in Abraham's later years.

It was the Midianites who sold Joseph to Potiphar, the Egyptian. And now it was the home for a man who had been brought up and educated in the court of Pharaoh and gained a reputation for being an excellent speaker and a man of action. Although he was brought up as an Egyptian there was no hiding the fact that he was a Hebrew, which meant an outsider. He was an Israelite descended from Levi, one of the sons of Jacob and Leah. He had a strong concern for his people and had wanted to lead and rescue them but all those hopes were dashed when one of his own people made it clear that they knew he had killed an Egyptian who had been beating a Hebrew and they didn't want him playing the judge and ruler in their lives. This shook him and he began to fear what might happen. When Pharaoh got to hear of it he became a wanted man who would face the death penalty if he were caught so he left Egypt quickly and entered the land of his distant relatives.

His heart was still for protecting the weak and when he saw some women being driven off from collecting water from a well by shepherds he became the man of action again and came to their rescue. Later, when the girls returned to their father they excitedly told him that an Egyptian rescued them and even drew water for them and watered the flock, he quickly told them "Don't leave him outside, invite him in and give him some food."

From the stranger being away from his home and without work, he was now given both. Jethro, a priest of Midian, who had seven daughters, gave him a home and one of his daughters to be his wife, her name was Zipporah and they had a son who Moses named Gershom, a name that reflected his position, as he had said, "I have become an alien in a foreign land."

His life now was to be different from what it had been. Now it would be simpler, he would eat, work, sleep and raise a family. He had wanted to lead his people but now he led a flock of sheep and grew to be content. It had been forty years since he left Egypt and to be an accomplished speaker wasn't needed in the rocky desert of southern Sinai.

Back in Egypt the Israelite's hardships increased as their oppressive work as slaves continued. God could both hear and see, as Hagar discovered long before, and his promise to Abraham, and Isaac and with Jacob was not forgotten.

It was just another day of seeing that the flock had food and protecting them from predators when a strange sight prompted Moses to get a closer look. He saw a bush on fire but the bush wasn't burning. As he came near he saw what must have been an angel and this being then addressed Moses personally from within the fire, "Moses! Moses!" "I'm here," he answered. "Don't come any closer and take your sandals off," the angel warned him, "you are standing on holy ground." The angel then spoke as God himself, "I am the God of your father, the God of Abraham, the God of Isaac and the God of Jacob." Moses was in a state of fear and didn't dare look at this being speaking as God.

Moses was then reminded of the misery of his people back in Egypt and that God had not only saw and heard their cries but was concerned over their suffering. God was now going to rescue his people and bring them to the land that had been promised them. Moses listened with his face to the ground when he heard God tell him that he was sending him to meet with Pharaoh and bring the Israelites out of Egypt. Moses had already tried this and it failed and that failure had a lasting effect on him so his first response was to express these strong self-doubts to God, "Who am I? I won't be able to go to Pharaoh and I can't release the Israelites."

"I will be with you," God said to him, "and when you've brought the people out, bring them here to worship God."

"If I go to the Israelites and tell them that the God of their fathers has sent me, they will ask me what your name is, what should I tell them?" Moses was beginning to panic.

"I am who I am, tell the Israelites, 'I am' has sent you. This is my name, and the name that is to be remembered for ever."

On one of the occasions that Jesus came close to being stoned, he had just said to the Jews, "I'm telling you the truth, if anyone keeps my word, he'll never see death." Unsurprisingly, they said, "Now we know that you're demon-possessed! Abraham died and so did the prophets, Are you greater than our father Abraham? He died, and so did the prophets. Who do you think you are?"

"If I glorify myself, my glory means nothing. My Father, whom you claim as your God, is the one who glorifies me. Though you don't know him, I know him. If I said I didn't, I'd be a liar like you, but I do know him and keep his word. Your father Abraham rejoiced at the thought of seeing my day; he saw it and was glad."

"You're not fifty years old, and you've seen Abraham!"

"I'm telling you the truth, before Abraham was born, I am!"

At this, they picked up stones to stone him, but he hid himself, slipping away from the temple grounds.

Moses wasn't sure he understood and his worries continued. God instructed him on what to do next: he was to get the leaders of Israel together and tell them God's purpose in rescuing them and bringing them into the highly populated and cultivated land of Canaan. After informing the leaders they would together go to Pharaoh and request a three-day journey into the desert to offer sacrifices to the Lord their God. God then told Moses that Pharaoh won't say yes to this unless something forces him to. It is then that God will strike the Egyptians with such force that Pharaoh will let them go.

Moses was taking this in while thinking of everything that could go wrong.

"What if they don't believe me and say that I've made it all up?"

"What's that you're holding?"

"A staff,"

"Throw it on the ground."

Moses threw it to the ground and it changed into a snake. He jumped away from it in fear and God said to him, "Pick it up by the tail." Moses picked it up and it changed back into a staff. "Do this and they'll believe what you say." Then Moses was told to put his hand into his jacket and when he took it out it was white and leprous. "Now put it back into your jacket," Moses did as he was told and when he took it out it was completely restored.

"If they don't believe the first miracle then do the second, but if they don't believe either then take some water from the Nile and pour it onto dry land and they'll see it change into blood."

After being shown these signs and given encouragement from God Moses still doubted.

"O Lord, I've never been eloquent, and in fact, I now stutter a lot."

"Who gave man his mouth? Who makes him deaf or speechless? Who gives him sight or makes him blind? I do that. Go; I will help you speak and I'll teach you what to say."

"O Lord, please send someone else to do it." Moses considered himself too much a failure to accept the mission and gave in to his fears.

God was now angry at Moses' refusal.

"What about your brother, Aaron? I know he's a good speaker. He's on his way to meet you and he's looking forward to seeing you. You speak to him and tell him what to say and I'll help both of you and I'll teach you what to do. He will be your spokesman, and take that staff with you so that you can perform miraculous signs with it." God also told Moses to tell Pharaoh, who will resist and not let the Israelites go, that Israel is God's firstborn son, and you must release his son so that he may worship God.

When Moses got back to Jethro he asked to be able to go back to Egypt to see how his people are, Jethro said, "Of course, my best wishes go with you." God had told Moses that all the people in Egypt who wanted him dead are dead, so that reassured him. A short time later he met with Aaron at the mountain of God and they kissed. Moses told him everything and then they moved back into Egypt.

Once there they brought together all the Israelite leaders and Aaron had told them why they were there Moses showed them the signs with the staff and his hand they believed. Knowing of God's concern for them they bowed their heads and worshipped.

Now it was time to meet with Pharaoh.

5

Resistance

A meeting between two representatives of a slave people and the most powerful leader in the world is going to be a memorable event. Aaron and Moses presented their request to Pharaoh and they weren't surprised by his answer, "Who is the Lord, that I should do what he says. I will not let Israel go." Moses and Aaron followed God's instructions and said to Pharaoh that their God has met with them and commanded them to take a three-day trip into the desert so that they could sacrifice to the Lord their God, and then they added that God may strike them with plagues or with the sword. Pharaoh responded by accusing the two of taking the people away from their work which was a serious charge.

When Moses and Aaron had left, Pharaoh gave the order to those who supervised the slaves not to supply them with straw for making bricks but order them to collect their own. But the number of bricks made must not drop. "They're lazy, that's why they're crying out to be released. Make them work harder and don't pay any attention to their lies."

This ruling was enforced and caused the people to move out in all directions in search of straw. The result was that they couldn't meet the same quota as before and the Israelite foremen were beaten for not reaching the target. The foremen appealed directly to Pharaoh about the unfairness of the order and Pharaoh turned on them with the charge that they were lazy and that they wouldn't get any straw but they still had to make up the full quota of bricks. This meant serious trouble for the work force and they knew who to blame for their extra difficulties—Moses and Aaron!

When they later met the two brothers they were angry and said to them, "God will judge you! You have made us a stink to Pharaoh and his officials and this latest rule is like a death sentence for us."

Moses could see this plan to free the slaves was crumbling before his eyes, and he prayed, "O Lord, why have you brought trouble on this people? Is this why I was chosen? From the start things have got worse not better, and there's no sign of your people getting released, quite the opposite."

The Lord then spoke to Moses, "Now you're going to see my power unleashed. Pharaoh will not only release the people, he'll drive them out of his country. Don't forget who I am, I've not forgotten the covenant I made with Abraham, Isaac and Jacob. This is not going to be done by human power, tell the Israelites that I am the Lord, and I will bring you out of slavery. I will take you as my own people, and I will be your God. I will bring you to the land I promised to Abraham and give it to you to own."

Moses told the leaders what God had told him but because they were so discouraged they didn't listen to him. Then the Lord said to him, "Go and tell Pharaoh to let the Israelites out of his country." Moses replied, "The Israelites won't listen to me, so why should Pharaoh listen, I still stammer."

The lord reminded Moses that Aaron would speak for him; "It would be as if you were God and Aaron your prophet, that's how it will be when you are before Pharaoh."

Pharaoh had made up his mind, it was decided and nothing would change it, and God informed Moses that he would set even harder Pharaoh's mind that when miraculous signs are done he still won't listen to him, until it comes to breaking point for them and they realise that the God of Abraham, Isaac and Jacob is God.

Moses was eighty years old at this time and Aaron was three years older and on their next visit to Pharaoh when his response was just as negative Aaron threw his staff down in front of them and it became a snake but when Pharaoh brought in his magicians they were able to do the same thing but with one big difference, Aaron's snake swallowed up their snakes and he picked it up and it returned to being a staff again. Pharaoh was not impressed and refused to listen.

The next morning Pharaoh went to the edge of the Nile and Aaron and Moses were there waiting for him. And Moses told Aaron what to say to Pharaoh which was that the God of the Hebrews has sent me to say to you, Let my people go, but you have not listened so watch and see what God can do. Aaron hit the water of the Nile and it turned to blood, the fish died and the river stank. All the water sources were contaminated so the Egyptians had to dig along the Nile to find fresh supplies of water. But again, the Egyptian magicians were able to do the same. Pharaoh didn't even take it seriously. He just turned around and went back into his palace.

A week passed and God told Moses to go back to Pharaoh and give him the same message, and add that if he didn't listen his whole country will be covered in frogs, and they'll be everywhere. After speaking to Pharaoh Aaron pointed the staff over the waters and the frogs came and were everywhere. Again the magicians were able to do the same, but Pharaoh did summon Moses and Aaron to pray to God so that the frogs would go away, and if you do this, he told them, I'll let your people go and offer sacrifices to the Lord.

"I leave it up to you to decide when you want me to pray for you and all your people." Moses waited for Pharaoh's reply. "Tomorrow," Pharaoh said. "It will be done as you say, so that you know that there is only one living God," Moses answered. Moses prayed and God answered, the frogs died where they were and where collected and piled into heaps that stank, but as soon as Pharaoh saw what happened his attitude hardened again, just as God said it would.

Aaron was then told to hit the ground with the staff and the dust of the ground became gnats that got in and on everything. This, Egypt's magicians were not able to copy. Pharaoh was told by his magicians that this was the finger of God, but he didn't listen to them either.

Moses was instructed to get up early next morning and confront Pharaoh as he goes to the waters' edge and say to him that he must let the Israelites go and if he doesn't he and all of his people will experience swarms of flies to fill your houses and everywhere, but where my people live, in the land of Goshen, there will be no swarms of flies because I'll make a distinction between my people and yours. This will happen tomorrow, and it did.

The dense swarms of flies got everywhere and the land was ruined. Pharaoh let Moses and Aaron know that the people could sacrifice to their God, but it must be done here and not out of the country. Moses replied that it wasn't possible and that they must take the three-day journey into the desert. "That's what we've been commanded to do."

Pharaoh conceded a little and gave permission for them to leave but not to go very far, "Now, start praying for me!" Pharaoh insisted. Moses prayed, the flies disappeared and Pharaoh changed his mind. The cycle was repeated yet again. Once more Moses was sent to Pharaoh to tell him what would happen if he refused again to let the people go. This time a deadly disease would strike all their livestock, but not those in Goshen, every animal would be infected. The next day God did it, all the livestock of the Egyptians died, but none belonging to the Israelites died. Even when Pharaoh got all the facts he still refused to let the people go.

Somehow both Moses and Aaron were still able to go and speak to Pharaoh and the next time they saw him they had handfuls of soot to throw into the air while Pharaoh looked on. "This," they told him, "will become fine dust over the whole land of Egypt and men and animals will find festering boils on them. This happened and the magicians found themselves with boils as well and had no power to stop it happening, even so, Pharaoh didn't change his mind.

Full force is threatened next if Pharaoh doesn't relent and let God's people go. In doing this, the Egyptian leader is told, they will know that there is no-one like the Lord in all the earth. God could have killed every last one then if he chose but, as Moses told Pharaoh, God has raised him up for the purpose of showing his power and that his name might be proclaimed throughout the earth. "As you are setting yourself up against God's people" Moses continued, "by this time tomorrow Egypt will experience its worst hailstorm in all of its history. For the protection of your people and their livestock, give the order that they all find a place of shelter because if they are outside when it comes they'll die."

Those officials who did take what Moses said seriously went out quickly and got their slaves and livestock under shelter, those who didn't left their slaves and livestock where they were.

Moses was told to stretch out his arm and point the staff towards the sky. The sky darkened and the lightning flashed to the ground and the hail began to beat down over Egypt. Trees were stripped bare and crops were flattened, the only place it didn't hail was in Goshen. Very soon Moses and Aaron got the call to see Pharaoh. When they arrived Pharaoh told them "This time I've sinned. The Lord is right and we are wrong, pray to the Lord, because we cannot take any more of this dreadful hail. You don't have to stay here anymore, your people can go."

Moses told Pharaoh that when he leaves the city he will pray to God and this storm of thunder and hail will stop so that you will know who the true God is, but I know that you and your officials do not fear God.

A short time later when the storm had ceased Pharaoh reverted back to his hardened position, and he once more refused their release.

Moses was told to go back to Pharaoh as what was going to happen will be told down through the generations as an example of the greatness of God.

Once more Moses and Aaron stood before Pharaoh and conveyed God's message to him, "How long will you refuse to humble yourself before me? Release my people so that they can worship me, and if you refuse you will see your country covered by locusts—there will be so many of them that you'll be unable to see the ground and they'll eat what remains of your crop. It will be more severe than anything seen in this country before."

As Moses and Aaron were leaving, Pharaoh's officials urged him to reconsider as Egypt was now ruined. Pharaoh relented and Moses and Aaron were brought back and asked "Who among the Israelites needs to go on this three-day trip into the desert?" Moses replied, "All of us, without exception." "That's not possible" a sternly faced Pharaoh stated, "only the men will be allowed to go. That's my decision." Moses and Aaron were then thrown out.

God again told Moses to stretch out his staff over Egypt and the locusts will come and eat up everything that remains from the hail storm. An east wind blew all that day and night and by the morning they had arrived and covered the land with a living blackness. Pharaoh got the two brothers back without any delay and implored them to forgive him and pray to their God to take this deadly plague away. After Moses prayed a strong west wind picked up the locusts and carried them off to the sea and then they were all gone, very much like Pharaoh's regret over sinning against the Hebrew's God. The problem was lifted and so his heart was hardened.

Yet again Moses was told to stretch out his hand towards the sky and a deep and total darkness descended over the land. It was so dark that they couldn't see anything around them, but the Israelites still had light. This lasted for three days. In this darkness Pharaoh called back Moses and told him that he and everyone else could go but not their livestock, they have to remain behind. Moses protested that their animals must go with them because they don't know how many will be needed in their worship. "We can't leave anything behind." Moses insisted. Pharaoh immediately cancelled his offer and said that none of them can go. "Get out of my sight!" Pharaoh shouted at them, "The next time you see me it'll be death for you."

"I will not come before you again," Moses replied.

The Israelites had seen miracle after miracle and were observers of the battering and distress of the Egyptians. Now they were to be told that they need to do something themselves. "On the 10th day of what will be known as the first month in the Hebrew calendar, each man is to take a lamb for his family, one for each household. If any household is too small for a whole lamb, they must share one with their nearest neighbour, having taken into account the number of people there are.

"You are to determine the amount of lamb needed in accordance with what each person will eat. The animals you choose must be year-old males without defect, and you may take them from the sheep or the goats.

"Take care of them until the 14th day of the month, when all the people of the community of Israel must slaughter them at twilight. Then they're to take some of the blood and put it on the sides and tops of the door-frames of the houses where they eat the lambs. That same night they're to eat the meat roasted over the fire, along with bitter herbs, and bread made without yeast. Don't eat the meat raw or cooked in water, but roast it over the fire—head, legs and inner parts. Don't leave any of it till morning; if some is left till morning, you must burn it. You're to eat it with your cloak tucked into your belt, your sandals on your feet and your staff in your hand. Eat it in haste; it's the Lord's Passover.

"On that same night," the Lord informed Moses and Aaron, "I will pass through Egypt and strike down every firstborn—both men and animals—and I'll bring judgment on all the gods of Egypt. I am the Lord. The blood will be a sign for you on the houses where you are; and when I see the blood, I will pass over you. No destructive plague will touch you when I strike Egypt."

Then Moses summoned all the elders of Israel and instructed them to "Go at once and select the animals for your families and when you slaughter the Passover lamb take a bunch of hyssop, dip it into the blood in the basin and put some of the blood on the top and both sides of the door-frame. None of you must leave the house until morning. When the Lord goes through the land to strike down the Egyptians, he will see the blood on the top and sides of the door-frame and will pass over that doorway and he'll not permit the destroyer to enter your houses and kill you."

There were some further restrictions concerning the future observance of the Passover: "No foreigner is to eat it. Any slave you've bought may eat it only after you've circumcised him, but a temporary resident and a hired worker, isn't allowed to eat it.

"It must be eaten in one house, and none of the meat taken outside of the house. Do not break any of the bones. The whole community of Israel must celebrate it."

The day Jesus hung on the cross slowly dying was what was called a preparation day; this was because the following day was to be the first of the seven annual Sabbaths which was called the First day of Unleavened Bread. John called it 'a special Sabbath,' and the weekly Sabbath came three days later; towards the end of that Sabbath Jesus would have been dead for the period of time he said that would elapse before he rose from the dead. John records that as 'the Jews didn't want the bodies left on the crosses during the Sabbath, they asked Pilate to have the legs broken and the bodies taken down. The soldiers (one or two of them working from both sides as Jesus was in the middle of the three) came and broke the legs of the first man who had been crucified with Jesus, and then those of the other, but when they came to Jesus and found that he was already dead, they didn't break his legs' (some believe that a soldier's spear thrust happened before his death and was the cause of Jesus' early death; this, they say, was the reason he cried out in a loud voice before dying) 'The man who saw this testifies that it's true (the sudden flow of blood and water). These things happened so that the scripture would be fulfilled: "Not one of his bones will be broken," and, as another scripture says, "They will look on the one they have pierced."'

Moses had been told, and he had told Pharaoh, as well as all the Israelites, that God was about to perform a miracle that will be worse than anything that has happened before or that will happen in the future. It will create such grief throughout the land that Pharaoh will want every Israelite and all that they have to leave the country as quickly as possible.

At midnight an angel charged with this destruction of the firstborn, arrived and looked at every door of every house and where there was no blood on the sides and top of the door the firstborn in that house would die, human and animal, rich or poor, free or slave and every house had a death within it. But those houses that did have blood around the door were spared, the destroying angel passed over it.

Pharaoh and all his leading men got up while it was still night and they could hear the heart-rending cries all around then and from within the palace itself.

It was still night when Pharaoh summoned Moses and Aaron, not to kill them as he had threatened, but to say, "Go now! Go, and do what you want to do, just as you've asked. Take everything you have and we will all give you gold and silver and whatever else you want, as long as you go, and take this deadly plague away from here."

With some urgency the Egyptians helped the Israelites to leave as they were sure that if they stayed any longer they'd all be dead. There were about 600, 000 men of military age, not counting the women and children, plus many other people went with them, and all their livestock of sheep and cattle. The number of people leaving Egypt may have been more than three million.

The prophet Hosea living about eight centuries later was to write, 'When Israel was a child, I loved him, and out of Egypt I called my son.' When Jesus was a child his parents were told by an angel to escape to Egypt and stay there until they were told that it was safe to return. After King Herod died they were told to go back to Israel 'for those who were trying to take the child's life are dead,' just as God had told Moses when he was in Midian to return to Egypt for all the men who wanted to kill him are dead, and so was fulfilled what God had said through his prophet long before Jesus was born, 'Out of Egypt I called my son.'

The shortest route back to Canaan was along the coast but because that way was heavily fortified and it would mean war and the people might easily change their minds and head back to Egypt, so God directed them through the desert route heading towards the Sea of Reeds. They would need to go through the Sinai Peninsula which in those days was known as the wilderness of Paran.

In the daytime there was a pillar of cloud to lead them and in the night time it changed into a pillar of fire to provide them with light. Moses received instructions from God to camp by the sea which would lead Pharaoh to think that the Israelites were not sure of where they were going, but God's purpose was to harden his heart so as to think he could destroy them even before they've left Egyptian territory. Pharaoh and his officials were already regretting letting them go as they constituted a massive slave force.

Pharaoh ordered his elite force of 600 chariots to be ready as well as all the other chariots they could gather. His infantry were also mobilised and ready to march. Moving much faster than the vast army of civilians with their belongings and livestock, the Egyptians were soon able to overtake them while they were camped by the sea near Pi Hahiroth, opposite Baal Zephon.

When the Israelites saw the Egyptian army and that their backs were to the sea they were terrified and bitterly complained to Moses for leading them to that indefensible position, "Was it because there were no graves in Egypt that you brought us out here to die? We told you when we were in Egypt, 'leave us alone; let's serve the Egyptians' that would have been better than to die in the desert." Moses, full of confidence in God, said to the people, "Don't be afraid, stay firm and you will see how great our God is. Those Egyptians that you see about to attack will soon be dead. God is the one who will fight for you. All you have to do is watch."

God told Moses to lift his staff and stretch it towards the sea. This is what Moses did, and all that night a very strong east wind parted the waters making a pathway for the people to cross on dry land. Travelling at the front of Israel's masses was an angel and he moved to being behind them so that he was between the Egyptians and the Israelites. The pillar of cloud now was in front of the Egyptians and through the night they couldn't see through it to attack the Israelites, but on their side they had light so that they could see their way forward over the seabed. Just before the dawn came the darkness lifted and the Egyptians began their attack. They followed the same route as the Israelites; on the freshly dried land with the sea on both sides of them like two great walls.

The first the Egyptians knew that something seriously was going wrong was their chariot wheels getting stuck and as they were in the lead it held up all the other chariots and troops behind them. They now began to fully realise who they were really fighting against and made strenuous efforts to turn around which was near impossible with the whole army behind them, but by then it was too late for them to escape, they were trapped.

Moses was told to stretch out his staff over the sea again and this time millions of tons of water crashed down onto the Egyptians. It was daybreak and the surging waters flooded over all the Egyptians. Not one of them survived and some of their dead bodies were later seen on the shore line.

From over three million throats the noise of ecstatic celebration broke out. Some couldn't stop laughing, others fell to their knees in gratitude and praise that they were no longer slaves. Their bondage had ended at last, they were free. The cheers, shouting and springing into the air turned to singing as they realised what had been done for them, or, in spite of them.

The apostle Paul, looking beyond physical slavery, spoke of the slavery that everyone is born into without even realising that this is their natural condition. Addressing Christians in Rome he wrote, 'What then? Shall we sin because we are not under law but under grace? By no means! Don't you know that when you offer yourselves to someone to obey him as slaves, you are slaves to the one whom you obey—whether you are slaves to sin, which leads to death, or to obedience, which leads to righteousness? But thanks be to God that, though you used to be slaves to sin, you wholeheartedly obeyed the form of teaching to which you were entrusted. You have been set free from sin and have become slaves to righteousness.'

Jesus talked of that real freedom when he spoke to those who opposed him, 'To the Jews who had believed him, Jesus said, "If you hold to my teaching, you are really my disciples. Then you will know the truth, and the truth will set you free."

Ignoring their own history they answered him, "We are Abraham's descendants and have never been slaves to anyone. (Don't mention the Egyptians and Assyrians and Babylonians!) How can you say that we shall be set free?"

"I tell you the truth, everyone who sins is a slave to sin. Now a slave has no permanent place in the family, but a son belongs to it forever. So if the Son sets you free, you will be free indeed. I know you are Abraham's descendants. Yet you are ready to kill me, because you have no room for my word. I'm telling you what I've seen in the Father's presence, and you do what you have heard from your father."

"Abraham is our father."

"If you were Abraham's children then you would do the things Abraham did. As it is, you are determined to kill me, a man who has told you the truth that I heard from God. Abraham didn't do such things. You are doing the things your own father does."

"We aren't illegitimate children. The only Father we have is God himself."

"If God were your Father, you would love me, because I came from God and I'm here now. I haven't come on my own, I've been sent. Why is it that what I say to you isn't clear? It's because you can't hear what I'm saying. You belong to your father, the devil, and you want to carry out your father's desire. He was a murderer from the beginning, and he didn't hold on to the truth, because there's no truth in him. When he lies, he speaks his native language—he's a liar and the father of lies. Yet because I tell the truth, you don't believe me! Can any of you prove me guilty of sin? If I'm telling the truth, why don't you believe me? He who belongs to God hears what God says. The reason that you don't hear is that you don't belong to God."

The people now that they saw with their own eyes what happened to the Egyptians put their trust in God and in his servant Moses, but it wasn't to last.

Moses led them from the Sea of Reeds to the Desert of Shur and for three days they didn't find any fresh water. When they did arrive at some water they found it to be bitter and undrinkable so the place was called *Marah* meaning bitter. This brought up more criticism against Moses who entreated God for the water they needed and he was told to select a part of a particular tree and throw it into the water, and then the water became sweet; problem solved.

They next came to Elim where there were twelve springs and seventy palm trees, so they camped there. From there they came to the Desert of Zin, which is on the way to Sinai. This was thirty days after they came out of Egypt and the grumbling started again. This time they were thinking back, perhaps with a little embellishment, of all the good food they had in Egypt. "We're all going to starve to death in this desert," they complained. Moses received from God what they're to do, but first he told the people that God was fully aware of their grumbling against Moses and Aaron which was the same as grumbling against God.

"In the evening," Moses told them, "God will give you meat to eat and in the morning he will give you bread from heaven. Each morning you are to gather enough for that day and on Friday prepare twice as much as you do on other days. While Aaron was going over the details, and addressing their negative attitude with the people, they noticed a strange cloud in the distance.

That evening a flock of migrating quail landed amongst the Israelites and they were promptly caught, killed, plucked, cooked and eaten. The next morning, once the dew was gone, they saw thin flakes like frost on the ground and they asked each other, "What is it?" and that question became the name of this new food source: *manna*. Moses told them that this manna is going to be bread for them and they gathered it up, just what they needed for that day and no more. Having been told not to keep it till the next morning, some of them paid no attention and did keep it longer than they should have and it became smelly and full of maggots. Moses was angry that they wouldn't obey a simple command.

The manna that was collected on Friday didn't go bad on the Saturday, and they were able to bake or boil it just as they did during the week days. This was because the last day of the week was a day of rest, and no work was to be done. Human nature being what it is, some people did collect the manna on that day, or tried to, as there wasn't any there! God said to Moses, "How long will these people refuse to keep my instructions and commands?" The people were reminded what they were to do, and not do, and so they complied.

The manna tasted like wafers made with honey, and Moses instructed Aaron to keep a small amount in a jar and put it in a safe place as a reminder for future generations. They didn't know at the time but they were to eat this manna for the next forty years before they were allowed to enter the land of Canaan.

The subject of this bread came up when crowds of people who had their food provided free to them by the teacher from Nazareth eventually found him and asked, "What miracle will you do so that we can believe you? Our forefathers ate manna while they were in the desert, as it says, 'He gave them bread from heaven to eat,' Jesus told them that it wasn't Moses who gave this special bread from heaven, "but it is my Father who gives you the true bread from heaven. This bread of God is he who comes down from heaven and gives life to the world." Without comprehending what he was talking about, they pictured a continual free supply of bread and said to him, "Give us this bread from today onwards." "I am the bread of life," Jesus told them, "He who comes to me and believes in me will never go hungry or thirsty. But as I told you, you've seen me and you don't believe. Later in the conversation he began speaking about eating his flesh and drinking his blood, and people feeding on him, and that those who did would live forever. This form of speaking was disgusting and repugnant to the people that were following him, and because of what he taught at that time, many of them left him.

They moved camp and came to Rephidim where no water was found, and the people argued with Moses and demanded that he get them the water they needed. They brought up the same arguments as before, saying, "what was the point of coming out here where we'll all die of thirst." This wasn't an imaginary problem as their children and livestock would need more water if they were going to survive, yet it did show that after all that God had done for them in liberating them from slavery and destroying the Egyptian army how little trust they had in God and how quick they were to complain.

"You shouldn't put God to a test," Moses told them. And to God he said, "I don't know how to handle these people, they look ready to kill me." God then told him what to do. "Take the staff and bring together some of the elders of Israel and walk on ahead of the people to the rock at Horeb, I'll stand there by you. Hit the rock with your staff and enough water will come out for the people to drink." This happened as he was told it would and he called the place Massah and Meribah, which means testing and quarrelling. The people were even asking if God is among them or not. In later years Moses would write about this episode and set a warning before Israel not to test the Lord their God as they did at Massah.

When Jesus was being tempted by the being that invisibly controls this world to do something stupid and trust that God would come to the rescue, he quoted those words of Moses not to put God to the test. God was to be trusted, not tested.

While at Rephidim the Amalekites attacked them. They were descendents of Esau and this was their territory. Joshua, the assistant to

Moses, was told to choose the men to go and fight. The next day Moses stood on top of a hill with the staff of God in his hands. As the fighting was between thousands on each side the outcome was uncertain, but as long as Moses held up his hands the Israelites were winning but when, through tiredness, he lowered his hands they began to lose. Aaron and Hur, who were with Moses, saw what was happening and helped him. As he tired they took a large stone and had Moses sit on it, and they each supported Moses' arms so that by sunset the Amalekites were beaten. Years later Moses was to write, 'Remember what the Amalekites did to you along the way when you came out of Egypt. When you were tired and worn out, they came to you as you journeyed and killed those who were lagging behind; they had no respect for God. When God gives you rest from all the enemies around you in the land that is your inheritance, you destroy all the Amalekites. Don't forget!'

In Cecil B. DeMille's 1956 film, 'The Ten Commandments' the last scene is where Charlton Heston, playing the aged Moses, is seen walking up Mount Nebo where he will die and he turns, with a glorious sky behind him and the soaring music of Elmer Bernstein bringing tears to our eyes (or my eyes at least) and says to those watching, "Go, and proclaim liberty (or was it peace?) to all nations." Moving as this scene was, it was a complete misrepresentation of what the Israelites were to do, in that they were commanded to kill all the Canaanites in the land and move into their homes. It wasn't because they were better or more righteous people than the Canaanites, but that God was bringing judgement onto them and was employing the Israelites to do it, just as later he would use the Assyrians and Babylonians to punish the two nations of Israel and Judah for their sins and rebellion.

Moses warned the people that when they move into their ready-made homes not to think that God had brought them there because of their righteousness. "No," he wrote, "it's on account of the wickedness of these nations that the Lord is going drive them out of the land. It's not because of your righteousness or your integrity that you will own the land; but on account of the wickedness of these nations they are being driven out, and that is so God's promise to Abraham, Isaac and Jacob can be accomplished. So understand, that it's not because you are righteous, or better than them, for the fact is that you are a stiff-necked people. Remember this and never forget how you provoked the Lord your God to anger in the desert. From the day you left Egypt until you arrived in this land you have been rebellious against the Lord."

It was after the battle with the Amalekites that his father-in-law, Jethro, on hearing what God had done for Moses came to visit him in the desert, with him was Moses' wife, Zipporah, and his two children, Gershom, which sounds in Hebrew like *an alien there*, and Eliezer, meaning *my God is helper*. They were camped near to what was known as the mountain of God. This was in the third month after they had left Egypt.

They greeted each other warmly and Jethro was thrilled to hear first-hand about their liberation from the Egyptians. Jethro watched on the next day as Moses sat as a judge for the people which lasted for the whole day as people brought their problems and disputes before Moses for him to make a decision on. Jethro told Moses that he's going to wear himself out doing this on his own, so he suggested that selected men who could represent the people be given the responsibility of being judges themselves, some over ten people, some over fifty, others over a hundred and those who are to be over a thousand. Any problem that they can't handle they can take to the next level and if the top level can't solve it they can then come to you. If you do this, Jethro said, it will take a huge weight off your shoulders.

Moses recognised the wisdom in this advice and he implemented it straight away. Then Jethro returned to his own country.

6

At the Mountain of God

From the mountain God called Moses to come up and there he received a message for the people of Israel. It has been calculated (Alec Motyer; The Message of Exodus, p195) that Moses made seven ascents of the mountain and that the people were camped in that area for close to a year.

Part of that message was that the people of Israel were to fully obey God and so be his treasured possession. They were also to be a kingdom of priests; those who could teach others about God and that they collectively were to form a holy nation, a people reflecting God's character. They were also to be an example to other nations that would provoke them, because of their many blessings, to be allied with Israel and follow in the same obedience to God.

Christians have been given a very similar calling. Peter wrote, 'But you are a chosen people, a royal priesthood, a holy nation, a people belonging to God, that you might declare the praises of him who called you out of darkness into his wonderful light. Once you were not a people, but now you are the people of God; once you had not received mercy, but now you have received mercy.'

Moses went back to the people and told the leaders all God had said and they replied, "We will do everything the Lord has said," and Moses took their reply back up the mountain where God told him that in three days he will come down to him in a dense cloud and the people will actually hear him speaking with Moses and put their trust in him. Moses was to prepare the people for this momentous event. They were to wash their clothes and have no sexual contact and they were also to erect a barrier around the mountain and forbid any one to touch it. If anyone did they would be killed.

The third day came with the mountain covered by dark clouds and there was thunder and lightning along with a very loud trumpet blast which made all the people tremble with fear. Moses led them to the base of the mountain where they were to meet with God. The sound grew louder and the ground began to tremble as fire like a furnace descended on the mountain. Black smoke rose from the top of the mountain as the divine force was descending.

Out of this thunder and fire a voice spoke to Moses calling him to come up. When he got to the top he was told to go back down and warn the people not to try and get a closer look or they will die, no matter who they are. Moses said to the Lord that the people couldn't get any closer because they had followed his instruction to put limits around the mountain. "Go down" the Lord told him, "and bring Aaron up with you, but nobody else." The peoples' fear increased as they heard the voice of God and they moved further away. Moses was entreated by the people to speak to them himself and they would listen, but if God speaks anymore to them they thought they would die. Moses said to them, "Don't be afraid, this fear you have should stay in your minds so that the reality of God and that he is a consuming fire will stop you sinning."

In writing to Christians the author of Hebrews says, 'You haven't come to a mountain that is physical and is burning with fire; to darkness gloom and storm; to a trumpet blast or to a voice that when it was heard the people begged that it would stop. If anyone or an animal touched the mountain it would die and everyone, including Moses, was trembling with fear, so terrifying was the sight.

'But you have come to Mount Zion, to the heavenly Jerusalem, the city of the living God. You've come to multiple thousands of angels together in joy, to the church of the firstborn, whose names are written in heaven. You've come to God, the judge of all men, to the spirits of righteous men made perfect, to Jesus the mediator of a new covenant, and to the sprinkled blood that speaks a better word than the blood of Abel.' (The blood of Abel spoke of vengeance and retribution, while the blood of the mediator, Jesus, speaks of grace and pardon)

Moses again approached the darkness where God was and received his words that he was to pass on to the Israelites, "You have had direct evidence that God has spoken to you from above. Do not make anything in resemblance to him because when God spoke to you out of the fire you didn't see any kind of shape or form, you only heard his voice, so do not make anything of gold or silver and then call that god." While he was there he was given more rules, regulations and laws that would make Israel into the only nation on earth who would have God as their King. Amongst these laws was one that said, "Do not oppress an alien; you yourselves know how it feels to be aliens, because you were aliens in Egypt."

God further told him that he would be an enemy to your enemies and will oppose those who oppose you. But there are conditions to these great blessings; when they do enter the land where the Amorites, Hittites, Perizzites, Canaanites, Hivites and Jebusites live and they are finally removed, "you are not to worship their gods or follow their way of life.

You must demolish all their sacred sites and only worship the Lord your God. His blessing will be on what you eat and drink and he will take away sickness from you. None, human or animal, will miscarry or be barren in your land, and you will enjoy a full life span."

When Moses was back in the camp God called him back to the mountain, but this time accompanying him would be Aaron, Nadab and Abihu, two of his sons, and seventy of the leaders of Israel plus Joshua, the assistant to Moses. But before this selected group were to go up to the Lord Moses went and told the people the laws God had revealed to him and they all responded with a resounding agreement that everything the Lord had said they would do. Moses, as his custom was, wrote it all down so that it would be clearly remembered.

Early the next morning he built an altar of natural rocks at the foot of the mountain and set up twelve stone pillars representing the twelve tribes of Israel, then he sent young Israelite men, and they offered burnt offerings, symbolizing the holding of nothing back from God and fellowship offerings or peace offerings, symbolizing fellowship with God. Then Moses took half of the blood and put it in bowls and the other half he sprinkled on the altar. He then read from the Book of the Covenant to the people and they all said, "We will do everything the Lord has said; we will obey." Moses took the blood and sprinkled it over the people saying that the blood represented the covenant God has made with you.

Over 1,300 years later the author of the letter to the Hebrews wrote, 'When Moses had proclaimed every commandment of the law to all the people, he took the blood of calves, together with water, scarlet wool and branches of hyssop, and sprinkled the scroll and all the people. He said, "This is the blood of the covenant, which God commanded you to keep." In the same way, he sprinkled with the blood both the tabernacle and everything used in its ceremonies. In fact, the law requires that nearly everything be cleansed with blood, and without the shedding of blood there is no forgiveness.'

Moses was also commanded to "anoint Aaron and his sons and consecrate them so they may serve me as priests, "Say to the Israelites, 'This is to be my sacred anointing oil for the generations to come. Don't pour it on men's bodies and don't make any oil with the same formula— it's sacred and you're to consider it sacred. Whoever makes perfume like it and puts it on anyone other than a priest must be cut off from his people." The details of how to make this special perfume were given to Moses for the exclusive use of the priesthood.

Paul taught the Christians of Ephesus to 'be imitators of God as dearly loved children and live a life of love, just as Christ loved us and gave himself up for us as a fragrant offering and sacrifice to God.' The priests were set apart by a special perfume and Jesus by his unique sacrifice was a fragrant offering to God and his followers, by sharing in the life of Christ, are a lovely aroma to those who are being saved but to those who are perishing they are 'the smell of death.' Death and life are compared to aromas, the one, a dreadful stink and the other, a beautiful perfume.

Then this group of seventy-five men went up and actually saw the God of Israel, but as the record only says that they saw his feet and what appeared to be below his feet which looked like a blue pavement clear as the sky, it could be that they had quickly bowed to the ground. God did nothing against these men; they saw God, the record tells us, and they ate and drank.

Moses received God's call to come to where God was and he would be given tablets of stone with the law and commands engraved on them. Moses told the elders to wait there for them, as he was taking Joshua with him, until they get back. Aaron and Hur were with them so if there's any problem they were to go to them with it.

A cloud covered and settled on the mount and it lasted for six days and the two of them remained where they were until the seventh day when Moses was called from within the cloud. From below the Israelites saw what looked like a consuming fire. Moses went up and entered the cloud and he stayed on that mountain for forty days.

7

Quick to Forget

A group of people gathered round Aaron and told him the situation needs a solution. Moses hasn't come back and everyone is getting restless. "We need a focus for the people," they explained to him. Nobody, including Aaron, knew what had happened to Moses; perhaps he had died up there in the smoke and fire; the whole mountain was dangerous to everyone but something must be done to calm the people.

"Let's make a god that we can follow, something all can see, as for Moses we don't know what's happened to him," they demanded of Aaron. Unexpectedly Aaron then asked for any gold people had. The Egyptians had given them plenty of gold before they left and he used what they gave him to make a cast in the shape of a calf. When it was finished the people were told that this was their god who brought them out of Egypt. Aaron also built an altar and announced a holy festival for the next day where they can make all sorts of offerings to their Lord. Perhaps he thought he was buying some time until Moses hopefully would return.

The first king of Israel, Saul, was told by Samuel, the last of the leaders that led Israel before the institution of the monarchy, who was a prophet of God, to wait at Gilgal for a week until he comes and makes offerings to God and gives Saul further instructions. But conditions at Gilgal had deteriorated with the Philistines about to attack and Saul's men quaking with fear. He waited the seven days but Samuel never came and Saul's men were beginning to scatter so he took matters into his own hands and made the offerings himself and just as he finished Samuel turned up. Saul went to greet him and Samuel asked, "What have you done?"

"When I saw the men scattering and you hadn't come at the set time, and the Philistines were preparing to attack I figured that I should seek the Lord's favour so I felt compelled to offer the burnt offering."

"You've acted foolishly. You've not kept the command the Lord your God gave you; if you had, he would have established your kingdom over Israel for all time, but now your kingdom will not last; the Lord has found a man after his own heart and appointed him leader of his people because you've not kept the Lord's command."

The Lord said to Moses, "Go back down, your people have corrupted themselves and made an idol and bowed down to it and sacrificed to it. They are a stubborn and arrogant people and I will destroy them and I'll make you into a great nation."

"O Lord, if you do this the Egyptians are going to say that was your intention all along; to get them into the desert and destroy all of them. Remember your sworn promise to Abraham, Isaac and Israel that you would make their descendents like the stars for number and that Canaan will be theirs forever. And the Lord held back from destroying the people.

Moses started on his way back to the camp. He carried two tablets of stone made by God and written on both sides by God. As he neared the base of the mountain he met with Joshua and they both heard noise coming from the camp. Joshua thought it sounded like war but Moses said it was neither the sound of victory or defeat they could hear but singing.

When Moses got close to the camp he saw the calf and the dancing and became so angry that he smashed the tablets at the foot of the mountain. He had the idol burned and ground to powder which he scattered on the water and made the Israelites drink it. He asked Aaron what was done to him to make him do such a stupid thing and Aaron replied, "Don't be angry, my lord, you know what these people are like. They said to me that they didn't know what had happened to you and that they needed a god to lead them so I asked for all their gold jewellery and I threw it into the fire, and out came this calf!" It's not recorded what Moses said to Aaron next.

Moses saw that Aaron had allowed the people to get out of control and they were running wild, so he stood at the entrance to the camp and called out, "Whoever is on the Lord's side, come to me." The Levite men rushed to him, and he told them to each get a sword and go through the whole camp and kill those who are directly involved in this idol worship, and don't hold back because they're friends or family members. They did as they were told and about three thousand people died. As a result Moses told them that they as a tribe would be set apart from the other tribes, and God blessed them. The priesthood would be theirs forever.

Moses returned to the Lord saying what a great sin these people have committed by making themselves a god of gold, but please forgive their sin, he asked, but if not, then take me out of your book.

God answered Moses, "I will choose who is blotted out of my book, now go and lead this people. My angel will go before you, and when the time comes for me to punish, I will do it." A plague then struck the people because of their idolatry.

It was now time to leave and go up to the land promised to Abraham, Isaac and Jacob, "But I will not go with you," God told Moses, "because they're a stiff-necked people and I'm likely to destroy them on the way."

This was bad news for the people who were distressed by what they were told, and all ornaments came off.

Moses had pitched a tent outside of the camp and called it the 'tent of meeting.' Anyone could go to this tent, the later Tabernacle would be sited in the centre of the camp and was highly regulated as to who entered it, but the distance from the camp suggests the separation between sinful humans and the holy God. God would, at his choosing appear at the tent. When Moses went out to the tent all the people stood outside their tents and watched as he entered the tent. When that happened a cloud would come down and stay at the entrance. The Lord would speak to Moses as a friend talks to his friend, face to face. Joshua remained at the tent.

The tent of meeting was where seventy of Israel's leaders were given some of the same spirit that Moses had and so were able to help him in leading the people. It was also the place where Aaron and Miriam were corrected by God for criticising Moses over his Cushite wife, and was where Joshua was commissioned to take over on the death of Moses.

The New Testament writer of the letter to the Hebrews notes that 'Jesus also suffered outside the city gate to make the people holy through his own blood. Let us, then, go to him outside the camp, bearing the disgrace he bore. For here we do not have an enduring city, but we are looking for the city that is to come.'

That God had said he would not go with the Israelites greatly troubled Moses who now wanted to know who it would be that leads them because, as Moses expressed, "If your Presence doesn't go with us, it would be better to stay here. How will anyone know that you are pleased with me and with your people unless you go with us? We would be no different from any other nation." The Lord said to him, "I will do the very thing you have asked, because I am pleased with you and I know you as a friend."

"Let me see your glory."

"I will cause all my goodness to pass in front of you, and I will proclaim my name, the Lord (Yahweh/ "I am who I am") before you. I will have mercy on whom I will have mercy, and I will have compassion on whom I will have compassion. But, you cannot see my face. No-one can see me and live."

Then the Lord said, "There's a place near me where you can stand on a rock, and when my glory passes I will put you in a cleft in the rock and cover you with my hand until I've passed, then I'll take my hand away and you will be able to see my back; but my face must not be seen."

Before Moses returned to the mount he chiselled two stone tablets like the ones he broke because the Lord had told him that he would write on them the same words that were on the first. No-one was to come with him this time. Early in the morning he went up the mountain carrying the two tablets in his hands. The Lord came down in a cloud and stood there with him and said, "My name is Yahweh. And he passed in front of Moses proclaiming his character. The compassionate and gracious God, slow to anger and abounding in love and faithfulness, maintaining love to thousands, and forgiving wickedness, rebellion and sin. Yet he doesn't leave the guilty unpunished; he punishes the children and their children for the sin of the fathers to the third and fourth generation."

The rebellious attitude and the disobedience shown by many of the Israelites did have a very real consequence for the next generation in that they had to go through many years of hardship due to what their parents did, but through the prophet Ezekiel we read that people were using this proverb; 'the fathers eat sour grapes, and the children's teeth are set on edge?' God responded to this complaint by saying, "As surely as I live, declares the Sovereign Lord, you'll no longer quote this proverb in Israel. For every living person belongs to me, the father as well as the son—both alike belong to me. The person who sins is the one who will die . . . . Yet you ask, 'Why doesn't the son share the guilt of his father?' Since the son has done what is just and right and has been careful to keep all my decrees, he will surely live. The person who sins is the one who will die. The son will not share the guilt of the father, nor will the father share the guilt of the son . . . Do I take any pleasure in the death of the wicked? Rather, am I not pleased when they turn from their ways and live?"

Moses was later to write, 'Fathers shall not be put to death for their children, nor children put to death for their fathers; each is to die for his own sin.'

Immediately Moses bowed to the ground and worshipped. "O Lord, if I please you then let the Lord go with us, even though this is a stiff necked people, forgive our wickedness and our sin, and take us as your inheritance."

"I am making a covenant with you. All of you will see great things never before done in any nation. Obey what I command you today and be careful not to make a treaty with any of those who now live in the land where you are heading for, or you will become ensnared by their religions. Break down their altars, smash their sacred stones and cut down the poles erected to the goddess Asherah (described as the mother of most of the 'younger' gods, including Baal). Don't worship any other god because the Lord is a jealous God."

After giving more instructions to Moses, God told him to write it all down for future generations to read. He also engraved on the stone tablets the Ten Commandments. In all he was there for forty days, neither eating, or drinking.

When Moses returned to the camp he was unaware of how he looked, and when people started to back away from him in fear he had to call them back so that they, and he, could understand what had happened. The face of Moses radiated light and when the leaders got over the shock of how he looked Moses explained all the commands God had given him. So that speaking to Moses wouldn't be too unsettling he put a veil over his face and kept it on until he entered the tent of meeting, then he took it off in the Lord's presence.

The apostle Paul saw a great significance in that veil, and wrote about it in his second letter to the Corinthians, 'God has made us competent as ministers of a new covenant—not of the letter but of the Spirit; for the letter kills, but the Spirit gives life.

'Now if the ministry that brought death, which was engraved in letters on stone, came with glory, so that the Israelites could not look steadily at the face of Moses because of its glory, fading though it was, will not the ministry of the Spirit be even more glorious? If the ministry that condemns men is glorious, how much more glorious is the ministry that brings righteousness! For what was glorious has no glory now in comparison with the surpassing glory. And if what was fading away came with glory, how much greater is the glory of that which lasts!

'Therefore, since we have such a hope, we are very bold. We are not like Moses, who would put a veil over his face to keep the Israelites from gazing at it while the radiance was fading away. But their minds were made dull, for to this day the same veil remains when the old covenant is read. It has not been removed, because only in Christ is it taken away. Even to this day when Moses is read, a veil covers their hearts. But whenever anyone turns to the Lord, the veil is taken away. Now the lord is the Spirit, and where the Spirit of the Lord is, there is freedom. And we, who with unveiled faces all reflect the Lord's glory, we are being transformed into his likeness with ever-increasing glory, which comes from the Lord, who is the Spirit.'

All the Israelites were assembled to listen to Moses as he underlined again the importance of treating the seventh day as holy and not to do any work on that day. Then he moved on to a massive project that they all could have a part in through contributions and their individual skills. This was the making of a portable tent, to be known as the Tabernacle. Moses gave an invitation for all skilled workers to get involved in the many elements that would make up this mobile centre of worship.

Moses told them that a man of Judah, Bezalel, grandson of Hur, has been given God's Spirit to enable his natural gifts to be increased in the areas of working with gold, silver and bronze, in cutting and setting stones, working with wood and all kinds of artistic craftsmanship. Bezalel and Oholiab, a Danite, had been given the ability to teach others. This team would include designers, craftsmen, embroiderers and weavers, all of them masters of their craft. The construction of this sanctuary was to be carefully monitored as it needed to be exactly as Moses had been told it should be. Day after day contributions kept coming in until there was more than enough to finish the work, and so Moses gave the order that no more offerings were needed.

The Tabernacle consisted of an enclosed sacrificial courtyard and an inner sanctuary. The outer perimeter, which was 75 x 150 ft, was encircled by linen curtains hung on 56 pillars 7½ ft. tall which hid the interior from view. The entrance faced east, covered by a screen of fine blue, purple and scarlet linen suspended on four columns. The Tabernacle itself was positioned in the west half of the courtyard. Between the sanctuary and the main entrance lay the large bronze-horned altar of sacrifice and the bronze basin for washing, Aaron and his sons had to wash their hands and feet from the basin whenever they entered. If they didn't they would die; such was the strictness of the procedures they needed to follow.

When the apostle Peter realised that Jesus was about to wash his feet he refused saying, "No, you'll never wash my feet." And Jesus answered him, "Unless I wash you, you have no part with me."

Hearing what Jesus said Peter quickly replied, "If that's the case Lord, then wash my hands and head as well as my feet!"

"A person who has had a bath," Jesus said to all of them, "needs only to wash his feet; his whole body is clean, and you are clean, though not every one of you." He knew who was going to betray him and that's why he said not everyone was clean."

David had written, 'Wash away all my iniquity and cleanse me from my sin . . . cleanse me with hyssop (used by the priests in the purification ritual for infectious skin disease) and I shall be clean; wash me and I shall be whiter than snow.'

Ezekiel compared the evil the people were doing as like a filthy defilement for which God promises a 'washing' with clean water so to cleanse them from all their impurities. Sin is compared to dirt and it's not dirt we can remove ourselves. Jeremiah wrote, 'Although you wash yourself with soda and use plenty of soap the stain of your guilt is still before me, declares the Lord.'

John wrote, 'If we freely admit that we have sinned, we find God utterly reliable and straightforward—he forgives our sins and makes us thoroughly clean from all sin (J.B. Phillips).

'Do you not know,' Paul wrote to the Corinthians, 'that the wicked will not inherit the kingdom of God? Neither the sexually immoral nor idolaters, adulterers, male prostitutes, homosexual offenders, thieves nor the greedy, drunkards, slanderers and swindlers will inherit the kingdom of God, and that is what some of you were, but you were washed, you were sanctified, you were justified in the name of the Lord Jesus Christ and by the Spirit of our God.'

Those who have been washed can draw near to God with a sincere heart in full assurance of faith, having their hearts sprinkled to cleanse them from a guilty conscience and having their bodies washed with pure water.

How clean we are is important to God. There is only so much we can do ourselves but to have a part with Jesus we must allow him to wash us.

The inner sanctuary was a series of linen curtains and hide coverings placed tent-fashion over an inner acacia wood frame. They made 20 frames for the south side and 40 silver bases to go under them—2 bases for each frame. For the other side, the north side of the tabernacle, they made 20 frames and 40 silver bases—2 under each frame. They made 6 frames for the far end, that is, the west end of the tabernacle, and 2 frames were made for the corners. The frames were 15ft.by27inches and each was set in 2 sockets of silver and supported by other frames interlocking them together.

This sanctuary measured 45x15 ft. and was divided into two rooms by a skilfully worked veil of linen. The outer room, the Holy Place (30x15 ft.), contained the incense altar, the table to hold twelve loaves of bread, in two rows of six, on it. The table would be made of acacia wood, about 3 ft. long, and about 2¼ ft. high. It was overlaid with pure gold and had gold moulding around it. There was a lamp stand of pure gold which had flowerlike cups, buds and blossoms all part of one piece. It had six branches extending from the sides, three on one side and three on the other side. Three cups shaped like almond flowers with buds and blossoms were on one branch, three on the next branch and the same for all six branches extending from the lamp stand. They made the lamp stand and all its accessories from a 75 pound brick of pure gold.

The inner room, named the Holy of Holies (15x15 ft.) contained the ark. Bezalel made it of acacia wood, and it was about 3¾ ft. long and 2¼ ft. wide and high. He overlaid it with pure gold, both inside and out, and made a gold moulding around it. He cast four gold rings for its four feet and then he made the poles of acacia wood and overlaid with gold. These poles were inserted into the rings on the side of the ark, as everything had to be disassembled each time they moved. The cover of the ark, called the atonement cover, was made of pure gold. He made two cherubim—powerful angels, one for each end of the cover, they had outstretched wings and faced each other but their heads were looking down towards the cover.

The total amount of gold used in the sanctuary was about 1 metric ton, the silver amounted to about 3.4 metric tons, and the bronze came to about 2.4 metric tons. The priestly clothes were specially woven from the finest materials, using blue, purple and scarlet fabrics, and were very detailed and specific in what went where. Everything had significance and a profound meaning; for the priests it was a matter of life and death that they used the tabernacle in the correct way and also prepared themselves in the way they were instructed. For Christians today we understand that the way to God is open to every individual that God calls while at that time under the first covenant it was strictly restricted because of who was allowed to enter and when that entrance could be made.

As the author of Hebrews tells us, 'When everything had been arranged like this, the priests entered regularly into the outer room to carry on their duties, but only the high priest entered the inner room, and that only once a year, and never without blood, which he offered for himself and for the sins the people had committed in ignorance. The Holy Spirit was showing by this that the way into the Most Holy Place had not yet been disclosed as long as the first tabernacle was still standing. This is an illustration for the present time, indicating that the gifts and sacrifices being offered were not able to clear the conscience of the worshipper.

'They are only a matter of food and drink and various ceremonial washings—external regulations applying until the time of the new order. When Christ came as high priest of the good things that are already here, he went through the greater and more perfect tabernacle that isn't man-made, that is to say, not a part of this creation. He didn't enter by means of the blood of goats and calves; but he entered the Most Holy Place once for all by his own blood, having obtained eternal redemption.'

When it was finished Moses came to inspect it. He examined the tent and all the furnishings, clasps, frames, crossbars, posts and bases; the covering of ram skins dyed red, hides of sea mammals, and all the curtains. He checked the gold lamp stand and the oil for the light, the gold altar, the anointing oil, the fragrant incense, the bronze altar with its bronze grating, the ark of the Testimony with its poles and atonement cover, all the poles to move the contents of the tabernacle, the basin with its stand, ropes and tent pegs for the courtyard, the woven clothes for those serving in the sanctuary and the special clothes for Aaron the priest and his sons.

Moses congratulated them on doing the work well and faithfully following all the instructions to the letter. When it was all erected the glory of God in a cloud settled on it. During the night the cloud had the appearance of fire. Whenever the Israelites had to move they would know because the cloud would be lifted but as long as the cloud remained there they would stay.

Two special silver trumpets were made for calling the community together and for having the camps move out. This is how they were used: When both sounded the whole community was to assemble at the entrance to the Tent of Meeting, if only one is sounded just the leaders and heads of the tribes of Israel were to assemble. When a trumpet blast was sounded the tribes camped on the east were to set out, when a second blast was given the camps on the south were to set out. It was the responsibility of the sons of Aaron, the priests, to blow the trumpets. If they were going out to battle the trumpet would sound. Also at the times of their appointed feasts they were to sound the trumpet.

Paul wrote of a time when the trumpet will sound and the dead will be raised imperishable, and we, whether alive or dead, will be changed. And John wrote of the seven angels who had each a trumpet and were prepared to sound them. 'The seventh angel sounded his trumpet, and there were loud voices in heaven, which said: "The kingdom of the world has become the kingdom of our Lord and of his Christ, and he will reign forever."'

On the 20th day of the 2nd month of the 2nd year, the cloud lifted from above the tabernacle. The Israelites then set out from the Desert of Sinai and travelled from place to place until the cloud came to rest in the Desert of Paran. Those chosen to carry the tabernacle moved out first so that it could be set up before the others arrived, this heavy responsibility was shared amongst the tribes.

Moses said to Hobab, the grandson of Jethro, his father-in-law, "We're setting out for the promised land. Come with us and we'll treat you well, God has promised good things to Israel."

"No, I won't go; I'm going back to my own land and to my own people."

"Please don't leave us, you know this area, you can be our eyes and you can tell us where it's best to camp. If you come with us we can share with you all the good things God gives us."

He agreed and they set off and travelled for three days. The ark of the covenant took the lead and the cloud of God was above them as they travelled.

When the ark would set out Moses would say, "Rise up, O Lord! May your enemies be scattered; may your foes run from you." And when it came to rest he would say, "Return O Lord, to the countless thousands of Israel."

All the Israelites, twenty years old and above, who were able to serve in the army were counted and the total number was 603,550.

About this time the people complained about the difficult conditions they were enduring, and because the Lord was angry at what they were saying he sent fire among them which resulted in some fatal casualties on the outskirts of the camp. Moses prayed to the Lord and the fire died down. They then called the place Taberah meaning *burning*.

Further trouble broke out when they demanded different food, "If only we had meat to eat," they complained, "We remember the free fish we used to eat in Egypt and the cucumbers, melons, leeks, onions and garlic; but now all we get is this manna!"

The Lord was extremely angry and Moses made his complaint as well, "Why have you brought this trouble on me? What have I done to displease you and have the burden of all these people on me? Did I conceive all these people? Did I give them birth? Why is it me that has to carry them like a nurse maid? Where am I going to get meat for all these people? They keep complaining to me, "Give us meat to eat!" This is too much for me, it's too heavy. If this is what I should expect, put me to death right now, you'll be doing me a favour."

The Lord said to Moses, "Bring me seventy men known to you as respected leaders and make them come to the Tent of Meeting and I will come down and speak to you there. I will take that Spirit that is in you and share it with them so that they can help you carry the weight of the people and you won't have to carry it alone."

Seventy of the leaders came and stood round the tent, then the Lord came down in the cloud and spoke to him, and he took of the Spirit that was on him and gave it to the seventy leaders and they immediately began speaking about God. However, Eldad and Medad, who were numbered with the seventy weren't there, they had stayed in the camp, yet the Spirit also came to them and they started speaking about God. A young man ran and told Moses what had happened and Joshua said to Moses, "My Lord, stop them!"

But Moses replied, "Are you trying to protect my position? I wish that all the Lord's people were prophets and that the Lord would put his Spirit on them!"

"Tell the people," God told Moses, "Get ready for tomorrow; you're going to eat meat! And it won't be just for one or two days, but for a whole month—until you're stuffed with it and are sick of the sight of it. Because you regretted leaving Egypt and you've rejected me through all your complaints."

But Moses said, "There's over 600,000 adult men here and we don't have enough flocks and herds to feed them, even if we killed all of them. I doubt if we'd have enough even if we caught all the fish in the sea."

"Is the Lord's arm too short?" God answered. "You will now see whether or not what I say will come true for you."

A strong wind drove quail in from the sea and brought them down all around the camp to a depth of about three feet and covered the whole area as far as a day's walk in any direction. For the next two days the people were out gathering quail and everyone had more than they needed. But even while they were in the process of gorging themselves on the meat the Lord in his anger struck them with a severe plague. They called the place Kibroth Hattaavah meaning *graves of craving* because it was there that they buried those who craved other food.

This critical attitude went to the very top when Aaron and Miriam were talking against Moses because he had married a Cushite, a person of a different ethnic background. "Is Moses the only person God speaks through?" they said to each other, "He's spoken through us as well." And the Lord heard this private conversation. The Lord called all three of them to come to the Tent of Meeting and he came down in a pillar of cloud at the entrance to the Tent and asked Aaron and Miriam to step forward, "Listen to what I say," he said. "When one of my prophets is with you, I reveal myself to him in visions and dreams. But this isn't true regarding Moses, who is faithful in all my house. With him I speak face to face, clearly and not obscurely; he sees my form. Why weren't you afraid to speak against my servant Moses?"

Then the Lord who was angry left them.

Being critical of others is normal; being critical of leaders is to be expected as their flaws and failings may be know of by so many more people. All humans get criticised and the well known names in the Bible are no exception. 'All have sinned' wrote Paul, 'and fall short of the glory of God.' In one of David's psalms, which are prayers to be set to music, circumstances were getting the better of him and he wrote that he felt he was up to his neck in water and sinking; he was worn out calling for help, and God didn't seem to be near at all. There were more people who hated him without reason, he wrote, than the number of hairs on his head.

A man who faced aggressive criticism almost non-stop was Jesus, and that came to him mainly because he exposed the religious hypocrites for what they were and he also condemned their traditions as being more man-made than God-given. In speaking to his disciples about the reaction they should expect from this world, including much of what would come to be called the Christian world, he said, "If the world hates you, keep in mind that it hated me first. If you belonged to the world, it would love you as its own. As it is, you do not belong to the world, but I have chosen you out of the world. That is why the world hates you. Remember the words I spoke to you: 'No servant is greater than his master.' If they persecuted me, they will persecute you also. If they obeyed my teaching, they will obey yours also.

"They will treat you this way because of my name, for they do not know the One who sent me. If I had not come and spoken to them, they would not be guilty of sin. Now, however, they have no excuse for their sin. He who hates me hates my Father as well. If I had not done among them what no-one else did, they would not be guilty of sin. But now they have seen these miracles, and yet they have hated both me and my Father.

But this is to fulfil what is written in their Law: 'They hated me without reason.'"

When the cloud lifted above the Tent, Miriam stood there white or more accurately flaky, like snow, Aaron looked open mouthed at her leprous condition and he turned to Moses saying, "Please my lord, we've been so foolish in our sin; don't let her remain in this frightful condition." Moses too was shocked at what happened to Miriam and he called to the Lord, "O God, please heal her!"

And the Lord told Moses, "If she had been spat in the face by her own father, she still would need to go outside the camp for a week. Her condition demands that she be removed and confined outside the camp for the same time; after that she can be brought back."

The camp didn't move until Miriam was brought back in.

After that the people left where they were and encamped further north, near the border of Canaan.

Philip H. Eveson in his book, 'The beauty of Holiness' a commentary on Leviticus writes, 'Aaron did not want his leprous sister Miriam to be like one born dead with their flesh half eaten. Nothing so unwholesome was fit to exist in the clean camp, and a person associated with such an unclean state was disqualified from worshipping the holy God who is set apart from all that is unclean and unwholesome.' A few pages later Eveson writes, 'These outward requirements reminded the people of what happened when the first human couple sinned and were removed from the paradise of God.'

Aaron's eldest sons, Nadab and Abihu, who were consecrated for priestly work took their censers, put fire in them and added incense and then offered it to the Lord. There were regulations on exactly how and when it should be done and they knew what these rules were. In some way the two of them on that day did it differently; what it was we don't know, but that alteration cost them their lives when a blast of fire killed them both.

Aaron was speechless and Moses organised two relatives to remove the bodies and take them outside the camp. Then Moses said to Aaron and his two remaining sons, Eleazar and Ithamar, "Don't let your hair become unkempt, and don't tear your clothes (demonstrating grief over a death), or you will die and the Lord will be angry with the whole community. But your relatives, all the house of Israel, may mourn for those the Lord has destroyed by fire and don't leave the entrance to the Tent of Meeting or you will die because the Lord's anointing oil is on you." So they did as Moses said.

Then the Lord said to Aaron, "You and your sons are not to drink wine or other fermented drink whenever you go into the Tent of Meeting, or you will die. You must distinguish between the holy and the common, between the unclean and the clean, and you must teach the Israelites all the decrees the Lord has given them through Moses."

The writer of the letter of Hebrews wrote that, 'The ministry Jesus has received is as superior to theirs as the covenant of which he is mediator is superior to the old one, and is founded on better promises.' What happened to Nadab and Abihu shouldn't be filed under 'no longer applicable' because God remains just as zealous for the truth and the honour of his name today as he was then. In the seven letters John was inspired to write and is contained in the book called Revelation there are extremely serious warnings addressed to the church, anywhere and anytime, although originally written for just seven churches in western Turkey.

There is a pattern to these letters that begins with some detail about the head of the church—Jesus, and acknowledgements of the good things they're doing, then a warning to the majority of them of their need to repent, then there follows a promise of what their reward will be if they remain faithful. If we focus on the need to repent within these short letters we'll see that its importance is even greater than doing the correct duty in the correct and proscribed way back in the days of the Tabernacle, and that brought a death sentence if it wasn't done correctly! These warnings refer to more than our physical lives.

To the church in Ephesus Jesus says, "Remember the height from which you have fallen! Repent and do the things you did at first. If you don't repent, I will come to you and remove your lampstand from its place (the lampstand made for the Tabernacle was stylized to look like a tree that gives out light from its seven lamps).

To the church in Smyrna Jesus says, "Be faithful, even to the point of death, and I will give you the crown of life."

To the church in Pergamum Jesus says, "Repent therefore! Otherwise, I will soon come to you and will fight against them (those holding to the teaching of Balaam, and the teaching of the Nicolaitans) with the sword of my mouth."

To the church in Thyatira Jesus says, "I have given her (that woman Jezebel, who calls herself a prophetess) time to repent of her immorality, but she is unwilling."

To the church in Sardis Jesus says, "So, remember what you've received and heard; obey it, and repent. But if you don't wake up, I will come like a thief, and you will not know at what time I will come to you."

To the church in Philadelphia Jesus says, "I am coming soon. Hold on to what you have, so that no-one will take your crown (as in the message to the church in Smyrna there is no call for repentance to the Christians at Philadelphia).

To the church in Laodicea Jesus says, "Those whom I love I rebuke and discipline. So be earnest, and repent."

The book of Revelation, as these letters show, is steeped in Old Testament references that are gleaned from Genesis and throughout the whole of the Old Testament. These short letters are written to encourage

Christians to be faithful and awake to the dangers that are always present just as it were for the ancient Israelites. The church is in the world but should not be a part of it; they represent another country and another government.

The repetition of the call to repentance is consistent with John the Baptist's call to "Repent, for the kingdom of heaven is near." And when Jesus began his preaching he said, "Repent, for the kingdom of heaven is near." Later he would add that "unless you repent, you too will all perish," and, as if for emphasis, he repeated it when he spoke of the eighteen who died when the tower in Siloan fell on them (Siloam was the location of a water reservoir for Jerusalem on the south and east walls of the city).

At the close of the letter to the Christians in Smyrna Jesus says, "He who overcomes will not be hurt at all by the second death." People are taught in their millions that the wicked will live in hell forever, but here we read of a second death, not a second life, which is exactly how Paul put it when he told the Romans, 'the wages of sin is death,' earlier he had written, 'whether you are slaves to sin, which leads to death . . .' Suffering in flames for ever is an alien import and needs to be deported back to the demon-inspired imaginations that have successfully made it a fundamental teaching for many. This teaching reflects the character of the enemy—the dragon and his fate and not God's character and the fate of the lost.

That second death is to be burned to ashes as Nadab and Abihu were, and was the fate of the people who in lived in the cities of the plain in the time of Abraham and Lot. If a branch is thrown into a furnace there is no need to wonder what happens to it, it's as obvious to us as it was to those who used it figuratively in Scripture as an illustration of what will happen to the wicked.

Jesus paid in full the death sentence that hung over us. He paid that debt instead of us, and what he did was acted out once a year for the Israelites in their desert home. On that special day of the tenth day of the seventh month Aaron was to offer a bull to cover his own, and his families' sins, then he was to bring two goats to the entrance to the Tent of Meeting, one of these goats was to be sacrificed for all the people and on the other goat he was to lay both hands on its head and confess over it all the wickedness and rebellion of the Israelites—it was as if all their sins were now on the goat's head—it now became the guilty one.

This goat, loaded down with the nations' accumulated sins, was taken away into the desert by a capable man and released out there far away from the camp. Both of these goats pictured what a high price Jesus paid to release us from God's righteous judgment on our sins; his life was taken violently from him and he was abandoned and far away from God, separated by the sins he carried; his relationship with his Father shattered. When it was all finished and done, his body taken down from the cross and placed in the new tomb where he remained there dead for three days and was then resurrected as the sun set on the Sabbath; he was the first to experience what still lies ahead for all who belong to him. 'The dead will hear the voice of the Son of God and those who hear will live.'

Paul, in his second letter to the Thessalonians, describes what will happen to those who are rebellious and disobedient, ' . . . They will be punished with everlasting destruction (this destruction is permanent and irreversible) and shut out from the presence of the Lord and from the majesty of his power.' Just as one goat was destroyed and the other taken far away in that ancient rite carried out once a year on the Day of Atonement, so the enemies of God will be both destroyed and completely shut away from God. Being dead will accomplish both of these sentences.

Christians are encouraged by those who teach eternal suffering to take the time to educate those they are sharing the gospel with into the theology of hell and to try to awaken them; here's a short extract, "Do you know what hell is like? There's weeping and gnashing of teeth, unending thirst, mind consuming pain, no ground or foundation (the sensation of always falling), and it lasts forever." This is from a booklet on how to share your faith. For a more detailed examination of what the Bible does teach about hell see the chapter on hell in my book 'The Dragon the World and the Christian.' Other commonly held beliefs held by millions are also addressed in that book.

8

Almost There

"Send a representative," Moses said, "from each of the twelve tribes to reconnoitre the land." these are their names:

1. Shammau from the tribe of Reuben, son of Jacob
2. Shaphat .... Simeon .... Jacob
3. Caleb .... Judah .... Jacob
4. Igal .... Issachar .... Jacob
5. Joshua .... Ephraim, the son of Joseph
6. Palti .... Benjamin .... Jacob
7. Gaddiel .... Zebulun .... Jacob
8. Gaddi .... Manasseh, the son of Joseph
9. Ammiel .... Dan .... Jacob
10. Sethur .... Asher .... Jacob
11. Nahbi .... Naphtali .... Jacob
12. Geuel .... Gad .... Jacob

It's commonly taught and understood that Moses, under God, led the Jews out of Egypt, this is true, but also misleading as the Jews (from the name Judah) were only from one tribe of Israel, and in the future history of Israel, after the nation split into two nations, there was ongoing conflict between Judah (Jews) and Israel (non-Jews). When the Jews returned from Babylonian captivity, they were comprised of three tribes; Judah, Levi and Benjamin, who were collectively known as Jews; the other tribes didn't return from their resettlement. No Jews existed before the tribe of Judah came into being.

"Go up through the Negev and on into the hill country," Moses told them. "Find out what the land is like and how populated it is, and where do they live? What kind of towns and cities are there—are they fortified or not? Is the soil good or poor? Do your best to bring back a sample of some of the fruit growing there."

They began their journey and came to Hebron where the descendents of Anak lived. These people, who were over nine foot tall lived in well fortified towns. In the Valley of Eshcol the twelve spies cut down a single cluster of grapes which they needed two men to carry it on a pole between them. At the end of forty days they returned to the people to give their report on what they saw.

Their report began very positively. It was indeed, they said, a land that flowed with 'milk and honey,' but, and it's a big but, we can't attack these people—they're too strong for us, the cities are fortified and large, just like the people who live there (these descendents of Anak and the Nephilim go back to the earliest times of mankind. The Moabites called them Emim, meaning the terrible or frightening ones—there were different names for the same people—some called them Rephaites but they were all giants of men). As well as these, the report went on. They saw the Amalekites, the Hittites, Jebusites and Amorites, not forgetting the Canaanites!

Then Caleb, unwilling to listen to any more of this defeatist talk spoke up and said, "We should go up and take this land. We can really do it!"

"We can't attack these people," the others who had explored the land said, "They're much stronger than us!" This negative news spread around the camp and before long they were raising their voices in despair and anger against Moses and Aaron who soon heard the people's opinion, "If only we had died in Egypt! Or in the desert! What's the point of God bringing us here only to be killed by the sword? Our wives and children are going to be taken captive—it would be better for us to return to Egypt than move forward to our deaths—let's choose a leader and go back to Egypt."

Moses and Aaron were shocked and lay face down on the ground in front of everyone, and Caleb and Joshua felt the same horror at what the people were saying and tore their clothes and said to all there, "This land we passed through is excellent land, and if the Lord is pleased with us he will lead us and give us this good land. But we mustn't rebel against the Lord—don't be afraid, it doesn't matter what we've seen, the Lord is with us, they don't have a chance of beating us; they have no protection against God."

The feeling of the people was so against moving into Canaan that they talked of killing those who were for it. At that moment the glory of the Lord appeared at the Tent of Meeting, and the Lord said to Moses, "How long will these people treat me with contempt? How long will they refuse to believe in me, in spite of all the miraculous signs I have shown them? I'll destroy all of them, and make you into a greater and stronger nation than them."

"Then the Egyptians will hear about it," Moses said to the Lord, "and all the other nations know that you are with this people, they know about the pillar of cloud by day and the pillar of fire by night, and if you put these people to death these other nations will say that you were not able to bring this people into the land that you had promised them on oath. You've revealed yourself as slow to anger, abounding in love and forgiving sin and rebellion. And you do not leave the guilty unpunished—you punish the children for the sin of the fathers to the third and fourth generation. Because of your great love, forgive the sin of these people, just as you've been doing since we left Egypt."

"I have forgiven them, as you asked, nevertheless, not one of the men who saw my glory and the miraculous signs I did in Egypt and in the desert, and then disobeyed me and tested me ten times—not one of them will ever see the land that I promised to their forefathers. No-one who has treated me with contempt will ever see it. Caleb and Joshua had a different attitude completely and they followed me with all their heart, I'll bring them into the land they explored, and their descendants will inherit it. Tomorrow morning, turn around and head back towards the Sea of Reeds."

The Lord spoke to Moses and Aaron and told them to tell "these wicked grumblers that as they had feared that they would die in this desert that is what will happen. Every one of you twenty years old or more and who has grumbled against me will die in this desert. And your children, that you said will be taken captive, they will enjoy the land that you rejected. You will be shepherds here for forty years, suffering because of your unfaithfulness, until the last of you are dead. For forty years—one year for each of the forty days you explored the land. You will suffer for your sins and know what it is like to have me against you."

Those men responsible for spreading the negative report were struck down with plague and died, only Joshua and Caleb survived.

When the Israelites learned of what happened they determined to make a change; first, by saying that they've sinned, and secondly, by strapping on their weapons and doing what they should have done before.

But Moses told them that it was reckless presumption to think that they could disobey the Lord's command and still be victorious. They went ahead anyway and faced the Amalekites and Canaanites who lived in the hill country and were soundly beaten and had to retreat all the way back to Hormah.

While the Israelites were in the desert, a man was found gathering wood on the seventh day. He was brought to Moses and was put into custody until they knew exactly what they should do with him. The Lord said to Moses, "The man must die. The whole assembly must stone him outside the camp." This was done as the Lord commanded. When Moses was with the Lord on the mountain he was given the rule that they must observe the Sabbath, because it is to be a different day from the other days. Anyone who deliberately ignores this ruling must be put to death, and he gave the example of a person working on that day having to be put to death because it was a sign between God and the Israelites that pointed back to creation where God himself stopped his work and rested.

One of the psalms speak of entering God's rest as a personal closeness with God, 'Today, if you hear his voice, do not harden your hearts as you did at Meribah, as you did that day at Massah in the desert, where your fathers tested and tried me, though they had seen what I did. For forty years I was angry at that generation; I said, "They are people whose hearts go astray, and they haven't known my ways." So I declared an oath in my anger, "They shall never enter my rest."

The writer of the letter to the Hebrews lays great stress on that 'rest,' he mentions it thirteen times and brings that old psalm into his contemporary context. Entering the Promised Land was to be a type of rest for the Israelites—no longer having to wander in the harshness of the desert, but there is coming a place and a time for an even greater rest that goes beyond just one nation. This is what he writes: 'Who were they who heard and rebelled? Were they not all those Moses led out of Egypt? And who was he angry with for forty years? Wasn't it with those who sinned, whose bodies fell in the desert?

'And to who did God swear to that they would never enter his rest— it was to those who disobeyed. So we see that they were not able to enter, because of their unbelief.

'The promise of entering God's rest still stands, so we need to be careful that we don't fall short of it. We've had the good news preached to us, just as they had, but the message they heard was of no value to them, because they didn't combine it with faith, but we who do believe enter that rest. The words spoken at the end of the creation of the world was, "And on the seventh day God rested from his work." And God said to the disobedient Israelites, "They shall never enter my rest," which was taken up by the psalmist, as quoted above.

'It still remains that some will enter that rest, and those long ago who had the good news spoken to them did not go in, because of their disobedience. So again God set a certain day, and he called it 'Today.' Many years later God spoke through David when he said, "Today, if you hear his voice, don't harden your hearts." If Joshua had given the people rest, God wouldn't have spoken later about another day.

'There still remains then a Sabbath-rest for the people of God, because anyone who enters God's rest also rests from their own work, just as God did from his. So let's make every effort to enter that rest, so that no-one will fall by following their example of disobedience.'

Those words, 'make every effort' were used by Jesus when he said, "Make every effort to enter through the narrow door, because many will try to enter and will not be able to." In a similar statement he said, "Enter through the narrow gate. Because the gate that leads to destruction is wide and broad and many go through it, but the gate that leads to life is small and narrow and only a few find it."

The word 'Today' isn't referring to a day of the week; people can be just as legalistic about Sunday worship as they can about Saturday worship, while at the same time saying that they are against legalism. They can recognise the legalism in others but rarely in themselves. The Sabbath lay at the heart of the old covenant, but that covenant is now obsolete ('By calling this covenant "new" he has made the first one obsolete; and what is obsolete and ageing will soon disappear'), and has been replaced by the new covenant of the Spirit rather than the letter. The 'Today' is now, this moment. Today, if you hear God's voice, don't harden your heart, listen and obey.

(Warning: this does not apply to voices from within, or the reasonable and authoritative voices of church leaders; this listening applies to an individual reading directly from God's word without the aid of anyone else. Two examples might help; Eve was not pressured or frightened into eating the fruit from the tree of good and evil, she was intellectually challenged to discover for herself whether she should or shouldn't eat it but the suggestion that prompted her action came from the 'evil one'. She was deceived by the serpent's cunning. Paul, very aware of Satan's schemes, wrote to the Corinthians for the second time saying, 'For such men (who were deceiving Christians) are false apostles, deceitful workmen, masquerading as apostles of Christ. And no wonder, for Satan himself masquerades as an angel of light. It is not surprising, then, if his servants masquerade as servants of righteousness. Their end will be what their actions deserve.')

The 'rest' we read of isn't idleness or going to heaven or a laid back attitude to life but the relief from a life that mirrors the history of the ancient Israelites who were in God's words, 'a disobedient and obstinate people.' We are prone to follow their example as we all share the same sinful nature which, however difficult it is to acknowledge, is hostile to God and does not submit to God's law, neither can it do so. Jesus expressed the radical change that comes to a person when God draws them to see that sinful nature for what it is.

"Blessed are the poor in spirit, for theirs is the kingdom of heaven," has nothing to do with how much money we have in our bank balance but in the attitude of our mind when we see our spiritual destitution. If we can acknowledge that spiritual poverty we can then say 'I was blind but now I see,' this is a spiritual comprehension that comes from God, just as "Blessed are those who mourn" isn't referring to the normal sadness and grief that humans experience but to the realisation of that sinful nature that stands against God, in ourselves and in others. Ezekiel wrote of a man with a writing kit at his side who was commanded by God to go throughout the city of Jerusalem and put a mark on the foreheads of those who grieve and lament over all the detestable things that are done in it. James wrote of sinners needing to grieve, mourn and wail; to change their laughter to mourning and their joy to gloom—to humble themselves before the Lord and he will lift them up.

Under the old covenant things had to be done by the right people, at the right time, in the right way and in the right place. This came from God and it was good. No other nation had God to lead and teach them. But their hearts were not in it. It became just outward ritual, and God knew that it was the heart that needed to change. The rituals pointed to something greater that was to come. As the writer of Hebrews tells us, 'The law is only a shadow of the good things that are coming—not the realities themselves.'

Paul also expressed this difference in the two covenants in his letter to the Colossians, 'So don't let anyone judge you over what you eat and drink or in regard to a religious festival, a new moon celebration or a Sabbath day. These are a shadow of the things that were to come; the reality, however, is found in Christ.'

In the words of Jeremiah, 'The time is coming, declares the Lord, when I will make a new covenant with the house of Israel and with the house of Judah. It will not be like the covenant I made with their forefathers when I took them by the hand to lead them out of Egypt, because they broke my covenant, though I was a husband to them. This is the covenant that I will make with the house of Israel after that time. I will put my law in their minds and write it on their hearts. I will be their God and they will be my people.' Ezekiel compared this new covenant to being sprinkled with clean water, and given a new heart and a new spirit, in other words, a new and better mind and attitude, a different heart, as Caleb and Joshua had when they trusted that God would do what he had promised.

Jesus said, "Come to me, all you who are weary and burdened, and I'll give you rest. Put on my yoke and learn from me, for I'm gentle and humble in heart, and you will find rest for your life. Because my burden is easy and it's light." That is the rest we are called to in this life and beyond that, eternal life, but it's not rest in heaven but in a restored earth ruled over by the Messiah and all those whose heart God has washed and changed, the Joshuas and Calebs of the old covenant as well as the disciples of Christ.

9

Entry Denied

Korah, a Levite, and certain Reubenites—Dathan, Abiram and On became rebellious and opposed Moses and Aaron. There were 250 community leaders in support of them and they all came to Moses and Aaron and said, "You've gone too far!" All of us are holy, we're all set apart for God's work, so why do you set yourself above the rest of us?"

"In the morning," Moses said to Korah and those with him, "the Lord will show who belongs to him and who is holy, and he will make that person come near him. You Korah, and all your followers are to take censers and tomorrow put fire and incense in them before the Lord. You Levites have crossed a line! Who is Aaron that you should make this complaint against him, he's a Levite too and you Levites have been given the great responsibility and honour of serving in the Lord's tabernacle, but now you want the priesthood as well!"

Then Moses summoned Dathan and Eliab, but they refused to come. "We won't come! You brought us all this way into the desert to kill us and now you still want to be in charge? You haven't taken us into this new land where we can get fields and vineyards. You're just deceiving us! No, we're not coming!"

Moses filled with anger said to the Lord not to accept their offering, "I haven't taken anything from them or wronged them in any way."

Moses again said to Korah, You and your followers, and Aaron, are to present your censers before the Lord tomorrow morning.

The next morning Korah and his supporters met at the entrance to the Tent of Meeting where the glory of the Lord appeared to all of them. The whole assembly was there to see it. The Lord said to Moses and Aaron, "make some space between you and them. I'm going to kill them right now."

But Moses and Aaron fell face down and pleaded with God, "O God, God of the spirits of all mankind, will you kill everyone when only one man sins?"

God then told Moses to tell this massive crowd to move away from the tents of Korah, Dathan and Abiram. He knew that God intended to act violently and he walked to their tents where they stood outside the entrances of their tents with all their family members, and he said to everyone who could hear, "What you're going to see will convince you that God has sent me to do what I've done and that it wasn't my idea. What you see happen is because these men treated the Lord with contempt."

The next moment the earth beneath them began opening up and those three men and all who were with them as well as their tents disappeared into the ground, while everyone else stood back and ran as fast as they could believing that they too were going to be swallowed up, some turned and watched as the earth just as quickly closed up and silenced the screams that came from below. God's fire then came and incinerated the 250 men who had allied themselves with Korah. The records show that some of Korah's family did distance themselves from him because his family line didn't die out.

The Lord instructed Moses to tell Eleazar, Aaron's son, to go over the smouldering remains and retrieve the bronze censers from the men who sinned, because they were made for a holy purpose, and hammer them into sheets to overlay the altar, as they still will have a holy use. No-one except a descendant of Aaron was allowed to burn incense before the Lord or they'll end up like Korah and his followers.

More complaints erupted the next day when Moses and Aaron were charged with killing God's people. Their grumblings came to a halt when they saw the glory of the Lord covering the Tent of Meeting. Moses and Aaron went to the entrance and the Lord said to them, "Move away from this assembly so that I can put an end to them." And they fell face down.

Moses told Aaron, "Put incense on your censer and fire from the altar and run to the people so you can make atonement for them because the Lord is showing his anger and the plague has begun. Aaron stood between the living and the dead while he offered the incense and made atonement for them. The plague did stop but by then 14,700 people had died.

Atonement means restoring a relationship with God. It involves reconciliation and the sacrificial system practised under the old covenant was done to provide a regular reminder of sins, even though it's impossible for the blood of bulls and goats to take away sins it was required to be done in restoring that relationship. The writer of Hebrews quotes one of David's psalms where it says, 'Sacrifice and offering you did not desire, but a body you prepared for me; with burnt offerings and sin offerings you were not pleased. Then I said, "Here I am—it is written about me in the scroll—I have come to do your will, O God."'

'First he said, 'Sacrifices and offerings, burnt offerings and sin offerings you did not desire, nor were you pleased with them' (although the law required them to be made). Then he said, 'Here I am, I have come to do your will.' And by that will, we have been made holy through the sacrifice of the body of Jesus Christ once for all.'

He had earlier said, 'But now he has appeared once for all at the end of the ages to do away with sin by the sacrifice of himself. Just as man is destined to die once, and after that to face judgment, so Christ was sacrificed once to take away the sins of many people; and he will appear a second time, not to bear sin, but to bring salvation to those who are waiting for him.'

Paul, in his second letter to the Corinthians wrote 'that God was reconciling the world to himself through Christ, not counting men's sins against them. And he has committed to us the message of reconciliation. We are therefore Christ's ambassadors, as though God were making his appeal through us. We implore you on Christ's behalf: Be reconciled to God. God made him who had no sin to be sin for us, so that in him we might become the righteousness of God,'

It was time to put an end to this constant grumbling over what family should have responsibility for the work within the Tent of the Testimony. So Moses told the Israelites to collect twelve staffs from the leaders of the twelve tribes and write the name of each man on the staffs. The tribe of Levi would have Aaron's name on it. Moses was then to place all the staffs before the Lord in the Tent; and the staff belonging to the one God chooses will sprout. The next day Moses entered the Tent and saw that Aaron's staff had not only sprouted but budded and blossomed and actually produced almonds!

Moses brought all the staffs out so that each man could claim his own and that all saw what had happened to Aaron's staff. The Lord said to Moses, "Put Aaron's staff inside the Tent in front of the Testimony. This will put an end to their rebellious grumbling against me. So Moses put it there as a sign for the people.

The Israelites, knowing that God is dangerous if he is approached in the wrong way said to Moses that they thought that they'll all die, "We're lost; we're all lost! Anyone who comes near the Tabernacle of the Lord will die. Are we all going to die?" They'd seen many of the leaders of their people die, but had they learned the lesson? Did they understand?

10

Thirst

It was the first month of the year, Nisan, and the whole community of Israelites arrived at the Desert of Zin, south-east of Canaan. They stayed at Kadesh and it was there that Miriam died and was buried.

There was no water there and opposition to Moses and Aaron rose yet again. "If only we had died when our brothers fell dead before the Lord! Why did you bring us here into this desert—all of us are going to die here? Why did you bring us out of Egypt to this terrible place? It has no grain or figs, grapevines or pomegranates and there's no water to drink!"

Moses and Aaron went directly to the entrance of the Tent of Meeting and fell face down, and the glory of the Lord appeared to them, and Moses was told to take the staff and you and your brother gather everyone together then speak to the rock that's before them and it will pour out its water so that they and their livestock can drink.

When they all got to the rock Moses said to them, "Listen, you rebels, must we bring you water out of the rock?" Then Moses, instead of speaking to the rock, he struck it twice with his staff. Water gushed out and they and their livestock drank.

God then said to the both of them, "You didn't trust me enough to honour me as holy in front of everyone, so you will not bring the Israelites into the land that I'll give them." These were the waters of Meribah, which means quarrelling.

Near the end of his life Moses pleaded with the Lord, and recorded his words, "O Sovereign Lord, you've begun to show to me your greatness and your strong hand. For what god is there in heaven or on earth who can do the deeds and mighty works you do? Let me go over and see the good land beyond the Jordan—that fine hill country and Lebanon." But because of you the Lord was angry with me and wouldn't listen to me. "That's enough," the Lord said. "Don't speak to me anymore about this matter." Moses went on to say, "Don't add to what I command you and don't subtract from it, but keep the commands of the Lord your God that I give you." At Meribah he, in his anger, had added to what God had told him to do at great personal cost to him because God doesn't show favouritism.

From Kadesh Moses sent messengers to the king of Edom, saying: 'This is what your brother Israel says: You know about all the hardships that have happened to us. Now we're at Kadesh, a town on the boarder of your territory. Please let us pass through your country. We'll not go through any field or vineyard, or drink water from any well. We'll travel the king's highway and not deviate from that route until we've passed your territory."

Moses received the king's reply; "You are not to pass through here; if you try, we'll march out with our weapons and attack you."

The Israelites replied: "We'll go along the main road, and if we or our livestock drink any of your water, we'll pay for it. We only want to pass through on foot, nothing else."

They received a further answer; "You may not pass through."

The Edomites came out in a show of force, and since that way was closed to them, Israel turned and went in another direction. After travelling north a short distance they came to Mount Hor and the Lord told Moses to call Aaron and his son and take them up Mount Hor and when you're there take off Aaron's priestly clothes and put them on his son, Eleazar. Aaron died on top of the mount and Moses and Eleazar returned to the camp. When the people learned that Aaron was dead they mourned for him thirty days.

The Israelites continued north along the Way of the Atharim. The Canaanite king of Arad, which was further north, attacked the Israelites and captured some of them. At this, Israel made a vow to the Lord that if he delivers these attackers into their hands, they will totally destroy their cities. The Lord listened to their request and granted them victory and they completely destroyed them and their towns; so the place was named Hormah which means destruction.

11

Deadly Snakes

They travelled along the route to the Sea of Reeds, so that they could go round Edom, but this made the people very impatient and they spoke against God and against Moses. "Why have you brought us up out of Egypt to die in the desert? There's no bread! And there's no water! We detest this miserable food—manna!"

Later Moses was to write, 'Remember how the Lord your God led you all the way in the desert these forty years, to humble you and test you in order to know what was in your heart, whether or not you would keep his commands. He humbled you, causing you to hunger and then feeding you with manna, which neither you nor your fathers had known, to teach you that man doesn't live on bread alone but on every word that comes from the mouth of the Lord. Your clothes didn't wear out and your feet didn't swell during those forty years. So know in your heart that as a parent disciplines his child, so the Lord your God disciplines you.'

Poisonous snakes then began appearing in large numbers all over the camp. Its bite caused many people to die and they quickly came to Moses saying, "We've sinned. We shouldn't have been critical against the Lord and you. Pray that the Lord will take these snakes away from us." So Moses prayed for them, and the Lord said to him, "Make a bronze snake and attach it to a pole." When this was done those who were bitten by a snake were told to look at the bronze snake on the pole and when they did they were healed.

About six centuries later a king named Hezekiah ruled in Jerusalem, and he was quite different from most of the other kings in that he 'trusted the Lord, the God of Israel. There was no-one like him among all the kings of Judah, either before him or after him. He held fast to the Lord and did not cease to follow him; he kept the commands the Lord had given Moses. And the Lord was with him; he was successful in whatever he undertook.'

This commendation of his rule is a summary and it needs to be remembered that like everyone else he sinned and didn't always make wise decisions, but like David, he did what was right in the eyes of the Lord. He removed the high places, which were pagan worship sites; he smashed the sacred stones and cut down the Asherah poles, which had to do with the Canaanite goddess and the objects that represented her. He also broke into pieces the bronze snake Moses had made, because up to that time the Israelites had been burning incense to it, having completely distorted its temporary purpose they had made it an object of worship.

It was night-time when Nicodemus, a Pharisee and a member of the Sanhedrin, the supreme ruling council of the Jews came to speak with Jesus, he said, "Rabbi, we know you are a teacher who has come from God. No-one could do the miracles that you've done if God wasn't with him."

"I tell you the truth, no-one can see the kingdom of God unless he is born from above."

"How can a man be born when he's old? He certainly can't enter his mother's womb a second time to be born!"

"I tell you the truth, no-one can enter the kingdom of God unless he is born of water and the Spirit. Flesh gives birth to flesh, but the Spirit gives birth to spirit. You shouldn't be surprised when I say you, including everyone else, must be born again. The wind blows wherever it pleases—you hear its sound, but you can't tell where it comes from or where it's going. It's the same with those born of the Spirit."

"How can this be?"

"You are Israel's teacher, and you don't understand these things? I'm telling you the truth, we speak of what we know, and we attest to what we've seen, but you, and those who are the religious leaders still don't accept what we say. I've spoken to of earthly things and you don't believe; how will you believe if I speak of heavenly things?

"No-one has ever gone into heaven except the one who came from heaven—the Son of Man. Just as Moses lifted up the snake in the desert, so the Son of Man must be lifted up, that everyone who believes in him may have eternal life."

For most Christians going to heaven is their hope, their focus and their dream; it will remain a dream because, as we've just read, Jesus said, 'no-one has ever gone into heaven.' The focus and hope of the people of God, both in the Old Testament and the New is the establishment of the kingdom of God, which will not come until the king of that kingdom returns. It is to that divine city and country that the men and women of faith looked forward to, not to leaving this earth.

It's impossible to say whether Nicodemus understood the link between the bronze snake attached to the pole and Jesus being lifted up, or did the words of Isaiah come into his mind? 'He was pierced for our transgressions, he was crushed for our iniquities; the punishment that brought us peace was upon him.' Or perhaps the words of Zechariah came into his vision, 'They will look on me, the one they had pierced, and they will mourn for him as one mourns for an only child, and grieve bitterly for him as one grieves for a firstborn son.' It's unlikely that any of these texts came into his mind anymore than they entered the mind of the disciples. After the crucifixion of Jesus those who witnessed it and saw what took place 'beat their breasts and went away.' And it was only after the resurrection that Jesus opened the disciple's minds so that they could understand how the Law of Moses, the prophets and the Psalms spoke of him.

Whatever Nicodemus thought, he saw Jesus as a teacher from God, and he was there when Jesus died; helping Joseph carefully take the body down from the cross. He had bought about seventy-five pounds in weight of myrrh and aloes, which they used in wrapping the body in strips of linen; this was in accordance with Jewish burial customs.

The Israelites went from one location to the next and eventually came from the desert to the valley in Moab where the top of Pisgah overlooks the wasteland. It was in this same area that Moses was later to die.

Israel sent a request, like the others, to King Sihon, the Amorite, asking that they may have permission to travel through his territory, but the answer, except for the Ammonites and the descendants of Esau, was like the other requests, no. "Set out and cross the Arnon River," God told Moses, "Sihon will lose this battle, even though he has his whole army with him. From today I will begin to put the terror and fear of you on all the people in this land. They'll hear reports of you and they'll tremble with fear." Sihon marched his entire army against Israel and they came together at Jahaz, and Israel put everyone to the sword and took over his land, so the Israelites settled in the land of Amorites.

The campaign continued as they headed north on the road to Bashan, and Og, the king, met them with his army in battle at Edrei, near the Yarmuk River. The Lord said to Moses, "Don't be afraid of him, he's yours, and his whole army, do the same to him as you did to Sihon, the Amorite." Og was the last of the Rephaites, who were giants, his iron bed, which was kept, was more than thirteen feet long and six feet wide!

By the end of the battle there were no enemy survivors, and they took control of the land.

These explicit commands given to Moses, and later to Joshua, have been cruelly distorted by some who somehow were convinced that what God had decreed for that time of conquest could be high-jacked and used against indigenous people by a so-called civilised power. This mindset has also been effectively used by bishops of the church, such as Athanasius and Augustine of Hippo, who provided a template of oppression for later bishops to quell all divergence from the authorised theological position. This was done by Rome and continued by Protestant leaders after the reformation. They were both unified in dealing with what they called heresy as if the command to destroy the Canaanites was still in force.

However, the language of warfare and being fully armed, both defensively and offensively against a very real enemy is central to being a disciple of Christ. John wrote of only two groups of people; the children of God and the children of the devil, and that humanity is made up of those two groups. "We know," he wrote, "that the whole world is under the control of the evil one." As such, Christians are living in the enemies' territory and must, as Peter says, 'be self-controlled and alert. Your enemy the devil prowls around like a roaring lion looking for someone to devour. Resist him, standing firm in the faith, because you know that your brothers throughout the world are undergoing the same kind of sufferings.'

John was inspired to write about Satan, who is also called the dragon. This spiritual being is a real dragon that Michael and his angels fought against which resulted in the dragon and his angels being hurled to the earth. Jesus told his disciples that he witnessed that fall. This is good news for heaven but bad news for earth, 'Because of this victory rejoice, you heavens' (Which heaven? There are three: the earth's atmosphere, outer space and the spiritual domain; it doesn't really matter because he goes on to write) 'but woe to the earth and the sea, because the devil has gone down to you! He is filled with fury, because he knows that his time is short.'

That dragon is also called that ancient serpent, the devil and Satan. The next statement is often taken to apply to other faiths apart from Christianity, or heretical groups claiming to be Christian; it is neither of these. Here is what John wrote, 'Satan, who leads the whole world astray.' Jesus called him 'the prince of this world' at his last supper. Paul used a similar expression in his letter to the Ephesians: 'the ruler of the kingdom of the air, and 'the spirit who is now at work in those who are disobedient.' This 'prince' or 'ruler' uses deception to lead all people astray. It began with one woman in a garden, and now it's grown to include every single person on earth. This counterfeiting and distorting of what is true has continued in different guises from the beginning. And the church has been no exception. Remember what Paul told the Ephesian leadership; "I know that after I leave, savage wolves will come in among you and will not spare the flock. Even from your own number men will arise and distort the truth in order to draw away disciples after them. So be on your guard! Remember that for three years I never stopped warning each of you night and day with tears.'

The effectiveness of the dragon's deception is seen in that there are people who believe that Jesus is the Son of God and who rely on the love of God yet are divided through denominational differences. This division has set one brother in Christ against another who both claim the high ground in faithfulness to what God says, yet little realising that all fellowships have been affected and infected by the distortions that Paul warned of so long ago.

The Christian's relationship with God is through the person of Christ and isn't dependant on any ritual or date, time or place, as was the case under the old covenant, even though he was the one that led them, Paul wrote to the Corinthians saying, 'I don't want you to be ignorant of the fact that our forefathers were all under the cloud and that they all passed through the sea. They were all baptised into Moses in the cloud and in the sea. They all eat the same spiritual food and drank the same spiritual drink; for they drank from the spiritual rock that accompanied them, and that rock was Christ. Nevertheless, God was not pleased with most of them; their bodies were scattered over the desert.'

Under that covenant the people of God were given not only a 'Sabbath of rest, a day of sacred assembly', but seven annual Sabbaths that also were to be days of sacred assembly. These special days looked back to their liberation from slavery and forward to their entry into a country of their own. They were days of celebration for what was done for them and identified them as the people of God. These special days also prefigured the time when people of all races and backgrounds would be liberated from the slavery of sin and find spiritual rest in belonging to Christ. As well as this there is the sure hope of not just a new country, but a new world that will come at the sound of a greater trumpet than the Israelites had, yet they demonstrated time after time, through their rebellion and disobedience a heart and mind that was set against God, just as it naturally is for all of us, the Israelites were no exception.

The record of the Israelites show us that even when God intervenes directly on their behalf, they will, after a brief period of thankfulness, still rebel and quickly turn to other gods. One of the Psalms has, 'when our fathers were in Egypt, they gave no thought to your miracles; they didn't remember your many kindnesses, and they rebelled by the Sea of Reeds. Yet he saved them for his name's sake, to make his mighty power known. He rebuked the Sea of Reeds, and it dried up; he led them through the depths as through a desert. He saved them from the hand of the foe;

from the hand of the enemy he redeemed them. The waters covered their adversaries; not one of them survived. Then they believed his promises and sang his praise.

'But they soon forgot what he had done and didn't wait for his council. In the desert they gave in to their craving and in the wasteland they put God to the test so he gave them what they asked for, but added a wasting disease upon them. In the camp they grew envious of Moses and of Aaron, who was consecrated to the Lord. The earth opened up and swallowed Dathan; it buried the company of Abiram. Fire blazed among their followers; a flame consumed the wicked.

'At Horeb they made a calf and worshipped an idol cast from metal. They exchanged their Glory for the image of a bull, which eats grass. They forgot the God who saved them, who had done great things in Egypt, miracles in the land of Ham and awesome deeds by the Sea of Reeds. So he said he would destroy them—had not Moses, his chosen one, stood in the breach before him to keep his wrath from destroying them.

'Then they despised the pleasant land; they didn't believe his promise. They grumbled in their tents and didn't obey the Lord. So he swore to them with uplifted hand that he would make them fall in the desert and make their descendants fall among the nations and scatter them throughout the lands.'

The psalm continues but we need to return to when God was striking the leaders and the people of Canaan with fear as they heard what Israel was doing, and what one king decided to do to stop them.

12
Balak and Balaam

At the close of World War 1, as Winston Churchill noted, 'the world lifted its head, surveyed the scene of ruin, and victors and vanquished alike drew breath. In a hundred laboratories, in a thousand arsenals, factories, and bureaus, men pulled themselves up with a jerk, turned from the task in which they had been absorbed. Their projects were put aside unfinished, unexecuted; but their knowledge was preserved; their data, calculations, and discoveries were hastily bundled together and docketed 'for future reference' by the War Offices in every country.

'The campaign of 1919 was never fought; but its ideas go marching along. In every army they are being explored, elaborated, refined under the surface of peace, and should war come again to the world it is not with the weapons and agencies prepared for 1919 that it will be fought, but with developments and extensions of these which will be incomparably more formidable and fatal.'

The weapons available to the armies of 3,300 years ago were just as deadly, but basic in that they cut and smashed, but the end result was the same; the enemy was dead. When God fed the minds of those who were in the path of this tidal wave of Israelites with fear, they had to make their calculations as to their capability of going to war with these intruders.

King Balak of Moab knew what had happened to the two kings, Sihon and Og, and realised he needed extra help in defeating the Israelites because there were so many of them and the whole country was terrified. Both the Moabite and Midian leadership understood the danger their people were in so Balak came up with the idea of a new weapon that might accomplish what the sword couldn't. He was going to curse the Israelites, but this required a specialist, someone with a track record of successful curses.

Balak knew just the man for the job; his name was Balaam who lived at Pethor, near the Euphrates River. The invitation was delivered by a selection of Moabite and Midian princes who relayed the king's message to him, 'A people has come out of Egypt; they cover the face of the land and have settled next to me. Now come and put a curse on these people, because there're too powerful for me. Perhaps then I'll be able to drive them out of the country. I know that those you bless are blessed, and those you curse are cursed.'

There was also quite a substantial fee for Balaam and he invited them to spend the night at his house while he consulted the lord as to what he should do. But God said to Balaam, "Don't go with them. You mustn't put a curse on those people, because they're blessed."

The next morning Balaam told the princes, "Go back to your own country, because the Lord has refused to allow me to go with you." When the princes got back to Balak they told him that Balaam refused to come. Then Balak sent different princes, more higher ranking than the first, to persuade Balaam with an even greater financial incentive to come and curse the Israelites.

When Balaam received this second request he told his distinguished visitors, "Even if Balak gave me his palace filled with gold and silver, I still can't go beyond what God tells me, but stay the night and I'll find out if there's any more that God will tell me."

Balaam did receive a message from God which was that as these men had summoned him, he should go with them, "But only do what I tell you."

When Balaam set off with the princes of Moab, he couldn't, even with his special abilities, have foreseen what was about to happen. An angel of the Lord armed with a sword stood in his path, barring his way. The only eyes that saw the angel were those of the donkey who understandably veered out of the angel's way which annoyed Balaam who beat the donkey to get her back on the track. There was a narrow path between two vineyards with walls on both sides. When the donkey saw the angel she couldn't get away so she pressed herself against the wall hurting Balaam's foot and getting another beating. For a third time the angel positioned itself in a narrow place where it was impossible to change direction so the donkey just collapsed under Balaam and refused to move.

Balaam was so angry that he beat his donkey with his staff, and then, the Lord opened the donkey's mouth! "What have I done to you to make you beat me three times?"

"You've made a fool of me! If I had a sword I'd kill you right now."

"I'm your donkey that you've always ridden. I haven't done this before, have I?"

"No," Balaam answered.

Then Balaam's eyes were opened to see the armed angel standing in their way. Balaam quickly fell face down to the ground. The angel asked Balaam why he had beaten his donkey three times, "Your donkey saw me and if she didn't stop I would definitely have killed you, but I would have spared her." No record of what the donkey thought of this exists!

"I've sinned. I didn't realise you were there blocking our way. If you want me to go back, I will."

"Go with these men, but only say what I tell you to say."

When Jesus told his disciples how hard it is for a rich man to enter the kingdom of God, he was asked, "Who then can be saved?" and Jesus replied, "What is impossible with men is possible with God." "For nothing is impossible with God," as the angel told Mary about the child she would have even though she was a virgin. The dead were raised, peoples' sight and hearing were restored, storms were stilled, the hungry feed, the lame walked and lepers were healed, and a donkey spoke.

On hearing that Balaam was on his way, Balak went to meet him at the Moabite town on the Arnon border, at the edge of his territory. "I sent an urgent summons, why didn't you come?"

"Well, I'm here now." Balaam replied.

After sacrifices were done Balak took Balaam to a high point where they could see some of the Israelites. Balaam wanted seven altars built and seven bulls and seven rams where one of each was offered on each altar. Then Balaam said to Barak, "You stay here, I'm going to move away a distance and wait for the Lord to reveal to me what I should say and whatever I hear I'll tell you. God did speak to him and told him to take a message back to Balak. Balaam found Balak where he left him and told him what God had given him to say, "Balak, the king, took me from Aram. 'Come and curse Jacob, and denounce Israel for me.'

"How can I curse those whom God hasn't cursed? How can I denounce those whom the Lord hasn't denounced? From this height I can see them, and I see people who live apart and don't consider themselves one of the nations. They're too many to number. Allow me to die the death of the righteous, and may my end be like theirs!"

Balak was angry with Balaam for what he said, "What have you done to me? I brought you here to curse them and you've blessed them!"

"I can only speak what the Lord gives me to say."

Although Balak was frustrated by Balaam's words of blessing, he took him to another place where they had a view of the Israelites and there he built another seven altars and did just as they did before. And again Balaam asked him to wait there while he moved some distance away. Having received the second message he was asked by the king, with the princes standing with him, what it was that the Lord said? Balaam said to him, "Balak, get up and listen; God isn't a man, that he should lie or change his mind. Does he speak and not act? Does he promise and not fulfil it? I have received a command to bless; God has blessed, so I can't change it.

"No misfortune is seen in Jacob, no misery observed in Israel, the Lord their God is with them; the shout of the king is among them. God brought them out of Egypt; they have the strength of a wild ox. There is no sorcery against Jacob, no divination against Israel. It will now be said of Israel, 'See what God has done!' The people rise like a lioness, and like a lion that doesn't rest till he devours his prey and drinks the blood of his victims."

In exasperation Balak said to Balaam, "Don't curse them and don't bless them!"

"I told you I have to do what I'm told to do." Balaam answered.

For the third time Balak took him to another high place and again the seven altars routine was carried out, but by now Balaam knew that the Lord was pleased to bless Israel, and resorting to sorcery wasn't going to achieve anything. Balaam looked down at the vast camp site of the twelve tribes of Israel and the Spirit of God came upon him and this is what he said, 'The message of one who sees clearly and hears the words of God and sees a vision from the Almighty, who falls prostrate, and whose eyes are opened:

"How beautiful are your tents, O Jacob, your dwelling-places, O Israel!

"Like valleys they spread out, like gardens beside a river, like aloes planted by the Lord, like cedars beside the waters. Water will flow from their buckets; their descendants will have abundant water.

"Their king will be greater than Agag; their kingdom will be exalted.

"May those who bless you be blessed and those who curse you be cursed!"

Balak was so angry that he hit his hands together and said to Balaam, "I got you here to curse my enemies, but you've blessed them three times! Now leave and go home! I was going to reward you but the Lord has stopped you from being rewarded."

Balaam reminded the king that he couldn't do anything of his own accord, but only what the Lord says. "Yes, I'm going back to my people, but let me warn you what this people will do to your people in the coming days—

"The message of Balaam. As one who sees clearly and hears the words of God. I see him, but not now; I perceive him, but not near. A star will come out of Jacob; a sceptre will rise out of Israel. He will crush the foreheads of Moab, the skulls of all the noisy boasters. Edom will be conquered, but Israel will grow strong. A ruler will come out of Jacob and destroy the survivors of the city.

"As for the Amalekites; they were first among the nations, but they will come to ruin.

"As for the Kenites; who are close to both the Midianites and the Amalekites, and were not enemies of Israel, but were mostly neutral. Their living area is safe and secure but they will be destroyed when Asshur (the future military force of Assyria) takes them captive.

"Ah, who can live when God does this? Ships will come from the shores of Kittim (city of Cyprus) they will subdue Asshur and Eber, but they too will come to ruin."

Then Balaam got up and returned home and Balak went his own way. However, it was later learned that during the time they spent together Balaam had advised the Midianites and the Moabites of an effective way of turning the Israelites away from God—Baalism.

13

Baal of Peor

El was the general name of the supreme God, as in Israel and Immanuel and Samuel and Elijah which means 'My God is Yahweh', but under El was, for the Canaanites, Baal.

Regarded as the greatest of all Canaanite gods, his name means 'lord' 'master' 'owner' or 'husband.' The name Baal became commonly used for places and even as part of the names of people. He was the god of fertility and was linked to the weather, particularly storms. Baal was supposed to have defeated the dragon Yamm, who was the source of chaos and confined it to the sea. He was believed to have been defeated by Mot (Death), but reappeared later victorious over death which happened at the coming of spring. Asherah or Ashtart was described by the Canaanites as 'holiness' and 'queen' and was both sister and consort of Baal.

This female deity was also a goddess of fertility and war whose name was closely associated with the Canaanite goddess Astarte, and several variations of her name were in use depending on the area, also known by the Babylonians as Ishtar the Queen of Heaven, goddess of love and fertility. Interestingly very few would question why a leading Christian festival should still openly bear the name of its pagan origins (Our word Easter is derived from *Eostur*, the Norse word for 'spring'. It was the Council of Nicaea in A.D. 325 that fixed the date of Easter on a set Sunday against those who still were observing the Passover on the biblical date of the 14th of Nisan, whatever day it fell on, which was given to Moses).

The Canaanites practised 'sacred' prostitution as part of their worship which would take place in their shrines to Baal. This was seen as an encouragement to the deities for the fertility of their crops, livestock and their families. Their gods needed to see this 'devotion' actively engaged in before they poured out their blessings. And for some the worship demanded the sacrifice of a child.

As the Israelites were camped very close to the Moabites the men began to have sex with the Moabite women and because of those relationships they became Baal worshippers themselves and God burned with anger against them.

God ordered Moses to take the ring-leaders, execute them and hang them somewhere where they can be seen, so that his anger turns away from Israel. Moses instructed Israel's judges to execute any who have joined in worshipping Baal of Peor.

Zimri, a son of the leader of a Simeonite family walked openly to his tent in front of Moses and others who were weeping at the entrance to the Tent of Meeting, and with him was Cozbi, the daughter of a Midianite leader.

Many people were dying of some plague at this time and Phinehas, grandson of Aaron, saw this couple go to the tent and taking a spear hurried after them. When he reached them he drove the spear right through both of them. Then the plague stopped. But by then 24,000 people had died.

After the plague a census was ordered of all the men twenty years old or more who were able to serve in the army. The first census, after they came out of Egypt counted 603,550 men twenty years and above, this second census of men came to 601,730. All the male Levites a month old or more numbered 23,000, but they weren't counted along with the other Israelites because they received no inheritance of land among them.

God said to Moses, "Phinehas has turned my anger away from the Israelites; because he was zealous as I am for my honour among them, so tell him that I'm making a covenant of peace with him and his descendants will keep their jobs in the priesthood because he was zealous for the honour of his God and made atonement for the Israelites."

God also said to Moses, "Treat the Midianites as enemies and kill them, because they treated you as enemies when they used deception in turning so many people away from me." God had earlier said through Moses, "Be careful not to make a treaty with those who live in the land; because when they prostitute themselves to their gods and offer sacrifices to them, they'll invite you and you'll eat what they've sacrificed. And the next thing will be marriages between your sons and their daughters, and they'll lead your sons to be involved in the same worship as them."

"Take vengeance on the Midianites," God told Moses, "After that, it'll be time for you to die." So Moses told the people to arm a thousand men from each tribe, and they were sent into battle, along with Phinehas who took some articles from the sanctuary as well as the two silver trumpets for giving the signals.

They fought against Midian and killed every man, including five kings of Midian. Balaam was also killed there, so he didn't make it back to his home. The Israelites spared the women and children, and took their livestock and goods as plunder. They torched all the places where the Midianites had settled and they brought all their plunder to Moses and Eleazar at their camp on the plains of Moab near the River Jordan.

Moses was angry at the army officers and said to them, "Why have you allowed the women to live? Now kill all the boys, and kill all the women who have slept with a man, but save for yourselves every young girl. And all those who have killed anyone, or touched anyone who was killed must stay outside of the camp for a week. On the third and seventh days you must wash yourselves and your captives, as well as your clothes, and everything made of leather, goat hair or wood." Eleazar told them that "if anything can withstand fire then it's to be put through fire, and everything else cleaned by water. After your wash on the seventh day you can come back into the camp."

The apostle Paul laid out what was to be the correct behaviour for the Christian in his letter to the Romans, 'Bless those who persecute you; bless and don't curse. Rejoice with those who rejoice; mourn with those who mourn. Live in harmony with each other. Don't be proud, but be willing to associate with people who don't have your living standard. Don't be conceited.

'Don't repay anyone evil for evil. Be careful to do what is right in the eyes of everybody. If it's possible, as far as it depends on you, live at peace with everyone. Don't take revenge, my friends, but leave room for God's wrath, for it is written, "It is mine to avenge; I'll repay," says the lord.' Christians are to behave differently from the world, 'If your enemy is hungry, feed him; if he's thirsty, give him something to drink. In doing this, you'll heap burning coals on his head. Don't be overcome by evil, but overcome evil with good.'

God does punish evil directly and sometimes, as he did in the old covenant, he uses other people to do it, both for his people and against them. Each were punished for their own sins.

One of the psalms has, 'they yoked themselves to the Baal of Peor and ate sacrifices offered to lifeless gods; they provoked the Lord to anger by their wicked deeds; and a plague broke out among them. But Phinehas stood up and intervened, and the plague was checked. This was credited to him as righteousness for endless generations to come.

'By the waters of Meribah they angered the Lord, and trouble came to Moses because of them; for they rebelled against the Spirit of God, and rash words were spoken by Moses.

'They didn't destroy the peoples as the Lord had commanded them, but they mingled with the nations and adopted their customs. They worshipped their idols, which became a snare to them. They sacrificed their sons and daughters to demons.

'They shed innocent blood by sacrificing their children to the idols of Canaan, and the land was desecrated by their blood. They defiled themselves by what they did; by their deeds they prostituted themselves.'

It is so easy to adapt and adopt the customs of those close to us and make them our own, to go with the flow and not stand out as different. The closer we are the more difficult it becomes not to conform to what those around us are doing and consider as right and normal. Paul, in his second letter to the Corinthians said, 'Don't be bonded together with unbelievers. For what does righteousness and wickedness have in common? Or what connection can light have with darkness? Is there harmony between Christ and Satan? What does a believer have in common with an unbeliever? What agreement is there between the temple of God and idols? We are the temple of the living God. As God has said, "I will live with them and walk among them, and I will be their God, and they will be my people."

While Moses was with the people he passed on to them what God had given him regarding all aspects of their lives, from what is good for food and good to wear to taking care of their surroundings so that in every way they would cause other nations 'who will hear about all these decrees and say, "Surely this great nation is a wise and understanding people." What other nation is so great as to have their gods near them the way the Lord our God is near us whenever we pray to him? And what other nation is so great as to have such righteous decrees and laws I am setting before you today.'

The longest psalm includes this devotion to God's laws, 'Oh, how I love your law! I meditate on it all day long. Your commands make me wiser than my enemies, for they are ever with me. I have more insight than all my teachers, for I meditate on your statutes. I have more understanding than the elders, for I obey your precepts. I have kept my feet from every evil path so that I may obey your word. I have not departed from your laws, for you yourself have taught me. How sweet are your words to my taste, sweeter than honey to my mouth! I gain understanding from your precepts; therefore I hate every wrong path.'

Here is a small example of God's laws:

Don't steal

Don't lie.

Don't deceive each other.

Don't swear falsely by my name and so profane the name of your God.

Don't defraud your neighbour or rob him.

Don't hold back the wages of a hired man overnight.

Don't curse the deaf or put a stumbling-block in front of the blind, but fear your God.

Don't pervert justice; don't show partiality to the poor or favouritism to the great, but judge your neighbour fairly.

Don't go about spreading slander among your people.

Don't do anything that endangers your neighbour's life.

Don't hate your brother in your heart. Rebuke your neighbour frankly so that you will not share in his guilt.

Don't seek revenge or bear a grudge against one of your people, but love your neighbour as yourself. I am the Lord.

The king of Israel was expected to make for himself a copy of the law and read it every day of his life, and in one of King David's psalms he writes, 'The law of the lord is perfect, reviving the soul. The statutes of the

Lord are trustworthy, making wise the simple. The precepts of the Lord are right, giving joy to the heart. The commands of the Lord are radiant, giving light to the eyes. The fear of the Lord is pure, enduring forever. The ordinances of the Lord are sure and altogether righteous. They are more precious than gold, than much pure gold; they are sweeter then honey, than honey from the comb. By them is your servant warned; in keeping them there is great reward.'

While they were still in Moab Moses summoned all the Israelites and said to them:

"You saw all that God did in Egypt; the miracles and wonders to free you from slavery. But to this day the Lord has not given you a mind that understands or eyes that see or ears that hear."

Miraculous signs and great wonders are considered by many as effective ways of convincing unbelievers that God exists, and thousands of Christians will travel far to be in a service where signs and wonders are being seen, yet even having experienced many miraculous events the majority of the people of Israel 'didn't have a mind that understands or eyes that see or ears that hear.' This is because that kind of mind, which understands, sees and hears, comes only from the Lord. It isn't a matter of human intelligence and wisdom, or a better education than the next person, but whether God has given that mind or not.

Paul explained this in his first letter to the Corinthians, 'The Spirit searches all things, even the deep things of God. For who among men knows the thoughts of a man except the man's spirit within him? In the same way no-one knows the thoughts of God except the Spirit of God. We've not received the spirit of the world but the Spirit who is from God, *that we may understand what God has freely given us.*

'This is what we speak, not in words taught us by human wisdom but in words taught by the Spirit, expressing spiritual truths in spiritual words.

'The man without the Spirit doesn't accept the things that come from the Spirit of God; to him they're foolish, and he can't understand them, because they are spiritually understood.' On the other hand, the spiritual man can better evaluate the things in the world, even though the world will not understand him, and will misjudge him.'

Paul then quotes from the book of Isaiah, 'Who has understood the mind of the Lord, or instructed him as his counsellor?' And Paul closes this section with the words, 'But we have the mind of Christ.' Later in the letter he writes, 'I think that I too have the Spirit of God.'

The terms 'the mind of the Lord' 'the mind of Christ' 'the Spirit of God' all mean the same thing, just as the mind of the Lord can be read as the Spirit of the Lord. Paul speaks of the man's spirit within him by which he knows his thoughts; that is a way of speaking of our minds, which is much more than just a brain. And in the same way God's Spirit is his mind, his thoughts and his nature. God is Spirit, and his Spirit coming to our spirit enables us to understand, as Paul said, and as Moses said, this was not given to the Israelites. Man's spirit is his mind and God's Spirit is his mind. God is the Holy Spirit. 'There is only one God,' as Paul wrote to the Romans—one Spirit, not two, or three. One Lord, one faith and one hope. There is one body: the church is one and we are all members of his body no matter what denomination we attend or even outside of a particular fellowship—we are united by that one mind and Spirit which is God.

"You shall not make for yourself in the form of anything in heaven above or on the earth beneath or in the waters below. You shall not bow down to them or worship them; For I, the Lord your God, am a jealous God." Not long after these words thundered into the hearing of the Israelites terrifying them as they and everything around them shook, they could be seen bowing down to the golden calf as their saviour.

Today the 'golden calf' is still with us and Christians are bowing down to it. They have taken something good and made an idol with it, and it all seems so reasonable and logical, just as the serpent presented the eating of the forbidden fruit as something to make one wise so millions of Christians have been led to recite and remember as the most important truth of the Christian message which is that the mind of God, his Holy Spirit is in fact another person, and we have worshipped this person from one generation to another in ignorance and forgetfulness that God's Spirit is God himself. In Peter's second letter he writes of God's divine power, his glory and his goodness, and that we can actually share in that divine nature—that holy Spirit, not through a third person, but directly and personally by belonging to God through and in Christ.

While every tribe were to be given a large area of land to settle in, the Levites were given the priestly duties as their inheritance but they had to live somewhere so the Lord said to Moses, "Command the Israelites to give the Levites towns to live in from their own tribal areas. They are to give them pasture-lands around the towns and these pasture-lands will extend out about 450 metres from the town wall. Outside the town measure about 900 metres north, south, east and west of the town as their pasture-land.

Six of the towns you give the Levites will be places of refuge, to which a person who has killed someone can go to. In addition, give them forty-two other towns. The larger an land-area a tribe has, the bigger will be the proportion of towns that are given to the Levites.

These six towns of refuge, three on the east side of the Jordan and three on the west side, will be for anyone, Israelite or alien, to go to if they've killed someone accidently. When he gets to one of these towns, he is to stand at the gate and state his case to the elders before they admit him to the towns' protection and give him a place to live, until he could stand trial.

But if it wasn't an accident, and it was done on purpose, the person who did it is a murderer, and shall be put to death. The weapon that is used in the murder is irrelevant. If it was a genuine accident then he must be protected from anyone who's intent on taking the law into their own hands, but he must stay in that town of refuge, because if he goes out and is found by someone who wants revenge then the person who kills him will not be guilty of murder. The accused must stay inside the town until the death of the high priest, and only after the high priest's death can he return to his own property. It is for the assembly to judge between the avenger and the accused by gathering all the facts.

No-one is to be put to death for murder on the word of only one witness.

No ransom must be accepted in the case of a person guilty of murder; they must be executed. No ransom can be paid for a person who has gone into a town of refuge either.

'Bloodshed pollutes the land, and the only way atonement can be made for the land in the case of murder is the blood of the one who shed it because I, the Lord, live where you live.'

Jesus, in the letter to the church in Pergamum said, "I know where you live—where Satan has his throne. Yet you remain true to my name. You didn't renounce your faith in me, even in the days of Antipas, my faithful witness, who was put to death in your city—where Satan lives."

When certain emperors made it a law that everyone was to perform a short ritual, in which the emperor would be recognised as Lord and God, and then they were to collect a certificate as proof that you've made this affirmation; more Christians than could be processed hurried to get their certificate, and some gained a certificate by other means, while others were even led by their bishop to get it done. Some well-known bishops went into hiding and left their congregations to sort it out the best way they could. After these persecutions there was a great deal of heated debate as to what to do with all those who gave in and made the sacrifice to the emperor, whether bishop or layperson (see 'The Birth of the Church' Ivor J. Davidson. *The Monarch History of the Church*. Pages 322-338).

The state has always imposed its laws on their people, and Paul writes that 'everyone must submit to the governing authorities, for there is no authority except that which God has established. The authorities that exist have been established by God.' The emperor at that time was Nero, hardly a person who pleased God, but as sitting in that seat of power Christians were taught to be subject to him and all those in authority under him. Yet if there does come a conflict between what an authority orders us to do and what God tells us to do we must be prepared to accept whatever punishment the state decrees.

For much of the Church's history Christians of all persuasions have had to live in a world where the church shared the authority, if not dominated, of the state, and there was no freedom or safety for those who chose not to follow what the church of the day had decided was correct. In Brian Moynahan's book about William Tyndale 'Book of Fire' he writes, 'The Church could not itself carry out a burning. To do so would defy the principle that *Ecclesia non novit sanguine*, the Church does not shed blood. Pope Lucius III had bypassed this inconvenience in 1184 by decreeing that unrepentant heretics should be handed over to the secular authorities for sentence and execution.' In the eyes of both state and church to invite people to make up their own mind was to foster anarchy and destroy their unity as a Christian state, yet there has never been a Christian state, only Christian individuals.

This world, as the apostle John wrote, 'is under the control of the evil one.' Only individuals can be released from the dragon's control as they submit in faith to Christ. "All men will hate you because of me," Jesus told his disciples, "but he who stands firm to the end will be saved."

14

Final Words

After going through their shared history Moses said to the people, "Now what I'm commanding you today isn't too difficult for you or beyond your reach. It's not up in heaven, or across the sea, no, the word is close to you, you're familiar with it, so that you can obey it.

See, I set before you today life and prosperity, death and destruction. I command you today to love the Lord your God, to walk in his ways, and to keep his commands, decrees and laws; then you'll live and increase, and God will bless you in your new land.

But if your heart turns away and you are not obedient, and if you are drawn away to bow down to other gods and worship them, you will certainly be destroyed.

I call heaven and earth as witnesses against you that I've set before you life and death, blessings and curses. Now choose life, so that you and your children may live. Listen to God's voice, and hold fast to him. For God is your life."

"I am 120years old and I'm no longer able to lead you," Moses made this announcement to all of Israel. "The Lord has said to me, 'You shall not cross the Jordan.' God himself will cross over ahead of you, and he will destroy those nations that are ahead of you, and you'll take their land.

"Joshua will lead you, and the Lord will do to them what he did to Sihon and Og, the kings of the Amorites. Be strong and courageous. Don't be afraid or terrified because of them, for God goes with you; he will never leave you nor forsake you."

Moses wrote down what we call the Pentateuch—the first five books of the Bible and he gave it to the priests saying, "At the end of every seven years, in the year for cancelling debts, during the Feast of Tabernacles, when all Israel comes to the place that he will choose, you shall read this law to the men, women, children, and the aliens living in your towns— so that they can listen and learn to fear the Lord your God and follow carefully all the words of this law, they must hear it.

"Take this book," Moses commanded the Levites, "and place it beside the Ark of the Covenant of the Lord your God. There it will remain as a witness against you. For I know how rebellious and stiff-necked you are. If you've been rebellious against the Lord while I'm still alive and with you, how much more will you rebel after I die!

"Assemble all the elders and all your officials so that I can speak to them, because I know that after my death you're sure to become utterly corrupt and turn away from what I've commanded you."

The Lord said to Moses, "The day of your death is near. Call Joshua and present yourselves at the Tent of Meeting, were I will commission him. When they arrived at the entrance the Lord appeared in a pillar of cloud and said to Moses, "You're going to rest with your fathers (the words 'rest' and 'sleep' are used in both Testaments to mean death; it is never said that 'they've entered glory' or 'they're with the Lord' or 'they are in heaven;' the simple sequence is that we live, we sleep (die), and then comes the awakening at the resurrection), and these people will soon prostitute themselves to the foreign gods of the land they're entering. They will forsake me and break the covenant I made with them. At that time

I'll forsake them; I'll hide my face from them, and they will be destroyed. Many disasters and difficulties will come on them, and at that time they will ask, 'Haven't these disasters come to us because our God isn't with us?' And I will certainly hide my face at that time because of all their wickedness in turning to other gods."

To Joshua God gave this command, "Be strong and courageous, for you will bring the Israelites into the land I promised them on oath, and I myself will be with you."

God told Moses to write a song down and teach it to the Israelites and make them sing it, because when they've eaten their fill in this new land flowing with milk and honey they will turn to other gods and worship them and this song will testify against them because it won't be forgotten by their descendants." So Moses wrote down the song and taught it to the Israelites.

This is the song that they had to learn:

Listen, O heavens, and I'll speak; hear, O earth, my words and let my teaching fall like rain and my words descend like dew, like showers on new grass, like abundant rain on tender plants.

I'll proclaim the name of the Lord. Oh, praise the greatness of our God! He is the Rock, his words are perfect, and all his ways are just. A faithful God who does no wrong, he is upright and just.

They've acted corruptly towards him; to their shame they're no longer his children, but a warped and crooked generation. Is this the way you repay the lord, O foolish and unwise people? Is he not your Father, your Creator, who made you and formed you?

Remember the days of old; consider the generations long past. Ask your father and he'll tell you, your elders, and they'll explain to you. When the Most High gave the nations their inheritance, when he divided all mankind, he set up boundaries for the peoples according to the number of the sons of Israel. For the Lord's portion is his people, Jacob his allotted inheritance.

In a desert land he found him, in a barren and howling waste. He shielded and cared for him; he guarded him as the apple of his eye, like an eagle that stirs up its nest and hovers over its young, that spreads its wings to catch them and carries them on its pinions. The Lord alone led him; no foreign god was with him.

He made him ride on the heights of the land and fed him with the fruit of the fields. He nourished him with honey from the rock, and with oil from the flinty crag, with curds and milk from herd and flock and with fattened lambs and goats, with choice rams of Bashan and the finest grains of wheat. You drank the foaming blood of the grape.

Israel grew fat and kicked; filled with food, he became heavy and sleek. He abandoned the God who made him and rejected the Rock his Saviour. They made him jealous with their foreign gods and angered him with their detestable idols. They sacrificed to demons, which are not God—gods they had not known, gods that recently appeared, gods your fathers didn't fear. You deserted the Rock, who fathered you; you forgot the God who gave you birth.

The Lord saw this and rejected them because he was angered by his sons and daughters. "I will hide my face from them," he said, "and see what their end will be; for they're a perverse generation, children who are unfaithful. They made me jealous by what is no god and angered with their worthless idols. I will make them envious by those who aren't a people; I will make them angry by a nation that has no understanding. For a fire has been kindled by my wrath, one that burns to the realm of death below. It will devour the earth and its harvests and set on fire the foundations of the mountains.

"I will heap calamities on them and expend my arrows against them. I will send famine against them, pestilence and plague. I will send wild beasts and venomous snakes. In the street the sword will make them childless and in their homes terror will reign. Infants, young men and women, as well as the grey-haired will perish. I said I would scatter them and blot out their memory from mankind, but I dreaded the taunt of the enemy, lest the adversary misunderstand and say, 'Our hand has triumphed; the Lord hasn't done all this.'"

They're a nation without sense, there's no discernment in them. If only they were wise and would understand this and discern what their end will be! How could one man chase a thousand, or two put ten thousand to flight, unless their Rock had sold them, unless the Lord had given them up? For their rock isn't like our Rock, as even our enemies concede. Their vine comes from the vine of Sodom and from the fields of Gomorrah. Their grapes are filled with poison, and their clusters with bitterness. Their wine is the venom of serpents, the deadly poison of cobras.

"Haven't I kept this in reserve and locked it in my safe? It's mine to avenge; I'll repay. In due time their foot will slip; their day of disaster is near and their doom rushes towards them."

The Lord will judge his people and have compassion on his servants when he sees their strength is gone and no-one is left, slave or free. He will say, "Now where are their gods, the rock they took refuge in, the gods who ate the fat of their sacrifices and drank the wine of their drink offerings? Let them rise up to help you! Let them give you shelter!

Now see that I am He! There's no god beside me. I put to death and I bring to life, I've wounded and I will heal, and no-one can deliver out of my hand. When I sharpen my flashing sword and my hand grasps it in judgment, I'll take vengeance on my adversaries and repay those who hate me. I'll make my arrows drunk with blood, while my sword devours flesh: the blood of the slain and the captives, the heads of the enemy leaders."

Rejoice, O nations, with his people, for he'll avenge the blood of his servants; he'll take vengeance on his enemies and make atonement for his land and people.

When Moses with Joshua finished reciting all these words to everyone there, he said to them, "Take to heart all the words that I've told you today, and command your children to carefully obey all the words of this law. They're not just idle words—they're your life. Live by them and you'll have a long life in the land you're crossing the Jordan to own."

All the prophets who were yet to put pen to paper, or whatever they wrote on, spoke of God in the same terms as this song that the people of Israel were made to learn. Their aim was to remind the people of their history and what God had done for them, and then to warn them that if there was no repentance then even worse events would follow, including deportation into other lands. But though there would be punishments there would also be great promises, not only of a return to the land that had been promised to Abraham and his children; but of a righteous king who would rule over them and that rule would include all other nations as well.

The prophet Isaiah wrote, 'Nevertheless (there's a lot before this), there will be no more gloom for those who were in distress. In the past he humbled the land of Zebulun and the land of Naphtali (tribal areas in the north of Israel), but in the future he will honour Galilee of the Gentiles (it was a ethnically mixed and highly populated area), by the way of the sea, along the Jordan—The people walking in darkness have seen a great light; on those living in the land of the shadow of death a light has dawned.

'You've enlarged the nation and increased their joy; they rejoice before you as people rejoice at the harvest, as men rejoice when dividing the plunder. For as in the day of Midian's defeat, you've shattered the yoke that burdens them, the bar across their shoulders, the rod of their oppressor. Every warrior's boot used in battle and every garment rolled in blood will be destined for burning, will be fuel for the fire.

'For to us a child is born, to us a son is given, and the government will be on his shoulders. And he will be called Wonderful Counsellor, Mighty God, Everlasting Father, Prince of Peace. Of the increase of his government and peace there will be no end. He will reign on David's throne and over his kingdom, establishing and upholding it with justice and righteousness from that time on and forever.'

A little later Isaiah tells us more about this person, 'A shoot will come up from the stump of Jesse; from his roots a Branch will bear fruit (Jesse was the father of David, from the tribe of Judah). The Spirit of the Lord will rest on him—the Spirit of wisdom and of understanding, the Spirit of counsel and of power, the Spirit of knowledge and of the fear of the Lord—and he will delight in the fear of the Lord.

'He will not judge by what he sees or decide by what he hears; but with righteousness he will judge the needy, with justice he'll give decisions for the poor of the earth. He'll strike the earth with the rod of his mouth; with the breath of his lips he will kill the wicked. Righteousness will be his belt and faithfulness the sash round his waist.'

As a king he would have been called, like all the kings of Israel who were anointed with oil on coming into office were called, 'the Lord's anointed.' This means *Messiah* in Hebrew and *Christos* in Greek.

When Andrew had Jesus pointed out to him by John the Baptist, who called him, "the Lamb of God," Andrew and another disciple of John started to follow Jesus who became aware that he was being followed, so he turned round and asked them, "What do you want?" and they said, "Rabbi, where're you staying?" and Jesus replied, "Come and you'll see." So they went with him and saw where he was staying and spent the day with him. It was about four in the afternoon.

Andrew, who had a brother called Simon, went and found his brother and told him, "We've found the Messiah," and he brought Peter to Jesus, who looked at him and said, "You're Simon son of John. You'll be called Peter (in Aramaic it's *Kepha*, a word meaning rock. This was the form (*Cephas*) by which Paul commonly named him, adding a final—s to adapt it to the Greek tongue and in Greek (*Petros—Peter*) it means rock.

On the same day that Moses taught the song to the Israelites God told him, "Go up into the Abarim Range to Mount Nebo in Moab, across from Jericho, and view Canaan, the land I'm giving the Israelites as their own possession. On that mountain you will die and join the rest of the dead, just as your brother Aaron died on Mount Hor and was gathered to his people. This is because both of you broke faith with me in the presence of the Israelites at the waters of Meribah Kadesh in the desert of Zin and because you didn't uphold my holiness in front of the people. So, you'll only see the land from a distance; you won't be allowed to enter."

Moses climbed Mount Nebo and there the Lord showed him the whole land—from Gilead to Dan, all of Naphtali, the territory of Ephraim and Manasseh, all the land of Judah as far as the Mediterranean Sea, the Negev and the whole region from the Valley of Jericho, the City of Palms, as far as Zoar. Then the Lord said to him, "This is the land I promised on oath to Abraham, Isaac and Jacob when I said, 'I will give it to your descendants.' I have let you see it, but you won't cross over into it."

So Moses died there in Moab, and the Lord buried him in the valley opposite Beth Peor, but to this day no-one knows where the grave is. The devil wanted Moses' body, perhaps so that he could lead the Israelites into worshiping at the site of his grave; as we've seen their keeping of the bronze snake attached to the pole became a snare for them and should have been destroyed, but was kept for centuries. The archangel Michael didn't use slander against Satan but said to him, "The Lord rebuke you!" and Satan sulked off without getting his hands on the body of God's servant.

15

A New Leader

Joshua was now the new leader and God encouraged him by saying that, "No-one will be able to stand up against you all the days of your life. As I was with Moses, so I will be with you; I will never leave you nor forsake you. Be strong and courageous, because you'll lead these people to inherit the land I promised to their forefathers."

Joshua ordered the officers to go through the camp and tell everyone to get all their supplies ready because in three days time they're going to cross the Jordan. He had earlier sent two young men to find out what they could about the route they were to take and make a careful check on the main city ahead of them, Jericho.

The gate of the city was open in daylight time and the two Israelites were able to walk though with other people without being halted. Much of the city wall had business properties built along the top and the two men entered a prostitute's house whose name was Rahab, but the men had been recognised as Israelites and were seen going into her home. She received a message from the king of Jericho telling her that these two men are spies and she must bring them out so that they can be arrested. She sent back a message saying that the spies had been in her house but they left before the gates would be shut, and told the king that if his men went quickly after them they should catch up with them.

But they hadn't left the city; she had hidden them on the roof because she needed to speak to them urgently. She went up on to the roof and said to them, "I know that the Lord has given this land to you and a real fear of you has come to all of us. We've heard how the Lord dried up the water of the Sea of Reeds for you when you came out of Egypt, and what you did to the two kings of the Amorites east of the Jordan, and when we heard that you completely destroyed them our hearts sank and we're all scared of what's going to happen to us. Your God is God, so please, because I've shown you kindness, be kind to my family and spare their lives. Give me a sign that you'll save us from death."

"Our lives for your lives," they said to her, "that is, if you don't tell anyone what we're doing we'll treat you kindly." They gave her a scarlet cord and told her to tie it from the window so that it could be seen from outside, and warned her that if any family member goes outside into the street they won't be protected, but everyone who stays in the house will be safe.

"I agree," she said, and she let them down by a rope through the window and advised them to hide in the hills for three days and then return to their people. When they had left she tied the scarlet cord to the window.

Three days later the two crossed the river back to their camp. They told Joshua everything that had happened and said, "The Lord has definitely given the whole land into our hands because all the people are really fearful of us."

The next morning the officers told everyone that, "When you see the ark of the covenant and the priests carrying it, that's the time to move from your positions and follow it, but keep a distance of about 900 metres between you and the ark; don't go near it."

And God said to Joshua, "Today I will begin to exalt you in the eyes of all Israel, so that they'll know that I'm with you as I was with Moses. Tell the priests who carry the ark that when they reach the edge of the Jordan's waters, to stand in the river." During this time of year the Jordan overflows its banks yet as soon as the priests carrying the ark stepped into the water the water from upstream stopped flowing and piled up in a heap a great distance away, while the water flowing down to the Dead Sea was completely cut off.

The priests who carried the ark stood firm on dry ground in the middle of the Jordan, while all Israel passed by. Twelve chosen men, one from each tribe, picked up a stone each from the middle of the river and put them down at the place they camped that night. This was because when someone in the future asks what these stones mean they can be told the story of their crossing and be a memorial to the people of Israel for ever.

As soon as everyone had crossed then the priests carrying the ark came to the other side. The men of Gad, Reuben and the half tribe of Manasseh, who were given lands east of the river, crossed over as well, that was about 40,000 armed men who were to assist the other tribes in conquering the lands west of the river.

As the priests came up out of the river the waters returned to the flood conditions as before. The people camped at Gilgal; this was the tenth day of the first month, and there they set up the stones.

When all the Amorite and Canaanite kings west of the Jordan heard what happened at the crossing their hearts melted and they didn't have the courage to fight the Israelites. At that time God commanded Joshua to make sharp flint knives and circumcise all those second generation Israelites who were born in the desert and hadn't been circumcised as yet. All those adult males who journeyed from Egypt forty years ago had died as God said they would because of their disobedience. When the circumcision was completed they remained where they were until they were healed. The place was known as the *hill of foreskins*.

On the evening of the 14th day they celebrated the Passover. The next day they ate some of the food of that land as well as unleavened bread and roasted grain. The Manna stopped that day. It had kept them alive, but it was no longer needed.

Joshua was near Jericho when he saw a man standing in front of him with a drawn sword in his hand. Joshua didn't recognise who he was so he approached him and asked, "Are you for us or for our enemies?" "Neither," he replied, "but as commander of the army of the Lord I've now come." Joshua fell face down to the ground in reverence and asked him, "What message does the Lord have for his servant?"

"Take off your sandals, the place where you're standing is holy."

"See, I've delivered Jericho into your hands," The Lord told him, "along with its king and fighting men. March around the city once with all the armed men, and do this for six days. Seven priests must each carry a ram's horn trumpet in front of the ark and on the seventh day march around the city seven times with the priests blowing on their trumpets.

"When you hear them give a long blast on the trumpets everyone is to give a loud shout; then the wall of the city will collapse and the people can go straight in."

Jericho was shut up tight and no-one came in or out.

The priests did has Joshua told them and they had an armed guard front and rear of them as they marched around the city each day, and then returning to the camp for the night.

On the seventh day they did exactly the same but this time, they circled the city seven times and on the last lap when the priests blew their trumpets everyone shouted and the wall collapsed, so every man charged in with orders to destroy everything every living thing in it, except for Rahab and her family who were taken to a safe place outside the camp of Israel by the two young men who she hid and the whole family remained close to the Israelites.

In the recorded genealogy of Jesus written by Matthew that goes back through King David to Abraham, the name of Rahab is found.

Joshua had also told them not to take any religious objects for themselves no matter how well made or costly it looked. "All the silver and gold," Joshua told them, "and the articles of bronze and iron are sacred to the Lord and must go into his treasury."

They burned the whole city and everything in it. At that time Joshua pronounced this curse on anyone who attempts to rebuild Jericho:

"Cursed before the Lord is the man who undertakes to rebuild this city, Jericho: At the cost of his firstborn son will he lay its foundations; at the cost of his youngest will he set up its gates."

The Lord was with Joshua, and his fame spread throughout the land. And he sent men from Jericho to Ai, west of their position, to get information on the city, and when they returned they said to Joshua, "You need only to send a few thousand men to take the city because it's not that well defended." But when this small force tried to take the city they were beaten back and chased away. About thirty-six of the Israelites were killed and when they heard the news everyone lost their confidence.

Joshua, who had expected a quick victory, tore his clothes and fell face down before the ark of the lord and stayed there till the evening, as did the elders of Israel, who threw dust on their heads.

Joshua prayed; "Ah, Sovereign Lord, why did you ever bring this people across the Jordan to deliver us into the hands of the Amorites to destroy us? If only we'd been content to stay on the other side of the Jordan! O Lord, what can I say, now that Israel has been routed by its enemies? The Canaanites and the other people of the country will hear about this and they'll surround us and wipe out all of us. What then will you do for your own great name?"

This wasn't the same as the many times the people of Israel complained about God. The difference was that Joshua was complaining *to* God, and not *about* God. David in the psalms brought many of his complaints to God directly, and Joshua was concerned over God's reputation and name. (See Dale Ralph Davis' 'Joshua: No Falling Words' page 61)

"Stand up!" the Lord said to Joshua, "what are you doing there down on your face? Israel has sinned; they have violated my covenant—they've taken some of the goods that should have gone into the treasury; they've stolen and they've lied. That's why the Israelites can't stand before their enemies; they turn their backs and run because they've made themselves an easy target. I'll not be with you anymore unless you destroy what is earmarked for destruction."

The lord told Joshua the people must get themselves ready for the next day when each tribe will come forward in turn to discover where the guilt lays. Early the next morning the tribe of Judah was selected, and the process of narrowing it down began; first the clans of Judah came forward and the Zarahites were selected, and from them it came to the families, and the family of Zimri was taken, then each man came forward one at a time and Achan, Zimri's grandson, was taken.

"My son," Joshua said to him, "give glory to the Lord, the God of Israel, and give him the praise. Tell me what you've done, and don't hide it from me."

"It's true! I have sinned against the Lord, the God of Israel. When I saw a beautiful robe from Babylonia I took it—and two hundred shekels of silver, and a wedge of gold weighing 1¼ pounds, I wanted them and took them, they're hidden in the ground inside my tent, with the silver underneath."

Joshua sent some men to check Achan's story, and they found it where he said it would be, and brought the stuff back to Joshua and spread them out before everyone.

They took Achan and his family, and all of his property to the Valley of Achor, and Joshua said to him, "Why have you brought this trouble on us? The Lord will bring trouble on you today."

Then all Israel stoned him, and after they'd stoned the rest, they burned them. Over the remains they heaped a large pile of rocks. The place has been called the Valley of Achor, meaning *trouble* ever since.

The Lord said to Joshua, "Don't be afraid and don't be discouraged. Take the whole army and go and attack Ai. You'll do to Ai and its king what you did to Jericho and its king, except this time you can carry off the plunder and livestock for yourselves," then the Lord gave him some tactical advice, "Set an ambush behind the city."

Joshua chose thirty thousand of his best fighting men and told them, "You're to set an ambush behind the city. Don't go very far from it. All of you stay alert, and all those with me will attack the city and when they come out against us, as they did before, we'll run from them, and as they pursue us you are to leave your hidden position and take the city, and when you've taken the city set it on fire. Do what the Lord has commanded, see to it; you have my orders."

Joshua sent them out at night and they found the place where they could lay in wait to the west of Ai, but Joshua spent the night with the people. He got his men together early the next morning and marched them to Ai. They set up camp north of Ai, with the valley between them and the city. He had about five thousand men with him and he joined the others in ambush west of the city. The soldiers took up their positions and that night Joshua went into the valley.

The king of Ai was aware of where Joshua's men were so early in the morning they stormed out through the gate to engage Israel in battle and as happened before the Israelites fell back and were eagerly pursued by all the fighting men of Ai. All this time the city gates were left open; then the Lord said to Joshua, "Hold out your Javelin towards Ai." As soon as he did this the men who were in hiding west of Ai got up from their position and rushed forward and entered the city and captured it, quickly afterwards they set it on fire.

The men of Ai who were pursuing the Israelites looked back and saw smoke rising from the city and Joshua and his men saw the smoke as well, so they turned and attacked the men of Ai. Once the fire was lit the men came out of the city and attacked the men of Ai from the rear. Israel cut them down leaving no survivors, but they captured the king alive and took him to Joshua.

When Israel had finished killing all the men of Ai in the fields and in the desert where they had chased them they returned to Ai and killed all that were left there. Twelve thousand men fell that day—all the people of Ai. Joshua then burned Ai and made it a permanent heap of ruins. As for the king, he was executed and then he was hung on a tree till evening when the body was taken down and thrown in front of the entrance to the city. They then raised a large pile of rocks over it, which is still there.

The hanging of the condemned man on a tree goes back to when Moses wrote, 'If a man guilty of a capital offence is put to death and his body is hung on a tree, you mustn't leave his body on the tree overnight. Be sure to bury him that same day, because anyone who is hung on a tree is under God's curse. You mustn't desecrate the land the Lord your God is giving you as an inheritance.'

The apostle Paul referred to this when, in his letter to the Galatians, he wrote, 'Christ redeemed us from the curse of the law by becoming a curse for us, for it is written: "Cursed is everyone who is hung on a tree." He redeemed us in order that the blessing given to Abraham might come to the Gentiles through Christ Jesus, so that by faith we might receive the promise of the Spirit.' Paul had just previously written that we should 'consider Abraham: "He believed God, and it was credited to him as righteousness" (from Genesis). Understand then, that those who believe are children of Abraham. The Scripture foresaw that God would justify the Gentiles by faith, and announced the gospel in advance to Abraham: "All nations will be blessed through you." So that those who have faith are blessed along with Abraham, the man of faith.'

Not long before the death of Moses he gave a command that when the people have crossed the Jordan they are to go to the area of Shechem which is between Mount Gerizim and Mount Ebal; half the tribes are to stand on, or in front of, one mount and the other six tribes on the other mount. The Levites had what seems the impossible task of raising their voices so that both sides could hear. Perhaps they all had copies of what they were to say and all said it at the same time; however it was accomplished what the people were to listen to were curses for disobedience and blessings for obedience.

Now the time had come to do what Moses had commanded, so Joshua and all Israel went to Shechem, where over four centuries before God had appeared to Abraham and said to him, "To your offspring I will give this land," and he built an altar there. Joshua built another altar, this time, on Mount Ebal, according to what is written in the Book of the Law of Moses—an altar of uncut stones, on which no iron tool has been used. On it they offered to the Lord burnt offerings and sacrificed peace offerings.

There, in the presence of the Israelites, Joshua copied on stones the law of Moses. All Israel, including women and children and aliens, were standing on both sides of the ark of the covenant facing the priests who carried it. The people, divided in two, were in front of these two mounts, as Moses had commanded.

Joshua began to read, along with the Levites, all the words of the law—the blessings and the curses—just as it's written in the Book of the Law:

"Cursed is the man who carves an image or casts an idol—a detestable thing to the Lord—and sets it up in secret."

Then all the people shall say, "Amen!" (Yes!)

"Cursed is the man who dishonours his father or his mother."

"Yes!"

"Cursed is the man who moves his neighbour's boundary stone."

"Yes!"

"Cursed is the man who leads the blind astray on the road."

"Yes!"

"Cursed is the man who withholds justice from the alien, the fatherless or the widow."

"Yes!"

"Cursed is the man who sleeps with his father's wife, because he dishonours his father's bed."

"Yes!"

"Cursed is the man who has sexual relations with any animal."

"Yes!"

"Cursed is the man who sleeps with his sister, the daughter of his mother and father."

"Yes!"

"Cursed is the man who sleeps with his mother-in-law."

"Yes!"

"Cursed is the man who kills his neighbour secretly."

"Yes!"

"Cursed is the man who accepts a bribe to kill an innocent person."

"Yes!"

"Cursed is the man who does not uphold the words of this law by carrying them out."

"Yes!"

'If you fully obey the Lord your God and carefully follow all his commands that I give you today, the Lord your God will set you high above all the nations on earth. All these blessings will come upon you and accompany you if you obey the Lord your God:

You'll be blessed in the city and in the country.

Your children will be blessed and your crops and the young of your livestock—the calves of your herds and the lambs of your flocks.

Your basket and your kneading trough will be blessed.

You'll be blessed when you come in and when you go out.

The Lord will grant that your enemies will be defeated before you. They'll come at you from one direction but run from you in seven.

The Lord will send a blessing on your barns and on everything you put your hand to. He'll bless you in the land he's giving you.

The Lord will establish you as his holy people, as he promised you on oath, if you keep his commands and walk in his ways. Then all the peoples on earth will see that you're called by the name of the Lord, and they'll fear you. The Lord will grant you abundant prosperity—in your children, your livestock and your crops—in the land he promised to your forefathers to give you.

The Lord will open the heavens, the storehouse of his bounty, to send rain on your land in season and to bless all the work of your hands. You'll lend to many nations but borrow from none. The Lord will make you the head, not the tail. If you pay attention to the commands of the Lord your God you'll always be at the top, never at the bottom. Don't turn aside from any of the commands I give you today, to the right or to the left, following other gods and serving them.

However, if you don't obey the lord your God and don't carefully follow all his commands and decrees I'm giving you today, all these curses will come upon you and overtake you:

You'll be cursed in the city and in the country.

Your basket and kneading trough will be cursed.

Your children will be cursed, as will the crops of your land, and your livestock.

You'll be cursed when you come in and when you go out.

The Lord will send on you curses, confusion and rebuke in everything you put your hand to, until you're destroyed and come to sudden ruin because of the evil you've done in forsaking him.

The Lord will plague you with diseases until he's destroyed from the land. He'll strike you with wasting disease, with fever and inflammation, with scorching heat and drought, with blight and mildew.

The sky over your head will be bronze, the ground beneath you iron. The Lord will turn the rain of your country into dust and powder; it'll come down from the skies until you're destroyed.

The Lord will cause you to be defeated by your enemies. You'll come at them from one direction but run from them in seven, and you'll become a thing of horror to all the kingdoms on earth. Your carcasses will be food for all the birds and beasts, and no-one will frighten them away.

The Lord will afflict you with the boils of Egypt and with tumours, festering sores and itching, from which you cannot be cured. He will afflict you with madness, blindness and confusion of mind. At midday you'll grope about like a blind man in the dark.

You'll be unsuccessful in everything you do; day after day you'll be oppressed and robbed, with no-one to rescue you. You'll be pledged to be married, but another will take her. You'll build a house, but you won't live in it. You'll plant a vineyard, but you'll not even begin to enjoy its fruit. Your ox will be slaughtered in front of you, but you'll eat none of it. Your donkey will be forcibly taken from you and will not be returned. Your sheep will be given to your enemies, and no-one will rescue them.

Your sons and daughters will be given to another nation, and you'll wear out your eyes watching for them day after day, powerless to lift a hand. A people that you don't know will eat the produce of your land and your labour, and you'll have nothing but cruel oppression all your days. The sights you'll see will drive you mad. The Lord will afflict your knees and legs with painful boils that can't be cured, spreading from the soles of your feet to the top of your head.

The Lord will drive you and the king you set over you to a nation unknown to you or your fathers. There you'll worship other gods, gods of wood and stone. You'll become an object of scorn and ridicule to all the nations where the Lord will drive you.

You'll sow much seed in the field but you'll harvest little, because locusts will eat it. You'll plant vineyards and cultivate them but you'll not drink the wine or gather the grapes, because worms will eat them. You'll have olive trees throughout your country but you'll not use the oil, because the olives will drop off. You'll have sons and daughters but you'll not keep them, because they'll go into captivity.

The alien who lives among you will rise above you higher and higher, but you'll sink lower and lower. He'll lend to you but you won't lend to him. He'll be the head, but you'll be the tail.

All these curses will pursue you and overtake you until you're destroyed, because you didn't obey the Lord your God and observe the commands and decrees he gave you. Because you didn't serve the Lord your God joyfully and gladly in the time of prosperity, so in hunger and thirst, in nakedness and dire poverty, you'll serve the enemies the Lord sends against you. He'll put an iron yoke on your neck until he's destroyed you.

The Lord will bring a nation against you from far away, from the ends of the earth, like an eagle swooping down, a nation whose language you won't understand, a fierce-looking nation without respect for the old or pity for the young. They'll eat the young of your livestock and the crops of your land until you're destroyed. They'll leave nothing behind and they'll lay siege to all your cities until the high fortified walls in which you trust fall down.

Because of the suffering your enemies inflict on you during the siege, you'll eat the children the Lord your God has given you. Even the most gentle and sensitive man among you will have no compassion on his own brother or the wife he loves or his surviving children, and he'll not give to one of them any of the flesh of his children that he's eating. It'll be all he has left because of the siege. The most gentle and sensitive woman among you will begrudge the husband she loves and her own son or daughter the afterbirth from her womb and the children she bears, for she intends to eat them secretly during the siege and in the distress that your enemy will inflict on you in your cities.

Then the Lord will scatter you among all nations, from one end of the earth to the other. Among those nations you'll find no rest, and the Lord will give you an anxious mind and tired eyes full of longing, and a despairing heart. You'll live in constant suspense, filled with dread both night and day, never sure of your life. In the morning you'll say, "If only it was evening!" and in the evening, "If only it was morning!"—because of the terror that will fill your hearts and what you'll see. The Lord will send you back in ships to Egypt on a journey I said you should never make again. There you'll offer yourselves for sale to your enemies as slaves, but no-one will buy you.'

Joshua read all the words of the law—the blessings and the curses—just as it's written in the Book of the Law. There wasn't a word that Moses had commanded that Joshua didn't read to the whole assembly of Israel.

The Tent of Meeting was set up at Shiloh. By then the country was brought under their control, but there were still seven Israelite tribes who had not yet received their inheritance, so Joshua said to them, "How long will you wait before you take the land that God has given you? Select three men from each tribe and I'll send them to make a survey of the land and write a description of it, and when they return you divide the land into seven parts. Judah is to remain in its place on the south and the house of Joseph in its territory on the north. After you've written descriptions of the seven areas, bring them here to me and I'll cast lots for you in the sight of the Lord our God. The Levites, remember, don't get any land because their inheritance is their priestly duties. And Gad, Reuben and the half-tribe of Manasseh have already received their inheritance on the east side of the Jordan."

Town by town the land was surveyed, and when they returned to Shiloh Joshua cast lots for them and distributed the land according to their tribal divisions.

After a long time had passed and the Lord had given Israel rest from all their enemies around them, Joshua, by then he was very old, summoned all the leaders and said to them, "You have personally seen everything God has done to all these nations for your sake; it was God who fought for you. Remember your inheritance and the land that still remains to be taken. God himself will drive them out of your way and you'll take possession of their land, as God has promised you.

"Be very strong; be careful to obey all that's written in the Book of the Law of Moses, without any deviation. Don't associate with these nations that remain among you; don't invoke the names of their gods or swear by them. You must not serve them or bow down to them. You're to hold tight to the Lord your God, as you have until now.

"God has driven out great and powerful nations before you and no-one has been able to withstand you. So be very careful to love the Lord your God.

"But if you turn away and ally yourselves with the survivors of these nations, and if you intermarry with them then you may be sure that God will no longer drive out those nations before you. Instead, they'll become snares and traps for you, whips on your backs and thorns in your eyes, until you perish from off this good land, which has been given you.

"Now I'm about to go the way of all the earth. You know with all your heart and soul that not one of all the good promises the Lord your God gave you has failed. Every promise has been fulfilled. But just as every good promise has come true, so the Lord will bring on you all the evil he has threatened, until he's destroyed you."

At Shechem Joshua said to all the leaders, "This is what the Lord, the God of Israel says: 'Long ago your forefathers, including Terah the father of Abraham and Nahor, lived beyond the River Euphrates and worshipped other gods. But I took your father Abraham from there and led him throughout Canaan and gave him Isaac, and to Isaac I gave Jacob and Easu. I assigned the hill country of Seir (south-east of the Dead Sea) to Easu, but Jacob and his sons went down to Egypt.

"'Then I sent Moses and Aaron, and I afflicted the Egyptians by what I did there, and I brought you out. When you came to the sea the Egyptians pursued you with chariots and horsemen as far as the Sea of Reeds where they cried to the Lord for help when he put darkness between you and them; he brought the sea over them and covered them, as you saw with your own eyes. Then you lived in the desert for a long time.

"'I brought you to the land of the Amorites who lived east of the Jordan. They fought against you, but I gave them into your hands, and you took possession of their land. When Balak, the king of Moab prepared to fight against you, he sent for Balaam to put a curse on you. But I wouldn't listen to Balaam, so he blessed you again and again, and I delivered you out of his hand.

"'Then you crossed the Jordan and came to Jericho, and they fought against you, as did the Amorites, Perizzites, Canaanites, Hittites, Girgashites, Hivites and Jebusites, but I gave them into your hands. So I gave you a land on which you didn't work and cities you didn't build; and you live in them and eat from vineyards and olive groves that you didn't plant.'

"Now fear the Lord and serve him with all faithfulness. Throw away the gods your forefathers worshipped beyond the river and in Egypt, and serve the Lord.

"But if serving the Lord seems undesirable to you, then choose for yourselves this day who you'll serve, whether the gods of your forefathers, or the gods of the Amorites, in whose land you're living. But as for me and my household, we'll serve the Lord."

The people answered,

"Far be it from us to forsake the Lord to serve other gods! We too will serve the Lord, because he is our God."

"You aren't able to serve the Lord," Joshua told them, "he is a holy God; he is a jealous God. He'll not forgive your rebellion and sins. If you forsake the Lord and serve foreign gods, he'll turn and bring disaster on you and make an end of you, after he's been good to you."

"No! We will serve the Lord." The people replied.

"You're witnesses against yourselves that you've chosen to serve the Lord."

"Yes, we're witnesses,"

"Now then, throw away the foreign gods that are among you and yield your hearts to the Lord, the God of Israel."

"We'll serve the Lord our God and obey him."

On that day Joshua made a covenant for the people, and there at Shechem he drew up for them decrees and laws. And he recorded these things in the Book of the Law of God. Then he took a large stone and set it up there under the oak near the holy place of the Lord.

"See! This stone will be a witness against us. It has heard all the words the Lord has said to us. It'll be a witness against you if you're untrue to your God."

16

It Gets Worse

After Joshua had dismissed the Israelites, they went to take possession of the land, each to his own inheritance. During the lifetime of Joshua and the elders who outlived him the people served the lord.

Joshua, the servant of the Lord, died at the age of a hundred and ten and they buried him in the hill country of Ephraim. Another generation grew up who knew neither the Lord nor what he had done for Israel. They did evil in serving the Baals and forsook the Lord who brought them out of Egypt. They served other gods of the people around them and they provoked God to anger because of their unfaithfulness in serving Baal and the Ashtoreths.

Joseph was in an Egyptian jail on a false rape charge when Pharaoh, who was troubled by two dreams he had, learned that a young Hebrew prisoner could interpret the dream for him. So he sent for Joseph and after being cleaned up he came before Pharaoh who told him his dilemma. Joseph was quick to tell him that he couldn't do it, but God could provide the answers that Pharaoh wanted.

After explaining clearly what the dreams meant and providing Pharaoh with a sound policy for dealing with a future famine Pharaoh and his advisors knew they had the right person to deal with this very real problem that they would soon face.

Pharaoh said to Joseph, "Since God has made all this known to you, there's no-one so discerning and wise as you. You'll be in charge of my palace, and all my people are to submit to your orders. Only with respect to the throne will I be greater than you." He went on to say, "I hereby put you in charge of the whole land of Egypt." Pharaoh took his signet ring from his finger and put it on Joseph's finger. He also dressed him in robes of fine linen and put a gold chain around his neck. Joseph rode in a chariot as Pharaoh's second-in-command and men ran ahead shouting, "make way!" and all would bow down. Pharaoh said to Joseph, "I'm Pharaoh, but without your word no-one will do anything. Pharaoh gave Joseph the name Zaphenath-Paneah and gave him Asenath, the daughter of Potiphera, priest of On to be his wife (Re was the sun god worshipped at On, a city which the Greeks later called Heliopolis, city of the sun. From Derek Kidner's commentary on Genesis, page 197).

Two sons were born to Joseph by Asenath, and he named the firstborn Manasseh and said, "It's because God has made me forget all my trouble and my father's household," he had been sold as a slave to the Ishmaelites (Midianites) by his own brothers instead of killing him. The second son he named Ephraim, "because," he said, "God has made me fruitful in the land of my suffering."

He was later reconciled to his brothers and by the time he and all that generation had died the Israelites had gone from seventy five people to a countless multitude so that the land was filled with them. Then a new Pharaoh came to power who didn't know about Joseph so he began to make the Israelites into slaves and they were made to build store cities for Pharaoh.

A new generation can be quite different the previous one, forgetting, or not knowing what went before.

Things change.

Winston Churchill reflected on the changes under the reign of Charles II:

'The Kings example spread its demoralisation far and wide, and the sense of relief from the tyranny of the Puritans spurred forward every amorous adventure. Nature, affronted, reclaimed her rights with usury. The Commonwealth Parliament had punished adultery with death; Charles scourged chastity and faithfulness with ridicule. There can however be no doubt that the mass of the nation in all classes preferred the lax rule of the sinners to the rigorous discipline of the saints.

'The people of England did not wish to be the people of God in the sense of the Puritan God. They descended with thankfulness from the superhuman levels to which they had been painfully hoisted. The heroic age of the constitutional conflict and of the Civil Wars and the grim manifestation of the Puritan Empire were no more. All shrank to a smaller size and an easier pace. Charles noticed how much weaker was the type of manhood of the new generation he found about him than the high-spirited Cavaliers and rugged Roundheads who were dying off' (from 'A History of the English-speaking Peoples' vol. 2. 1969 Edition).

In his anger the Lord handed them over to raiders who plundered them. He sold them to their enemies all around. Whenever Israel went out to fight, the hand of the Lord was against them and they were defeated, just as he had promised them. As a consequence they were in great distress.

Then the Lord raised up leaders for them, who saved them out of the hands of these raiders. Yet they wouldn't listen to their leaders but prostituted themselves to other gods and worshipped them. They were quick to turn from the way their fathers walked.

The Israelites lived among the Canaanites, Hittites, Amorites, Perizzites, Hivites and Jebusites. They took their daughters in marriage and gave their own daughters to their sons, and served their gods.

Every time God raised a leader up for them, he was with that leader to save them from their enemies because he had compassion on them as they groaned under the oppression and affliction that came to them. But when that leader died, the people returned to ways even more corrupt than those of their fathers and they refused to give up their evil practices and stubborn ways.

God's anger burned against Israel so that he sold them into the hands of Cushan-Rishathaim, king of Aram Naharaim (north-west Mesopotamia), to whom the Israelites were subject for eight years. But when they cried out to the Lord, he raised up for them a deliverer, Othniel, who was the son of Caleb's younger brother, who saved them. The Spirit of the Lord came on him, so that he became Israel's leader and went to war. He overpowered Cushan-Rishathaim king of Aram, so the land had peace for forty years, until Othniel died.

Once again the Israelites did evil and so the Lord gave Eglon, king of Moab, power over Israel. The Ammonites and Amalekites also joined him, and the Israelites were subject to him for eighteen years.

As was to be expected, the Israelites cried out to the Lord, and he gave them Ehud, a left-handed Benjamite. The Israelites sent him with tribute to Eglon king of Moab, and when he got to the king he presented the tribute to him and Eglon, who was a very fat man, received it and then Ehud sent those who had carried the tribute away while he turned back and said to the king that he had a secret message for him. The king called for quiet and all his attendants left him. Ehud then approached him while he was alone in the upper room and said, "I have a message from God for you." As the king rose from his seat Ehud reached with his left hand to his right thigh where a double-edged sword about a foot and a half long was strapped and drawing it out he plunged it into the king's belly so far that even the handle sank in after the blade, which came out of his back. Ehud didn't pull out the sword, and the fat closed in over it. Then Ehud shut and locked the doors of the upper room and made his escape.

Meanwhile the king's servants were becoming concerned about the doors being locked and thought that he might be relieving himself so they waited, and when they couldn't wait any longer they found another key and let themselves in and there they saw the king laying on the floor dead.

Their waiting gave Ehud the time to get away. He escaped to Seirah in the hill country of Ephraim where he blew a trumpet and all the Israelites came down from the hills and joined him as their leader.

"Follow me, for the Lord has given Moab, your enemy, into your hands." So they followed him down and taking control of the fords of the Jordan that led to Moab, they allowed no-one to cross over. At that time they killed about ten thousand strong Moabites, and none of them escaped. That day Moab was made subject to Israel, and the land had peace for eighty years.

After Ehud came Shamgar son of Anath (Anath was worshipped as the virgin sister and consort of Baal), who killed six hundred Philistines with an ox-goad. He too saved Israel even though we know nothing of him.

Over a thousand years later a baby was to be born having the name Jesus, which is the Greek form of Joshua, because, as the name signifies, he will save his people from, not the Moabites or the Philistines or even the Romans, but from their sins.

The Israelites once again went back to the gods of the people around them, so the Lord sold them into the hands of Jabin, a king of Canaan, who reigned in Hazor, ten miles north of the Sea of Chinnereth (later the Sea of Galilee). His commander of the army was Sisera, he had nine hundred iron chariots and cruelly oppressed the Israelites for twenty years. They cried to the Lord for help.

At that time Deborah was leading Israel. She held court between Ramah and Bethel in the hill country of Ephraim, and the Israelites came to her to have their disputes settled. She sent for Barak and said to him, "The Lord, the God of Israel commands you to take ten thousand men of Naphtali and Zebulun and lead the way to Mount Tabor. I'll lure Sisera to the Kishon River and give him into your hands."

"If you go with me, I'll go; but if you don't go with me, I'm not going," Barak replied.

"Very well, I'll go with you, but because of the way you're handling this, the honour will not be yours, because the Lord will hand over Sisera to a woman." So Deborah went back to Kedesh with Barak, where he summoned the ten thousand men.

Heber, who was a Kenite, and a descendant of Moses' father-in-law, left the other Kenites and pitched his tent by the great tree in Zaanannim near Kadesh, and his wife's name was Jael.

When Sisera was told that Barak had gone to Mount Tabor, he gathered his nine hundred iron chariots and all the men with him and headed towards to the Kishon River. Then Deborah said to Barak, "Go! This is the day the Lord has given Sisera into your hands, hasn't the Lord gone ahead of you?" So Barak and his ten thousand men went down Mount Tabor and advanced towards Sisera's forces. The lord routed Sisera and he abandoned his chariot and escaped on foot. The rest of his forces were cut down without any survivors.

Sisera reached the tent of Heber and felt safe as there were friendly relations between Jabin king of Hazor and the clan of Heber the Kenite. Jael went out to meet Sisera and invited him in, "Come right in, don't be afraid," and then she put a covering over him.

"I'm thirsty," he said, "please give me some water." She opened a skin of milk and gave him a drink, and then covered him up.

"Stand in the doorway of the tent, if someone comes by and asks you if there's anyone inside, say there isn't."

Sisera fell fast asleep as he was exhausted, and Jael picked up a tent peg and a hammer and moved quietly towards him. She bent over him and drove the peg through the flat part of his head between the forehead and his ear and the peg went right through into the ground.

Barak came looking for Sisera and Jael went out to meet him.

"Come, I'll show you the man you're looking for." He entered the tent and there lay Sisera, pegged to the ground, dead. On that day God subdued Jabin, the Canaanite king, and the hand of the Israelites grew stronger against Jabin, until they destroyed him.

At that time Deborah and Barak sang a new song, it began with; "When the princes of Israel take the lead, when the people willingly offer themselves—praise the Lord!

"Hear this, you kings! Listen, you rulers! I will sing to the Lord, I will sing; I will make music to the Lord, the God of Israel." Later in the song we read the words, "Most blessed of women is Jael, the wife of Heber the Kenite, most blessed of tent-dwelling women.

"He asked for water and she gave him milk; in a bowl fit for nobles she brought him curdled milk. Her hand reached for the tent peg, her right hand for the workman's hammer. She struck Sisera, she crushed his head, she shattered and pierced his temple. At her feet he sank, he fell, there he lay. Where he sank, there he fell—dead."

Then the land had peace for forty years.

But it wasn't too long before the people reverted to doing it their way. As a consequence of this return to evil God gave them into the hands of the Midianites for seven years, and because their rule was so oppressive the Israelites prepared shelters in mountain clefts, caves and strongholds.

Whenever they planted their crops the Midianites and Amalekites, as well as others, invaded the country. They camped on the land and ruined the crops all the way to Gaza and didn't spare a living thing for Israel— they came up with their livestock and tents like swarms of locusts. It was impossible to count the men and their camels. Midian so impoverished the Israelites that they cried out to the Lord for help.

God sent them a prophet, who said, "This is what the Lord, the God of Israel, says, "I brought you up out of Egypt, out of the land of slavery. I snatched you from the power of Egypt and from the hand of all your oppressors. I drove them from before you and gave you their land, I said to you, 'I am the Lord your God; don't worship the gods of the Amorites, in whose land you live.' But you have not listened to me."

Sitting down under the oak in Ophrah, that belonged to Joash the Abiezrite (a clan of the tribe of Manasseh), an angel said to Gideon, Joash's son, as he was threshing wheat in a winepress so as to keep it from the Midianites, "The Lord is with you, mighty warrior."

How shocked Gideon was, or wasn't, isn't recorded, but he answered respectfully, "Sir, if the Lord is with us, why has all this happened to us? Where are all the wonders that our fathers told us about when they said, 'Didn't the Lord bring us up out of Egypt?' But now the Lord has abandoned us and put us into the hand of Midian."

It seems that Gideon was told about all the good things God had done for them, but wasn't filled in on all the rebellion and idolatry that they regularly fell into. It's far easier to see the failings in others than recognise them in ourselves. The words: "You have not listened to me," have a lasting application.

The lord turned to him and said, "Go in the strength you have and save Israel out of Midian's hand. Am I not sending you?"

"But Lord, how can I save Israel? My clan is the weakest in Manasseh, and I'm the least in my family."

"I will be with you, and you will strike down all the Midianites together."

"If now I've found favour in your eyes, give me a sign that's it's really you talking to me. Please wait here while I prepare my offering and I'll come back and set it before you."

"I'll wait till you return."

Gideon went inside and made a big meal that must have taken some time and then brought it all out and offered it the angel sitting under the oak. The angel told him to take the meat and the unleavened bread and place them on a rock that was close by, and pour out the broth. When Gideon did that the angel touched the food with the tip of his staff and instantly a blaze of fire completely burnt the food up. And then the angel disappeared.

Now Gideon was afraid—"Ah, Sovereign Lord! I've seen of the Lord face to face!"

Gideon then heard the Lord say to him, "Be calm, don't be afraid. You're not going to die."

Gideon built an altar to the Lord there and called it, 'The Lord is Peace.' That same night the Lord told him what to do, "Take a mature bull from your father's herd, and tear down your father's altar to Baal, and cut down the Asherah pole next to it. Then build an altar in the correct way, natural uncut stones, on top of the ruins of the Baal altar—use the wood from the Asherah pole, and offer that bull as a burnt offering."

Gideon took ten of his servants and did as the Lord told him, but he did it at night-time because he was afraid of his family and the town's people.

He was right in his estimate of the towns' reaction to what he did. The next morning when they saw what had happened to the Baal altar and the Asherah pole they demanded to know who did it. It didn't take long before they were told it was Joash's son Gideon who was the guilty one. The townsmen confronted Joash and said, "Bring out your son, because of what he did, he must die."

"Are you trying to plead Baal's cause?" Joash replied to the hostile crowd around him, "Are you trying to save Baal? Whoever fights for him shall be put to death by morning! If Baal really is a god, he can defend himself when someone breaks down his altar." On that day they called Gideon 'Jerub-Baal' saying, "Let Baal contend with him," because he broke down Baal's altar.

The Midianites, Amalekites and other eastern peoples crossed over the Jordan and camped in the Valley of Jezreel, there was about 135,000 in total. Then the Spirit of the Lord came to Gideon, and he blew a trumpet, summoning the people of his clan to follow him, and he sent messengers throughout Manasseh, calling them to arms, and also into Asher, Zebulun and Naphtali, so they also came.

Gideon said to God, "If you will save Israel by my hand as you've promised—I'll place a wool fleece on the threshing-floor and if there's dew only on the fleece and all the ground is dry then I'll know that you will save Israel by my hand, as you've said." When Gideon rose early the next morning he squeezed the fleece and wrung out a bowlful of dew.

Gideon said to God, "Don't be angry with me for making just one more request, It's to do with the fleece, this time make the fleece dry and ground covered with dew."

That night God did it. The fleece was dry and all the ground was covered with dew.

We cannot hear God's voice as Gideon did, but we can read them, and still be uncertain as to whether they apply personally to us, or not. We can also easily misapply what we read and come to have false expectations of what God will do, or will not do. It can be difficult to be sure of what specifically applies to us individually. Isn't there something of Gideon in all of us in that we desire some sign of reassurance?

Jesus once said of all the people around him, "O unbelieving generation, how long shall I stay with you? How long will I put up with you?" they were no different from the people of ancient Israel, or us. A boy was possessed by a spirit that robbed him of speech and made him ill with seizures. "Bring the boy to me," Jesus said, and he asked the father of the boy, "How long has he been like this?"

"From childhood." He answered. "It's often thrown him into fire or water to kill him. But if you can do anything, take pity on us and help us."

"'If you can'?" Jesus said. "Everything is possible for him who believes."

"I do believe; help me overcome my unbelief!" When the Pharisees accused Jesus of using the power of Satan in driving demons out of the minds of those afflicted with them he confronted them with their faulty reasoning, "If Satan drives out Satan, he's divided against himself. How then can his kingdom stand? And if I drive out the prince of demons by whom do your people drive them out? But if I drive out demons by the Spirit of God then the kingdom of God has come to you." As long as Jesus was among them the kingdom of God was here on earth with its power and authority over everything that humans have no power to control. Seeing with their own eyes the good things that Jesus was able to do and ascribing the healing to demonic powers the Pharisees were left without any genuine excuse for accepting who he really was—and so they couldn't be forgiven.

Early in the morning Gideon, (who was also known as Jerub-Baal) and his men camped at the spring of Harod. The Midian camp was north of them in the valley near the hill of Moreh. "You've too many men for me to deliver Midian into your hands," the Lord told Gideon, "In order that Israel doesn't boast against me that her own strength has saved her, announce to the people that anyone who trembles with fear may turn back and leave Mount Gilead."

Once his men heard this surprising announcement, 22,000 men left, while 10,000 remained.

"There are still too many men." God told Gideon, "Take them down to the water and separate those who lap the water with their tongues like a dog from those who kneel down to drink."

300 men lapped the water with their hands to their mouths. All the rest got down on their knees to drink. The Lord said to Gideon, "With the 300 men that lapped I'll save you and give the Midianites into your hands. Let all the other men go home.

The camp of Midian lay below him in the valley. During the night Gideon had received his instructions, "Get up and go down to the camp, and if you're afraid, take your servant Purah, and listen to what they're saying. After that you'll be encouraged to attack the camp. In a short while Gideon and Purah were at the outposts of the camp just as a man was telling his friend about his dream. "I dreamed a round loaf of barley bread came tumbling into the camp and it struck the tent with such force that the tent overturned and collapsed."

His friend said, "This can be nothing other than Gideon' sword. God has given the whole camp into his hands."

When Gideon heard that he thanked God, and returning to camp he called out, "Get up!" The Lord has given the Midianite camp into our hands." The 300 were divided into three companies and each man was given trumpets and empty jars with torches inside.

"Watch me, and follow my lead. When I get to the edge of the camp, do exactly what I do. When the company I lead blow our trumpets, you blow yours and shout, 'For the Lord and for Gideon.'"

Gideon and his 100 men reached the edge of the camp at the beginning of the middle watch; they had just changed the guard. Gideon and his men blew their trumpets and broke the jars; the other two companies did the same and held the torches in their left hands and the trumpets in their right, they shouted, "A sword for the Lord and for

Gideon!" They all kept to their positions while panic broke out in the Midian camp as they then began to turn on each other and the blood flowed, but most of them headed off as fast as they could into the desert. The Israelites who were sent home were called out and they pursued the Midianites. Gideon then sent messengers throughout the hill country of Ephraim asking them to come down and seize the waters of the Jordan before the Midianites get there.

The men of Ephraim took the waters of the Jordan as far as Beth Barah and they also captured two of the Midianite leaders, Oreb and Zeeb. They were quickly put to death and their heads were taken to Gideon, who was by the Jordan. The Ephraimites were critical of Gideon for not calling them at the beginning and felt that they had been badly treated by him.

"What have I accomplished compared to you," Gideon said, "God gave the leaders into your hands, I didn't do that, you did well." At this, their resentment left. Gideon and his 300, exhausted as they were, kept up the pursuit and they crossed the Jordan and came to Succoth where he asked for bread for his troops as they were worn out.

But the officials of Succoth said, "Why should we give bread to your troops? Have you captured the other leaders and cut off their hands so we can see them?"

"Just for that," Gideon said to them, "when the Lord has given me those other leaders I'll return and tear your flesh with desert thorns and briers." From there he went up to Peniel and asked them for food, but they gave the same answer. So Gideon told them that when he returns in triumph, he'll tear down their tower.

Out of a force of 135,000, 120,000 had been killed, and the remaining 15,000 were in Karkor, which was on their way to their homeland. Their two leaders, Zebah and Zalmunna were with them. Gideon caught up with them when they thought they were safe and routed their whole army. The two kings of Midian escaped but were pursued and captured.

On his way back Gideon caught a young man of Succoth and questioned him, and the man wrote down the names of seventy seven officials and elders in Succoth. When he and his men got back to Succoth he confronted the leaders with his two Midianite prisoners, and did what he said he'd do because they refused to give bread to his exhausted men. He then moved on to Peniel and pulled down their tower and killed the men of the town.

Gideon asked Zebah and Zalmunna, "What kind of men did you kill at Tabor?"

"Men like you, each one with the bearing of a prince."

"Those were my brothers, my own mother's sons. As surely as the Lord lives, if you had spared their lives, I wouldn't kill you."

"Kill them!" Gideon said to his oldest son, Jether, but he didn't draw his sword because he was young and afraid.

"Come, do it yourself—if you're man enough." The captives said. Gideon stepped forward and killed them.

Now the Israelites wanted Gideon to rule over them, not only him, but his son and grandson—a new dynasty! But Gideon said to them, "I won't rule over you. The Lord will rule over you." He did have one request to make to them, "Each of you give me an ear-ring that you've picked up from the enemy."

"We'll be glad to give them." They spread out a cloak and they all threw a ring onto it. The weight of the gold rings came to 1,700 shekels (about 43 pounds), not counting the ornaments, pendants and the purple clothes worn by the kings of Midian, and the chains that were on their camel's necks.

With these things Gideon made a golden ephod, which he placed in his hometown Ophrah.

The ephod was part of the sacred clothes that the high priest was to wear whenever they entered the Tent of Meeting or approach the altar to serve in the Holy Place, if they wore those special clothes anywhere else they could incur guilt and die.

The instructions for the making an ephod, which was given to skilled craftsmen to do, was to make it 'of gold, and of blue, purple and scarlet yarn, and of finely twisted linen. It's to have two shoulder pieces attached to two of its corners, so that it can be fastened. Its skilfully woven waistband is to be like it—of one piece with the ephod and made with gold, and with blue, purple and scarlet yarn, and with finely twisted linen.' The instructions went on to describe the two onyx stones that had the names of the twelve tribes of Israel engraved on them, and these stones were fastened to the shoulders of the high priest, and there were two braided chains of pure gold, like a rope, linking one stone to the other.

There was no central government in Israel in those days and every tribe, clan and family did what seemed right to them at that time.

In making this ephod Gideon was setting up his own shrine to replace the altar to Baal that he destroyed, rather than pointing people to Shiloh where the Ark of the Covenant was kept, and where the authentic ephod was located.

It's recorded that all Israel prostituted themselves by worshipping this ephod at Ophrah, and it became a snare to Gideon and his family.

For the rest of Gideon's life there were no more attacks from the Midianites, and the land enjoyed peace for forty years. Gideon had seventy sons, because he had many wives. His concubine, who lived in Shechem, gave him a son named Abimelech.

The Baal centres of worship were quickly rebuilt and back up and running soon after Gideon's death and they forgot about the good things Gideon had done for them.

Gideon's son Abimelech spoke to his mother's clan, including the seventy other sons, "Ask the citizens of Shechem what's best for you: to have all seventy of Gideon's sons rule over you, or just one? Remember, I'm your own flesh and blood."

The citizens considered it a reasonable offer and gave him seventy shekels of silver from the temple of Baal-Berith. Abimelech used it to hire some mercenaries, who became his followers. He and his gang of hired hands went to his father's home in Ophrah and on one stone slaughtered his seventy brothers, except for one, Jotham, the youngest son of Gideon, who escaped being killed by hiding. Then all the people of Shechem and Beth Millo came together beside the great tree at the pillar in Shechem to crown Abimelech king; in the same spot that many years before Joshua spoke to all the leaders of Israel and commanded them to fear the Lord and serve him with all faithfulness.

Jotham, fearing for his life, went into exile to a remote place.

Abimelech had governed Israel for three years when God sent an evil spirit, or ill feeling, between Abimelech and the people of Shechem. These were people who belonged to Satan, and thought and acted as he does. God did this in order that the crime against Gideon's seventy sons—the shedding of their blood, might be avenged on their brother Abimelech and the people of Shechem, who had helped him commit these murders.

The people of Shechem opposed Abimelech by setting men on the hilltops to ambush and rob anyone who passed by, and this was reported to Abimelech.

Gaal and his brothers moved into Shechem and its people put their confidence in him. They were holding a festival in the temple of their god and cursing Abimelech when Gaal said, "Why should you serve Abimelech? If only this people were under my command! Then I'd get rid of him—I'd say to him, 'call out your whole army!'"

When Abimelech's deputy, Zebul, who was the governor of the city, heard what Gaal had said, he was angry and sent messengers secretly to Abimelech telling him that Gaal and his brothers were stirring up a rebellion against him. And he advised Abimelech to set up an ambush against Gaal and the city.

The next morning Gaal and Zebul were standing at the entrance to the city gate just as Abimelech and his soldiers came out from their hiding-place.

"Look!" Gaal said, "people are coming down from the tops of the mountains."

"You're mistaking the shadows of the mountains for men," Zebul replied.

"Look, people are coming down from the centre of the land, and a company is coming from the direction of the soothsayer's tree."

"Where's your big talk now, you who said, 'Who is Abimelech that we should be subject to him?' Aren't these the men you ridiculed? Go out and fight them!"

Gaal led out his men but they were soon overwhelmed and cut down. The next day, while the people of Shechem were working in the fields Abimelech attacked them with a part of his force while he rushed for the city gate. The fight went on all day until he finally captured the city and killed those within it, except for about a thousand men and women who took shelter in a strong tower. As soon as Abimelech heard of this he and his men collected branches from nearby trees and piled them at the base of the tower and set it on fire. Everyone within the tower died.

He then went to Thebez and besieged it and captured it. All the people of the city went to their tower for safety, locked themselves in and went to the roof. Abimelech intended to do the same as he had done in Shechem but as he approached the entrance of the tower to set it on fire, a woman dropped an upper millstone on his head and cracked his skull. Quickly he called his armour-bearer, "Draw your sword and kill me, so that they can't say, 'A woman killed him.'" His servant killed him with his sword, and when the Israelites saw that Abimelech was dead, they went home.

In this way God repaid the wickedness that Abimelech had done to his father by murdering his seventy brothers, and God also made the men of Shechem pay for all their wickedness.

Tola, a man of the tribe of Issachar, was the next to save Israel, and he led Israel for twenty-three years.

He was followed by Jair of Gilead, who led Israel for twenty-two years.

The Israelites continued to serve the Baals and the Ashtoreths, and the gods of Aram, Sidon, Moab, and the gods of the Ammonites and of the Philistines. Because of this God sold them to the Philistines and the Ammonites who for eighteen years oppressed all of Israel on the east side of the Jordan in Gilead, the land of the Ammonites, who crossed the Jordan to fight against the tribes of Judah, Benjamin and Ephraim; and Israel was in great distress. They cried out to the Lord, "We've sinned against you by forsaking our God and serving the Baals."

"After the many times I've saved you and you still served other gods now the time has come for you to cry out to these gods that you've chosen and let them save you!"

"We've sinned. Do whatever you think best to us, but please rescue us now."

They then got rid of the foreign gods among them and served the Lord. God couldn't bear Israel's misery any longer.

The prophet Isaiah wrote that: 'In all their distress he too was distressed, and the angel of his presence saved them. In his love and mercy he redeemed them all the days of old.'

Jephthah was a strong warrior of Gilead, but he was driven away by his own family because his mother wasn't the same mother they had. His father, whose name was also Gilead, went with a prostitute and the result was Jephthah. He was told that he'd get no inheritance in their family because he was the son of another woman. So he left and settled in the land of Tob, east of the Jordan. There he became the leader of a band of men.

Meanwhile the Ammonites were prepared for war and camped in Gilead, and the Israelites were camped in Mizpah, and they said to each other, "Whoever will launch the attack against the Ammonites will be the head of all those living in Gilead."

The elders of Gilead came to the decision that they wanted to go and get Jephthah from Tob. When they got to him they said, "Come and be our commander, so we can fight the Ammonites."

"Didn't you hate me and drive me from my father's house? Why do you come to me now, when you're in trouble?"

"Whatever, we're turning to you now. Come with us, and you'll be the head of all who live in Gilead."

"Suppose I do go back with you and fight them, and win, will I really be your head?"

"The Lord is our witness; we'll certainly do as you say."

So Jephthah became the head and commander over them. He then sent messengers to the Ammonite king, asking him his reason for attacking the country. The king's answer can back stating: "When Israel came out of Egypt, they took away my land from the Arnon to the Jabbok, all the way to the Jordan. Now give it back peacefully."

Jephthah sent his reply: "Israel didn't take the land of Moab or the land of the Ammonites. But when they came up out of Egypt, they went through the desert to the Sea of Reeds and on to Kadesh. Then they sent messengers to the king of Edom, asking for permission to go through his country, but he refused. They also sent to the king of Moab, but he too refused, so they stayed at Kadesh.

"Next they travelled through the desert, and skirting the lands of Edom and Moab, passed along the eastern side of the country of Moab, and camped on the other side of the Arnon. They didn't enter the territory of Moab. The Arnon was its border. Then Israel sent messengers to Sihon king of the Amorites, who ruled in Heshbon, asking him if they could pass through his country, but he refused and fought against Israel. But Israel defeated them and took over all his land.

"Now since the Lord, the God of Israel has driven out the Amorites, what right do you have to take it over? You take what your god Chemosh gives you, and we'll do the same. Are you any better than Balak, king of Moab, he didn't risk war with Israel. For three hundred years Israel occupied Heshbon and all the towns along the Arnon. Why didn't you retake them during that time? I've not wronged you, but you're doing me a wrong by waging war against me, Let the Lord, the Ruler, decide the dispute this day between the Israelites and the Ammonites."

No answer came back. Then the Spirit of the Lord came to Jephthah and he advanced against the Ammonites. It was then that he made a vow to the Lord that to our minds sounds the height of stupidity, but none of us can really get inside of the head of a person that would make such a rash and senseless promise. He said, "If you give the Ammonites into my hands, whatever comes out of the door of my house to meet me when I return in triumph will be the Lord's, and I'll sacrifice it as a burnt offering."

The war with the Ammonites was won and twenty towns were devastated.

Jephthah returned to his home in Mizpah, and coming out to meet him was his daughter, dancing to the sound of tambourines. She was his only child, and when he saw her he tore his clothes and said, "Oh! My daughter! I'm sick and wretched, because I've made a vow to the Lord that I can't break." Perhaps he was reminded by the words of Moses: 'If you make a vow to the Lord your God, do not be slow to pay it, for the Lord your God will certainly demand it of you and you will be guilty of sin. But if you refrain from making a vow, you will not be guilty. Whatever your lips utter you must be sure to do, because you made your vow freely to the Lord your God with your own mouth.'

"My father, you've given your word to the Lord. Do to me just as you promised, now that the Lord has avenged you of your enemies. But grant me two months to roam the hills and weep with my friends, because I'll never marry."

"You may go," he said. She and the girls went into the hills and wept because she would never marry. After two months, she returned to her father and he did to her as he had vowed.

The book of Proverbs speaks wise words to those who don't think well and long on making a vow: 'It is a trap for a man to dedicate something rashly and only later to consider his vows.'

The men of Ephraim crossed over to Zaphon with their forces and said to Jephthah, "Why did you go to fight the Ammonites without calling us to go with you? We're going to burn down your house over your head."

"I and my people were fully engaged with the Ammonites, and I did call you, but you didn't come—I took my life in my hands and crossed over to fight them, and the Lord gave me the victory over them. Now why have you come here today to fight me?"

Jephthah and the men of Gilead fought against Ephraim and hit them hard because the Ephraimites had said that the Gileadites were no longer a part of the family of tribes that lived in that area. The fords of the Jordan were captured by the Gileadites and each man who wanted the cross the river was given a pronunciation test to reveal where he was from and if it wasn't to the guard's satisfaction they were taken to one side and killed.

Forty-two thousand Ephraimites were killed at that time. Jephthah died having led Israel for six years and he was buried in a town in Gilead.

After him, Ibzan of Bethlehem led Israel for seven years.

Next was Elon from the tribe of Zebulun. He led Israel for ten years.

Then came Abdon from Pirathon, which was west of Shechem in the land of Ephraim. He led Israel for eight years.

Once more the Israelites did evil and so the Lord gave them into the hands of the Philistines for forty years.

17

Strength in Weakness

In the land of the Danites (Dan was one of the sons of Jacob by his wife's servant Bilhah, who was given to him because at that time Rachel couldn't bear any children for Jacob) Manoah and his wife, whose name we don't know, and who was childless, lived in the town of Zorah.

An angel came to her and said, "You're sterile and childless, but you'll have a son, and you must see to it that you don't drink any wine or other fermented drink and don't eat anything that by God's law is unfit to eat. This son that you will have must not have his hair cut because he's to be a Nazirite, set apart to God from birth, and he'll begin the deliverance of Israel from the Philistines."

Then the woman went and told her husband what had happened, and he prayed that the man of God would return and teach them how to bring this special boy up. A few days later, when the woman was out in the field, the angel of God returned, but her husband wasn't with her so she hurried to tell him that the angel is back. They both went to where the man was and Manoah asked him, "Are you the one who talked to my wife?"

"I am," he said.

"When what you've said happens, what rules must we follow for the boy?"

"I've told your wife everything she must do."

"We'd like you to stay while we prepare a young goat for you."

"Even if I do stay, I won't eat any of your food. But if you prepare a burnt offering, offer it to the Lord."

"What's your name, so that we may honour you when what you've said comes true?"

"Why do you ask my name? That's beyond understanding."

Manoah took the young goat and the grain offering and sacrificed it on a rock to the Lord. They stood there watching as the fire blazed up into the air and then this person who looked just like a man stepped into the fire and was lifted up in the flames, seeing this they both fell face down to the ground with a realisation of who they had been speaking with.

"We're going to die!" he said to his wife, "We've seen God!"

"If the Lord had meant to kill us," his wife said, "he wouldn't have accepted the burnt offering from us, nor tell us what's going to happen."

The woman gave birth to a boy and named him Samson.

Samson went down to Timnah and found a Philistine woman there that attracted him, so when he returned to his parents he bluntly told them to get her so she could be his wife.

"Isn't there enough good women among your relatives or your own people? Why go to the uncircumcised Philistines for a wife?"

"Get her for me. She's the one I want." (This hard-headedness actually came from the Lord who was laying the groundwork for conflict with the Philistines)

Samson and his parents went down to Timnah, and while he was some distance ahead of his parents a lion charged at him and the Spirit of the Lord powerfully came to him and he killed the lion as easily as if it was a young goat. He didn't tell his parents what had happened, and they eventually got to speak with the woman that Samson wanted to marry.

Sometime later, he went back to marry her he came across the carcass of the lion and saw in it a swarm of bees and some honey. He scooped some of it out with his hands and ate it as he walked along, when he rejoined his parents he gave them some, and they ate it too.

As was the custom, he made a feast there and another custom was that he was given thirty companions.

"Let me give you a riddle," he said to his new friends.

"If you can give me the answer within the seven days of the feast, I'll give you thirty items of clothing and thirty linen garments. If you can't tell me the answer, you give them to me."

"Tell us the riddle, let's hear it."

"Out of the eater, something to eat; out of the strong, something sweet."

They were unable to find the answer, so on the fourth day they said to Samson's wife, "Get your husband to tell you the answer or we'll burn your house with you and your family in it. Did you invite us here to get robbed?"

Samson's wife turned on the tears, "You hate me!" she said between sobs, "you don't really love me—you're giving my people a difficult riddle and you haven't even told me the answer."

"I haven't explained it to my parents, so why should I explain it to you?"

The crying continued until on the seventh day Samson's resolve cracked and he told her. Then she went and told her people.

Before sunset on that last day (they counted the day from sunset to sunset) the men of the town said to him, "What is sweeter than honey? What is stronger than a lion?"

"If you hadn't ploughed with my heifer, you wouldn't have solved my riddle."

Then the Spirit of the Lord powerfully came on him, and he went down to the coastal town of Ashkelon and struck down thirty men, stripped them of their clothes and gave them to those who explained the riddle. Full of anger he returned to his parent's home. His new wife was given to a friend who attended his wedding.

At the time of the wheat harvest, Samson took a young goat and went to visit his wife. He tried to get in but her father would not let him,

"I was sure that you really hated her," her father said, "so I gave her to your friend, her younger sister is attractive, isn't she? Take her instead."

"This time I have a right to get even with the Philistines—I'll seriously harm them." He caught three hundred foxes and tied them tail to tail, and put a torch to every pair of tails. After lighting the torches he released them into the standing corn of the Philistines, as well as the vineyards and olive groves.

"Who did this!" the outraged Philistines asked, "Samson, the Timnite's son-in-law, because his wife was given to his friend," they were told. The Philistines went directly to where they lived and burned her and her father to death. Samson let them know that because of what they've done he wouldn't stop 'til he got his revenge on them.

He attacked them viciously and slaughtered many of them. He then went and stayed in a cave in the rock of Etam, south of Bethlehem.

The Philistines moved in force into Judah, and the men of Judah asked them if they've come to fight them. "We've come to take Samson prisoner," they answered, "we'll do to him what he did to us."

Three thousand men of Judah came to Samson at his cave house and accused him of making the situation with their Philistine rulers worse.

"I merely did to them what they did to me," Samson said to them.

"We've come to tie you up and hand you over to the Philistines."

"Promise me that you won't kill me yourselves."

"We agree, we're only going to tie you up and hand you over, we're not going to kill you."

They tied him with two new ropes and led him out. When the Philistines saw him they came towards him shouting. At that moment the power of the Lord's Spirit came to him and the ropes binding his arms became like the stems of old flowers and the cord tied round his hands just fell off. He found a fresh jaw-bone of a donkey and with it struck down a thousand men.

Samson said, "With a donkey's jaw-bone I've made heaps of donkeys of them. With a donkey's jaw-bone I've killed a thousand men."

He threw away the jaw-bone and the place was called Ramath Lehi, which means *jaw-bone hill*.

Samson cried out to the Lord because of his thirst, "You've given your servant a great victory. Must I now die of thirst and my body taken by the uncircumcised?" God opened the hollow place in the hill and water came out of it. Samson drank and his strength returned. The spring was called En Hakkore, which means *caller's spring*.

Samson went down to the Philistine city of Gaza and saw a prostitute who he intended spending the night with. The people of Gaza got to hear that Samson was there and surrounded the place planning to kill him at dawn. But Samson got up in the middle of the night and tore the doors of the gate loose, including the two posts and the bar, and carried them on his shoulders to the top of the hill that faces east towards Hebron.

He later fell in love with a woman whose name was Delilah. The Philistine rulers encouraged her, with the offer of eleven hundred shekels of silver to find out how his great strength could be overcome.

"Tell me the secret of your great strength and how you can be restrained." Delilah asked him.

"If anyone ties me with seven fresh bow-strings that are still wet, I'll become as weak as the next man."

The seven fresh bow-strings were given to Delilah which she tied Samson with, and with men hidden close by she called out, "Samson, the Philistines are here!" But he easily snapped the bow-strings at which Delilah reproached him for making a fool of her, "You lied to me, please, tell me how you can be tied."

"If anyone securely ties me with new ropes that have never been used, I'll be as weak as the next man."

The new ropes were provided and Delilah tied him with them and made the same call, "Samson, the Philistines are here!" But he snapped the ropes as though they were cotton threads.

"All this time," Delilah complained, "you've been making a fool of me with your lies; now tell me how you can be tied!"

"If you were to weave the seven braids of my hair to the fabric on your loom and tighten it with the pin, I'll be no different to any other man."

While Samson was sleeping she attached his hair to the loom and tightened it with the pin, and again shouted, "Samson, the Philistines are here!" He woke and pulled up the pin and the loom with the fabric.

"How can you say, 'I love you,' when you won't confide in me? This is the third time you've made a fool of me and haven't told me your secret." Day after day she asked, nagged and prodded him until he broke and told her the truth.

"No razor has ever been used on my head," he said, "because since my birth I've been set apart as a Nazirite. If my head was shaved, my strength would leave me, and I would be the same as other men."

Delilah knew that this time she had the truth, so she called for the rulers of the Philistines to come back once more. When they came they had the money with them. She put Samson to sleep on her lap and called for a man who saved off his seven braids of hair, and as it was being cut his strength began to weaken.

When it was finished she called, as she had done before, "Samson, the Philistines are here!" He woke, not realising his hair had been cut, and that the lord had left him. When the Philistines ran in they quickly overpowered him and gouged his eyes out. Delilah received her payment and they took him down to Gaza and securing him with bronze shackles set him to grinding in the prison. But his hair began to grow again.

There came a day when the rulers of the Philistines assembled together to celebrate and offer a great sacrifice to Dagon their god. "Our god has delivered Samson, our enemy, into our hands." The rulers announced, and when the people saw him they praised their god, saying, "Our god has delivered our enemy into our hands, the one who laid waste our land and multiplied our dead."

While they were enjoying themselves, they shouted for Samson to be brought out to entertain them, so he was set before them. They stood him between the pillars and Samson asked the servant who held his hand to place him where he could feel the pillars that supported the temple. The temple was overcrowded with people as well as all the rulers, and on the roof there were about three thousand people watching Samson perform.

Then Samson prayed to the Lord, "O Sovereign Lord, remember me, O God, please strengthen me just once more, and let me with one blow get revenge on the Philistines for my two eyes." Samson reached towards the two central pillars on which the temple stood. His right hand was on one and his left hand on the other. His last words were, "Let me die with the Philistines!" Then he pushed with all his might, and the temple came down with all the people in and on it. He killed more when he died than when he was alive.

His brothers and his father's whole family went down to get him. They brought him back and buried him between Zorah and Eshtaol in the tomb of Manoah his father. He had led Israel twenty years.

Did Samson deserve God's help? He was both unwise and unfaithful in his use of the gifts he had been given but he knew the Philistines were the enemy and should be fought against, unlike the men of Judah who accepted the Dagon worshipper's rule. None of us deserve God's help—he does it because of who he is, not what we are.

18

A Priest for Hire

Micah, a man from the hill country of Ephraim, confessed to his mother that the 1,100 shekels of silver that were stolen from her, had, in fact, been taken by him. "I took it," he said, and then returned it to her.

"The Lord bless you, my son," she said to him. "I solemnly consecrate my silver to the Lord for my son to make a carved image and a cast idol. I'll give it back to you."

She took 200 shekels of silver and gave them to a silversmith, who made them into the image and the idol, and they were put into Micah's house which he had turned into a house of gods. Meanwhile the authentic 'house of God' was still at Shiloh.

Micah made an ephod and some teraphim (household gods; busts, masks, or full-figured representations of the human form whose primary function was to represent the family or clan deity) and installed one of his sons as his priest. Everyone was doing what they thought was right for them.

Arriving at Micah's house was a young Levite who had left Bethlehem in search of another place to stay.

"Where're you from?" Micah asked him.

"I'm a Levite from Bethlehem in Judah, and I'm looking for a place to stay."

"Live with me and be my father and priest—I'll give you 10 shekels of silver a year, plus clothes and food." Micah's offer is accepted by the young Levite and he became like a son to him. We don't know how this arrangement worked as Micah had already installed one of his sons as his priest. A real Levite, Micah thought, must be more advantageous to his worship than a person from a non-priestly tribe.

"Now I know," Micah said, "that the Lord will be good to me, since this Levite has become my priest." It all looked and felt right to him.

The tribe of Dan had not yet found the land of their inheritance so they sent five warriors from Zorah and Eshtaol to explore the land. On their journey through the hill country of Ephraim they came to the house of Micah and from outside they recognised the voice of the young Levite. "What are you doing here?" they asked him,

"Micah has hired me and I'm his priest."

"Please enquire to God," they asked, "whether our journey will be successful."

"Go in peace," he answered, "your journey has the Lord's approval."

After spending the night there they moved on and came to Laish, south-west of Zorah, where they saw that the people there seemed not to be concerned over defences or fortifications, but lived openly and safely without anybody controlling them.

"How did it go?" They were asked when they arrived back in Zorah and Eshtaol. "It's a good land, and we shouldn't hesitate to go there and take it over, the land doesn't lack anything," they reported.

Armed for battle 600 men from the tribe of Dan set out and came first to Micah's house because the five men who did the scouting told the others that Micah's house is full of household gods, which they could do with.

The young Levite greeted the men at the entrance to the gate, while the five Danites went inside the house and took the carved image, the ephod, the other household gods and the cast idol. When the priest saw what they were doing he protested but was told to be quiet and not say a word. "Come with us," they said to him, "and be our father and priest. Isn't it better that you serve a tribe and clan in Israel as priest than just one man's household?"

The priest was happy at the new job offer and he helped move all the idols from the house and went along with the people.

After they had gone some distance the men who lived near Micah joined him and went after the Danites. When they'd caught up with them the Danites turned and said to Micah, "Have you called out your men to fight?"

"You took the gods I made, and my priest, what else do I have? Why shouldn't I be angry?"

"Don't get angry with us, or some of our men will attack you, and you and your family will end up dead."

Micah could see that they were too strong for him so he reluctantly turned around and went back home.

The Danites arrived at Laish, the place where the people lived peacefully, and they attacked them and burned down their city. There was no-one to rescue them as they lived a long way from the Sidonians, a coastal people, and had little contact with anyone else. Their town was in a valley near Beth Rehob.

The Danites rebuilt the city and settled there. They named it Dan after their forefather, one of the sons of Jacob whose name was changed to Israel. There they set up their idols and the grandson of Moses, Johnathan, and later his sons, were priests for the tribe of Dan. All the time the house of God was in Shiloh.

Much later a king of Israel, Jeroboam, who split the Israelites from the house of David and brought about two nations at war with each other, made two golden calves and said to the people, "It's too much for you to go up to Jerusalem. Here are your gods, O Israel, who brought you up out of Egypt." One he set up in Bethel, and the other in Dan.

(These accounts of Israel during the time before the monarchy was established are not necessary in chronological order and some of the events could have been happening around the same period of time)

19

The Crime that shocked the Nation

A Levite who lived in a remote area of the hill country of Ephraim took a woman from Bethlehem in Judah to be his wife, but she was more like property to him. She became unfaithful and angrily left him and went back to her father's house in Bethlehem. After four months he went there to persuade her to return, he had with him a servant and two donkeys. She took him into her father's house and he gave him a warm welcome. The girl's father invited him to stay, and he stayed there for three days. When he was ready to go his father-in-law asked him to stay longer, so they both made themselves comfortable and ate and drank, and he stayed another night. This happened over the next few days until he was unwilling to stay any longer. It was getting late but the man saddled his donkeys and with his wife and servant went towards Jebus (Jerusalem).

When they were near Jebus and the sun was going down, his servant suggested that they spend the night in the town of the Jebusites, but his master said that they would go on to Gibeah, as the Jebusites weren't

Israelites. So they went on until they reached Gibeah in Benjamin. There they stopped and sat in the town square, but no-one took them in for the night.

It was late evening when an old man from the hill country of Ephraim, who was living in Gibeah, came in from his work in the fields. When the old man saw them he asked, "Where're you going? Where did you come from?"

He answered, "We're on our way from Bethlehem in Judah to a remote area in the hill country of Ephraim where I live. We've straw and fodder for our donkeys and bread and wine for ourselves—we don't need anything."

"You're welcome at my house. Let me supply whatever you need. Only don't spend the night here in the square."

So he took them in and fed his donkeys. After they'd washed their feet, they had something to eat and drink.

While they were comfortable and enjoying themselves, there came a pounding on the door. The house was surrounded and they were shouting to the old man to bring out the man who's with him so that they could have sex with him. This horrific demand reminds us of when the two angels, looking just like men, where inside of Lot's house in the city of Sodom. They rescued Lot, his wife and two daughters at that time from the total destruction that was about to fall on that city and the other cities of the plain. But there appeared no rescuing angels in Gibeah that night.

The old man went outside and said to them, "No, this man is my guest—don't be so disgusting in wanting to do such a vile thing. There are two women in the house; my virgin daughter and the man's concubine, I'll bring them out to you now and you can use them in any way you want. But you're not going to do this terrible thing to this man."

They wouldn't listen to him, so the man took his concubine and threw her outside to them, and they raped and abused her all through the night. At dawn they released her. She managed to get back to the house where her master was staying and fell before the door and lay there until daylight.

When her master opened the door, ready to continue on his way, he immediately saw his concubine laid at the door with her hands on the doorstep.

"Get up, let's go." He said to her, but there was no answer, she was dead. He lay her over his donkey and set out for home.

When he reached home he took a knife and cut her up, piece by piece, into twelve parts and sent them into all the areas of Israel. Everyone who saw it said, "Such a thing has never been done since the Israelites left Egypt. Something must be done. Think about it! What can we do?"

Then all the Israelites from Dan to Beersheba, and from Gilead east of the Jordan, assembled together before the Lord at Mizpah, approximately five miles north of Gibeah. This was a show of unity never before seen, there were 400,000 armed men there, except that the Benjamites weren't there, but they knew what was happening. Gibeah was a Benjamite city.

"Tell us how this awful thing happened." The Levite was asked, and he began to recount what had happened, slanting the account in his favour: "I and my concubine came to Gibeah in Benjamin to spend the night, and during the night the local men came after me and surrounded the house, intending to kill me. They raped my concubine and she died. I took her and cut her into twelve pieces and sent one piece to each tribe because they committed such a dreadful act in Israel. Now, speak and give your verdict."

"None of us," they all agreed, "will go home. We'll go up against Gibeah. We'll send for provisions first for the army, then, when the army gets to Gibeah we'll give them what they deserve. Men were sent throughout Benjamin to say, "What about this awful crime that was committed among you? Surrender those wicked men of Gibeah so we can put them to death and purge the evil from Israel."

But the Benjamites wouldn't listen to their brother Israelites. From their towns they came together at Gibeah to fight against the Israelites. They were quickly able to mobilise 26,000 swordsmen from their towns as well as 700 chosen men from Gibeah itself. Among the total number were 700 who were left-handed, each of them were experts in the use of the sling.

The Israelites went up to Bethel, which means, *the house of God* to enquire of God who should go first against the Benjamites. The answer came back: Judah.

The next morning the battle began and the Benjamites were able to kill 22,000 Israelites that day. The Israelites went up before the Lord and cried until the evening and they asked of the Lord if they should go up again against their brothers the Benjamites, the answer was yes, so they encouraged each other and again took up the same positions they had on the first day.

This time the Benjamites killed 18,000 armed Israelites. Then all the Israelite people went up to Bethel where they sat weeping before the Lord. They fasted till evening and offered sacrifices to the Lord. In those days the ark of the covenant of God was there, and Phinehas, grandson of Aaron was serving before it. They asked again if they should continue the fight, or not. The answer was for them to fight, "For tomorrow I'll give them into your hands."

This time Israel set an ambush, as Joshua did at Ai, and when the Benjamites came out of the city, as they'd done before, they began to inflict casualties on the Israelites as they'd expected to do, but this time, as they were saying, "We're defeating them again," the Israelites, who had lain in ambush and had been waiting until the Benjamites were far enough from the city, made a frontal attack on Gibeah with 10,000 of their finest troops. The fighting was so heavy that the Benjamites didn't realise how close disaster was. On that day 25,100 armed Benjamites were killed, and they knew that they were beaten.

The men of Israel had arranged with those who were in ambush that they would retreat before the Benjamites and so draw them out further, giving time for those attacking the city to get inside and after killing everyone set it on fire, once that was done the retreating Israelites would turn and attack the pursuing Benjamites. The Benjamites turned and saw their city on fire and were terrified as they realised that they had lost. Many of them ran for the desert, but they were cut down. They had surrounded them to the east of Gibeah and 18,000 Benjamites died there, all brave fighters, and 5,000 were killed on the roads and 2,000 more, further away. Only 600 men were left and they went into the desert to the rock of Rimmon, where they stayed for four months.

All those living in Benjamite towns were put to the sword, including the animals and everything else they found. Then the towns were set on fire.

The men of Israel had taken an oath at Mizpah: "Not one of us will give his daughter in marriage to a Benjamite."

They went to Bethel again and sat before God weeping bitterly, "O Lord the God of Israel, why has this happened to Israel? Why should one tribe be missing from Israel today?" they were grieving for their brothers, the Benjamites. Early the next day they built an altar and presented burnt offerings and peace offerings.

They then asked, "Who from all the tribes of Israel has failed to assemble before the Lord?" They had taken a solemn oath that anyone who failed to go to Mizpah certainly be put to death. They discovered that no-one from Jabesh Gilead, north and east of the Jordan had come to the camp for the assembly. 12,000 fighting men were ordered to go there and kill everyone they found, except for the women who were virgins. They found, after they had killed the rest, 400 young women and they took them to the camp at Shiloh.

An offer of peace was sent to the Benjamites at the rock of Rimmon. They accepted the offer and returned to be given the women of Jabesh

Gilead who had been spared. But there was still not enough for all of them.

There was now a gap in the tribes of Israel and the people grieved for Benjamin.

"With the women of Benjamin destroyed, how shall we provide wives for the men who are left?" The elders asked. "The Benjamite survivors must have heirs so that a tribe of Israel isn't wiped out. We can't give them our daughters as wives, since we've taken the oath that anyone who gives a wife to a Benjamite is cursed. But there is the annual festival to the Lord in Shiloh, to the north of Bethel."

They instructed the Benjamites to go and hide in the vineyards and watch. When they see the girls come out to join in the dancing, then rush in and grab a wife and return to your own land. When the fathers and brothers bring their complaints to us we'll say to them, "You didn't give your daughters to them so you're innocent of breaking the oath, be kind to us by helping them, because we didn't get wives for them during the war."

The Benjamites did as they were instructed and each man caught a girl, no doubt protesting vigorously, and carried her off to be his wife. When they returned to their own land they rebuilt their towns and settled in them.

There was no king in Israel then and everyone did what they wanted to do.

A Benjamite from Gibeah became the first king over Israel. Although he was a head taller than others he was, as it's written, 'small in his own eyes,' and even hid when the time came to publicly announce his appointment as king. Samuel presented him before the people and said, "Do you see the man the Lord has chosen? There is no-one like him among the people." Then all the people shouted, "Long live the king!" His name was Saul.

His reign began well, but it was soon apparent that he had little self control and had difficulty in following what God had commanded him. He was quick to admit his sins but was unable to master his strong emotions, his successor, David, was anointed privately while Saul was still alive. At the moment of David's anointing with oil the Spirit of God came on David in power, while the Spirit of the Lord had left Saul and an injurious spirit from the Lord troubled him.

There was another Saul, also a Benjamite. He belonged to the strictest religious group in Israel, then known as Judea, he was a Pharisee and as far as following the letter of the law and the traditions of the elders he was faultless. This sort of achievement induced a self righteousness in him which led naturally to an intolerant attitude towards all who didn't share the same degree of commitment and a hatred of those who were in any way critical of their teachings. Until one day when in his dedication to eradicating the followers of Jesus he and his small group travelled towards Damascus and when they were close to the city a stunning brilliant light caused him to fall blinded to the ground and a clear voice said to him, "Saul, Saul, why do you persecute me?"

"Who are you, Lord?" Saul asked.

"I'm Jesus, whom you're persecuting, now get up and go into the city, and you'll be told what you must do."

So deeply life-changing was this encounter with Jesus, that when his sight returned (after Ananias had placed his hands on him and said, "Brother Saul, the Lord Jesus has sent me so that you may see again and be filled with the Holy Spirit,") he spent a few days with the disciples in Damascus, then he began to preach in the synagogues that Jesus is the Son of God and all those who heard him were astonished that he was the same person who had caused havoc in Jerusalem for those who followed Jesus. Yet through his understanding of the Scriptures was able to prove that Jesus was the Messiah. Because of the many who came to believe him the Jews planned to kill him, but Saul learned of their plan and he was helped to escape by night by being lowered in a basket through an opening in the wall. He then, according to what he told the Galatians, 'didn't consult with any man, nor did I go up to Jerusalem to see those who were apostles before I was, but I went immediately into Arabia and later returned to Damascus.' It wasn't till three years later that he went to Jerusalem and met Peter and James, the brother of Jesus. Perhaps he needed more time to fully digest this shocking revelation and to relearn everything he had taken as true.

He later said, when he stood before King Agrippa, what else Jesus had said to him, "I have appeared to you to appoint you as a servant and as a witness of what you've seen of me and what I'll show you. I'll rescue you from your own people and from the Gentiles. I'm sending you to them to open their eyes and turn them from darkness to light and from the power of Satan to God, so that they may receive forgiveness of sins and a place among those who are sanctified by faith in me."

Saul, better known as Paul, preached to both Jews and Greeks that they must turn to God in repentance and have faith in the Lord Jesus. Previously he was convinced he was right when he was wrong and opposed the name of Jesus of Nazareth to the point of using his authority to imprison the saints, and when they were condemned to death, he cast his vote against them. From the time of his conversion he preached about the kingdom of God, explaining and trying to convince people who Jesus was, from the writings of Moses and from the Prophets.

20

On Mount Carmel

The Baal worshippers, numbering about four hundred and fifty, were beginning to tire. They had been passionately calling on the deities name from morning till noon. Around the altar they danced and shouted for Baal to answer them and even cut themselves with swords and spears, all to no avail, the heavens were silent. A rough looking prophet encouraged them to "shout louder!" and added, "Surely he's a god! Perhaps he's deep in thought or gone out for the morning." His suggestions didn't seem to help as their fervour and blood flowed out. Midday passed and they continued their urgent pleas for a divine response—but nothing happened, no-one answered, no-one paid attention.

It had been about three hundred and sixty-five years since the Benjamites carried off those screaming girls to a new life away from their people, and their tribe. Now was the time of the kings, both for Israel and Judah. The division of what was once one nation happened when King Rehoboam, Soloman's son, decided to go against the advice of the elders to lower the taxes and lessen the forced labour, in other words, to serve his people, and took the advice of the young men he'd grow up with to raise the taxes and maintain the forced labour.

At this Jeroboam, who had been in exile in Egypt, said to the king, "What share do we have in David? To your tents, O Israel! Look after your own house, O David!" So the Israelites went home, but for those Israelites who were living in the towns of Judah, Rehoboam still ruled over them.

This division came from God. Before Jeroboam went into exile he was met going out of Jerusalem by a prophet of Shiloh named Ahijah who was wearing a new cloak. They were alone and Ahijah took off this cloak and tore it into twelve pieces, and said to Jeroboam, "Take ten pieces for yourself, because this is what the God of Israel says, 'Watch, I'm going to tear the kingdom out of Solomon's hands and give you ten tribes. But for the sake of my servant David and the city of Jerusalem, which I've chosen out of all the tribes of Israel, he'll have one tribe. I'll do this because they've forsaken me and worshipped Ashtoreth the goddess of the Sidonians, Chemosh the god of the Moabites, and Molech the god of the Ammonites, and haven't walked in my ways, nor done what is right in my eyes, nor kept my statutes and laws as David, Solomon's father, did.

"'But I'll not take the whole kingdom out of Solomon's hand; I'll take the kingdom from his son's hand and give you ten tribes. I will take you, and you will rule over all that your heart desires—you'll be king over Israel, If you do whatever I command you and walk in my ways, as David my servant did, I'll be with you and build you a dynasty as enduring as the one I built for David. I'll humble David's descendants because of this, but not for ever.'"

That's when Solomon tried to kill Jeroboam, but he quickly left for Egypt and stayed there until Solomon's death.

There was splendour about Solomon's reign and his wisdom was acknowledged beyond the borders of Israel; King David, his father, saw that wisdom in him when he gave his final instructions on his death bed, "Be strong and show yourself a man," David said to him, "Observe what the Lord your God requires and walk in his ways." David asked Solomon to show kindness to the sons of Barzillai of Gilead "and let them eat at your table because they stood by me when I had to escape from your brother Absalom."

As was the custom for many leaders when passing on their last instructions David brought up the cases of two men, Joab and Shimei, who warranted the death sentence but were still alive. David told Solomon to deal appropriately with them which he did.

Solomon made an alliance with Pharaoh and married his daughter and later when he had finished building the temple of the Lord and the royal palace the Lord appeared to him for the second time and said to him, "I've heard the prayer you've made, and I've consecrated this temple which you've built by putting my name there forever—my eyes and my heart will always be there.

"As for you, if you walk before me in integrity of heart as David did and do all I command, I'll establish your royal throne over Israel for ever, as I promised to David. But if you or your sons turn away from me and go off to serve other gods then I'll cut off Israel from the land I've given them and will reject this temple. Israel will then become a byword and an object of ridicule among all peoples, and though this temple is now imposing, all who pass by will be appalled and will scoff and say, 'Why has the Lord done such a thing to this land and to this temple?' People will answer, 'Because they've forsaken the Lord their God who brought their fathers out of Egypt and have embraced other gods, worshipping and serving them—that's why the lord brought all this disaster on them.'"

After twenty years, during which Solomon built the temple of the Lord and the royal palace, he gave twenty towns in Galilee to the king of Tyre, Hiram, because he had supplied Solomon with all the cedar and pine and gold he wanted. When Hiram left Tyre to see for himself the towns that Solomon had given him he wasn't happy with what he saw. "What kind of towns are these you've given me, my brother? He asked, and he called them the Land of good-for-nothing, *Cabul*, a name they retained. Hiram had sent Solomon about four tons of gold.

Solomon conscripted forced labour in building the Lord's temple, his palace and other building projects and all the people left from the Amorites, Hittites, Perizzites, Hivites and Jebusites whom the Israelites hadn't killed were conscripted for this slave labour force. They built the walls of Jerusalem, Hazor, Megiddo and Gezer.

At the beginning of Solomon's reign Pharaoh had attacked and captured Gezer, about twenty miles west of Jerusalem. He burnt it and killed its Canaanite inhabitants and then gave it as wedding gift to his daughter, Solomon's wife.

King Solomon also built ships at Ezion Geber, which is near Elath in Edom, on the shore of the Sea of Reeds. Hiram sent his men who were sailors that knew the sea and to serve in the fleet with Solomon's men. They sailed to Ophir at the southern part of Arabia and brought back about fourteen tons of gold which they delivered to Solomon.

His fame spread to all the surrounding nations—he spoke 3,000 proverbs and his songs numbered 1,005. He described plant life, from the cedar of Lebanon to the hyssop that grows out of walls. He also taught about animals and birds, reptiles and fish. Men of all nations came to listen to Solomon's wisdom, sent by all the kings of the world who had heard of his wisdom.

When Jesus spoke of a future judgment to come on the people of his generation he said, "The Queen of the South (a ruler of a people called Sabeans who lived approximately where Yemen is today) will rise at the judgment with this generation and condemn it; for she came from the ends of the earth to listen to Solomon's wisdom, and now one greater than Solomon is here.

He was later to write, 'I thought to myself, "Look, I've grown and increased in wisdom more than anyone who has ruled over Jerusalem before me; I've experienced much of wisdom and knowledge." Then I applied myself to the understanding of wisdom, and also of madness and folly, but I learned that this too is a chasing after wind . . . I undertook great projects: I built houses for myself and planted vineyards. I made gardens and parks and planted all kinds of fruit trees in them. I made reservoirs to water groves of flourishing trees. I bought male and female slaves and had other slaves who were born in my house.

'I also owned more herds and flocks than anyone in Jerusalem before me. I amassed silver and gold for myself, and the treasure of kings and provinces. I acquired men and women singers, and, to the delight of man's heart, beautiful women for my bed. I became greater by far than anyone in Jerusalem before me. In all this I didn't lose my wisdom.

'I denied myself nothing my eyes desired; I refused my heart no pleasure. I took delight in all my work and all my hard work brought me this pleasure.

'Yet when I considered everything I've done and what I've worked to achieve, everything was without meaning, a chasing after the wind; I'd gained nothing.'

However, he was deeply attracted to many foreign women as well as Pharaoh's daughter, his wife; Moabites, Ammonites, Edomites, Sidonians and Hittites—these were from the nations that God had commanded the Israelites not to intermarry with 'because they will without doubt turn your hearts after their gods.' In spite of this command Solomon was addicted to them. He had 700 wives of royal birth and 300 concubines and as he grew old his wives turned his heart to other gods and he was no longer fully devoted to the Lord his God as David his father had been. He followed Ashtoreth the goddess of the Sidonians, and Molech the detestable god of the Ammonites. On a hill east of Jerusalem Solomon built a place of worship for Chemosh the god of Moab and for Molech, he did the same for all his foreign wives, who burnt incense and offered sacrifices to their gods.

The Lord became angry with Solomon because his heart had been led astray. God had appeared to him twice and he had forbidden him to follow other gods yet Solomon had turned his back on God's commandments. So the Lord said to Solomon, "Since this is your attitude and you've been disobedient to what I've commanded you I will tear the kingdom away from you and give it to one of your subordinates, but for the sake of David your father I'll not do it during your lifetime but I will do it to your son. I will not tear the whole kingdom from him but will leave him one tribe for the sake of David my servant and for the sake of Jerusalem, which I've chosen."

Solomon reigned in Jerusalem over all Israel for forty years and then he died and was buried in the city of David and Rehoboam his son succeeded him as king.

Jesus compared the message of the Kingdom of God as a seed and our individual reaction to hearing that message as soil: for some it will have no effect on their lives whatsoever because they are blind and deaf to the message; in other words the soil was hardened. Their spiritual father Satan takes it away from them so it's unable to take root. For others it'll be happily received but when problems and difficulties come it'll be dropped because the soil was too shallow, still others hear and believe the message but the worries of this life, the deceitfulness of wealth and the desires for other things come in and choke the word because the seed was sown among thorns—it got choked out. But for some the seed would penetrate the broken up and prepared soil so that they listened and trusted the source of the message and grew both in grace and in knowledge and were productive because 'the soil was good.'

He encapsulated this and other sayings of his with the words, "everyone who hears these words of mine and puts them into practice is a wise person—but everyone who hears these words of mine and doesn't put them into practice is a fool." Listening isn't enough.

Jeroboam, who Solomon tried to kill, created a counterfeit religious calendar with priests from different tribes, and made two golden calves to be worshipped, all designed to stop people going back to Jerusalem for the annual feasts.

Four kings of Israel later Ahab became king and he did more evil in the eyes of The Lord than any of those before him. He not only considered it trivial to repeat the sins of Jeroboam, but he also married the daughter of Ethbaal king of the Sidonians, and began to serve Baal and worship him. His wife's name was Jezebel and he set up an altar for Baal in the temple of Baal that he built in Samaria. He also made an Asherah pole and did more to provoke God than the kings of Israel before him.

The rough prophet wearing a coat of camel's hair with a leather belt round his waist said to Ahab, "As the Lord, the God of Israel, lives, whom I serve, there will be neither dew nor rain in the next few years except at my word." His name was Elijah and he was from Gilead.

"Leave this place," God told him, turn east and hide in Kerith Ravine, east of the Jordan. You can drink from the brook, and I've ordered the ravens to feed you there."

So he stayed there and the ravens brought him bread and meat in the morning and more of the same in the evening, and he drank from the brook.

Because there had been no rain the brook eventually dried up. The Lord told him to move to Zarephath, south of Sidon, on the northern coast, and stay there, "I have commanded a widow in that place to supply you with food."

When he came to the town gate he saw a widow gathering sticks, and he asked her, "Would you bring me a little water in a jar so I can have a drink?" As she was going to get it, he called, "And please, bring me a piece of bread."

"As true as the Lord your God lives," she replied, "I don't have any bread—only a handful of flour in a jar and a little oil in a jug. I'm gathering a few sticks to take home and make a meal for my son and myself. We'll eat it and die."

"Don't be afraid," Elijah said to her, "Go home and do as you said, but first make a small cake of bread for me from what you have and bring it to me, and then make something for you and your son, because the Lord, the God of Israel, says, 'The jar of flour will not be used up and the jug of oil will not run dry until the day the Lord gives rain on the land.'"

She went and did as Elijah had told her, and there was food every day for them. The flour wasn't used up and the oil didn't run dry.

Sometime later the woman's son became ill, and his condition worsened, until he stopped breathing. "What do you have against me, man of God?" she said to Elijah, "did you come to remind me of my sin and kill my son?"

"Give me your son," Elijah said, and he took him from her arms, and carried him to the upper room where he was staying and laid him on his bed. Crying out to the Lord, he said, "O Lord my God, have you brought tragedy also on this widow I'm staying with, by causing her son to die?" Then he stretched himself out on the boy three times and cried to the Lord, "O Lord my God, let this boy's life return to him!"

The Lord heard Elijah's cry, and the boy's life returned to him. Elijah picked him up and carried him downstairs and gave him to his mother, "Look, your son is alive!"

"Now I know that you are a man of God," she said to him, "and that the word of the Lord that you speak is the truth."

When Jesus was speaking in a synagogue to people who thought non-Jews (the Gentiles) were 'unclean' and should if possible be avoided, he said to them, "I assure you that there were many widows in Israel in Elijah's time when the sky was shut for three and a half years and there was a severe famine throughout the land. Yet Elijah wasn't sent to any of them, but to a widow in Zarephath in the region of Sidon. And there were many in Israel with leprosy in the time of Elisha the prophet, yet not one of them was cleansed—only Naaman the Syrian."

All the people in the synagogue were furious when they heard this, and got out of their seats and drove him outside. They took him to the brow of the hill on which the town was built so they could throw him down the cliff, but he walked right through the crowd and went on his way. This was in his home town of Nazareth.

This strong feeling of dislike towards the Gentiles came to the surface when Paul, who had been saved from an angry Jewish mob by the Romans, was allowed to speak to those who wanted to kill him. He talked about his personal history of being trained under Gamaliel in the law of his fathers and was just as zealous for God as they were. He told them of how he persecuted the followers of what was called 'the Way' to their death. He told them about the letters he had from the Jewish council to have the authority to arrest others who were in Damascus and bring them back as prisoners to Jerusalem for punishment.

He spoke of that blazing light that flashed around him, and the voice that was Jesus of Nazareth telling him that his persecution was against Jesus himself. He went on to speak of his sight returning and being baptised by Ananias, a devout observer of the law and highly respected by all the Jews living in Damascus, and a little later he came to the point when the Lord said to him, "Go; I will send you far away to the Gentiles," at the mention of this word the crowd who had been listening to him raised their voices and shouted, "Rid the earth of him! He's not fit to live!" As they were throwing off their cloaks and flinging dust into the air, the Roman commander ordered his men to protect Paul and take him into the barracks.

He would later in writing to the Thessalonians say to the Christians there, 'you suffered from your own countrymen the same things those churches (God's churches in Judea) suffered from the Jews, who killed the Lord Jesus and the prophets and also drove us out. They displease God and are hostile to all men in their effort to keep us from speaking to the Gentiles so that they may be saved.' Paul had written to the Romans saying, 'Then what shall we say? That the Gentiles, who didn't pursue righteousness, have obtained it, a righteousness that's by faith, but Israel, who pursued a law of righteousness, has not obtained it. Why not? Because they pursued it not by faith but as it were by works. They stumbled over the 'stumbling-stone,' as it's written: "See, I lay in Zion a stone that causes men to stumble and a rock that makes them fall, and the one who trusts in him will never be put to shame."

'Brothers,' Paul went on to write, 'my heart's desire and prayer to God is for the Israelites that they may be saved. For I can testify about them, that they're zealous for God, but their zeal isn't based on knowledge. Since they didn't know the righteousness that comes from God and sought to establish their own, they didn't submit to God's righteousness. Christ is the end of the law so that there may be righteousness for everyone who believes.' 'The law is good,' as Paul wrote to Timothy, 'if one uses it properly. We also know that the law is not for the righteous but for lawbreakers and rebels . . .' The expression 'end of the law' means the end of achieving righteousness through the law which is not possible because the law informs us of our guilt in breaking it and condemns us as lawbreakers, while righteousness and justification is given as a gift through faith in the righteousness and sacrifice of Jesus Christ who saved sinners by paying their penalty for lawbreaking himself.

Paul addressed the issue of this wall of hostility in his letter to the Ephesians: 'Remember that before you who are Gentiles by birth and called "uncircumcised" by those who call themselves "the circumcision" (that done in the body by the hands of men)—remember that at that time you were separate from Christ, excluded from citizenship in Israel and foreigners to the covenants of the promise, without hope and without God in the world.

'But now in Christ Jesus you who were once far away have been brought near through the blood of Christ.

'For he himself is our peace, who has made the two one and has destroyed the barrier, the dividing wall of hostility, by abolishing in his flesh the law with its commandments and regulations. His purpose was to create in himself one new man out of the two, thus making peace, and in the one body to reconcile both of them to God through the cross, by which he put to death their hostility. He came and preached peace to you who were far away and to those who were near. For through him we both have access to the Father by one Spirit.'

In the third year of no rainfall the Lord said to Elijah, "Go and present yourself to Ahab, and I'll send rain on the land."

The famine was severe in Samaria and Ahab had summoned Obadiah, who was in charge of his palace, to go through the land to find some grass to keep the horses and mules alive. So they divided the land they were to cover and Ahab went in one direction and Obadiah in another. Obadiah was a devout believer in the Lord. While Jezebel was killing off the Lord's prophets, Obadiah had taken a hundred of them and hidden them in two caves, fifty in each and had supplied them with food and water.

In Obadiah's search for grazing land Elijah met him. He recognised him at once and bowed down to the ground. "Is it really you, my lord Elijah?" he asked. "Yes, go and tell your master, 'Elijah is here'"

"What have I done wrong that you're handing your servant over to Ahab to be put to death? There's not a nation where my master hasn't sent someone to look for you, and he made them swear that you weren't there. But now you tell me to go to my master and say, 'Elijah is here.' I don't know where the Spirit of the Lord may whisk you off to when I leave here, and when I tell Ahab that you're here and he doesn't find you, he'll kill me!"

"As the Lord Almighty lives, who I serve, I will present myself to Ahab today," Elijah reassured him.

Obadiah met with Ahab, and the king went to meet Elijah. When he saw Elijah, he said, "Is that you, you troubler of Israel?"

"I've not made trouble for Israel, but you and your father's family have. You've abandoned the Lord's commands and have followed the Baals. Now summon the people from all over Israel to meet me on Mount Carmel or the mountain of Baal as you call it, and bring the four hundred and fifty prophets of Baal and the four hundred prophets of Asherah who your wife Jezebel takes care of."

Ahab sent word throughout all Israel and assembled the prophets on Mount Carmel and Elijah said to them, "How long will you waver between two opinions? If the Lord is God, follow him; but if Baal is God, follow him," the people said nothing.

"I am the only one of the Lord's prophets left, but Baal has four hundred and fifty prophets. Get two bulls for us, let them choose one and they can cut it in pieces and put it on the wood but don't light it. I'll prepare the other bull and put it on the wood and I won't light it either. Then you call on the name of your god, and I'll call on the name of the Lord. The god who answers by fire—he is God."

"What you say is good," all the people agreed.

The Prophets of Baal were first to start and soon had the bull prepared and stacked on the wood. They called on the name of Baal till noon, shouting for a response, and they danced around the altar but there was no response. By late afternoon they were all shouted out, but still no divine answer came.

"Come here to me," Elijah said to the people and they moved closer. He took twelve stones and placed them on the ruins of an old altar of the Lord, and he dug a trench round it. He arranged the wood, cut the bull into pieces and laid it on the wood. Then he said to them, "Fill four large jars with water and pour it on the offering and on the wood."

"Do it again," he said.

"Do it a third time," he ordered, and the water ran down around the altar and filled the trench.

At the time of the evening sacrifice, Elijah stepped forward and prayed: "O Lord, God of Abraham, Isaac and Israel, let it be known today that you are God in Israel and that I'm your servant and have done all these things at your command. Answer me, O Lord, answer me, so that these people will know that you, O Lord, are God, and that you're turning their hearts back again."

Instantly the whole offering was engulfed in fire, everything, including the water was sucked dry by the inferno that fell on that one small area. When all the people saw this they lay on the ground and cried, "The Lord—he is God! The Lord—he is God!"

The worshippers of Baal had prayed nearly all day; Elijah prayed for less than thirty seconds. There may not be any Baal worshippers today but there are many who think that the longer the prayer, plus the number of people praying the more effective it will be in getting God's attention. Jesus warned against this pagan approach to prayer when he said, "When you pray, don't rattle off long prayers like pagans, because they think they'll be heard if they go on long enough. Don't be like them; your Father knows what you need before you ask him."

Then Elijah commanded them to seize the prophets of Baal and not to let anyone escape. Elijah had them brought down to the Kishon Valley and there they were slaughtered. Elijah said to Ahab, "Go, and get some food—there's the sound of heavy rain. Ahab went off to eat while Elijah climbed to the top of Carmel and bent down to the ground with his face between his knees.

"Go and look towards the sea," he told his servant, who went up and looked.

"There's nothing there," he said.

"Go back and look again," Elijah told him; on the seventh time the servant reported a small cloud rising from the sea.

"Go and tell Ahab," Elijah said, 'hitch up your chariot and get down before the rain stops you.'" The sky grew black with clouds, and the wind rose. Heavy rain fell and Ahab rushed off to Jezreel, some seventeen miles away. The power of the Lord came to Elijah and tucking his cloak into his belt, ran ahead of Ahab all the way to Jezreel.

Ahab told Jezebel all that happened, so she sent a messenger to Elijah to say, "May the gods deal with me severely if by this time tomorrow I don't make your life like one of those you killed."

When Elijah saw that nothing had changed, Jezebel was still in control and even after what had happened on Mount Carmel—the evidence of the one and only God answering the prayer of his servant—nothing would change. The people, the nation, the world, all would continue as before. He had hoped that great changes and reforms would begin to turn the people back to God, but when he saw that it wasn't going to happen he then got away from that area as quickly as he could.

Jesus spoke of this unchanging world to his disciples: "As it was in the days of Noah, so it will be at the coming of the Son of Man. Because in the days before the flood, people were eating and drinking, marrying and giving in marriage, up to the day Noah entered the ark; and they knew nothing about what would happen until the flood came and took them all away.

"It was the same in the days of Lot. People were eating and drinking, buying and selling, planting and building. But the day Lot left Sodom, fire and sulphur rained down from the skies and destroyed them all. That's how it'll be at the coming of the Son of Man."

Individuals will continue to be drawn by God out of spiritual darkness and into his glorious light to become like Jesus and reflect his light and be ambassadors of his future kingdom, but the world, including many who call themselves Christian, will not change until change is imposed from above with the return of the King.

21

Back to the Mountain of God

When Elijah came to Beersheba in Judah, about one hundred miles south of Jezreel, he left his servant there and went a day's journey in to the desert where he came to a broom tree and sat under it.

"I've had enough Lord," he prayed, "take my life; I'm no better than my ancestors." Then he lay down and fell asleep. Elijah felt someone lightly shaking him and he heard a voice say, "Get up and eat." He looked around and saw a cake of bread baked over hot coals and a jar of water! He ate and drank and then lay down again.

"Get up and eat," the voice was there again, "for the journey is too much for you." He got up and had some more food and drink. Strengthened by that food he travelled for forty days, about two hundred miles south of Beersheba, until he reached Horeb, the mountain of God. He then went into a cave for the night.

"What are you doing here, Elijah?" The Lord said to him.

"I've been very zealous for the Lord God Almighty. The charge is that the Israelites have rejected your covenant, broken down your altars, and put your prophets to death. I'm the only one that's been public about my allegiance to you, and now they're trying to kill me too."

"Go out and stand on the mountain in the presence of the Lord, because the Lord is about to pass by."

When Moses had asked God to show him his glory, God had said to him, "I'll cause all my goodness to pass in front of you, but you cannot see my face, for no-one may see me and live." God then told Moses to stand on a rock and when his glory passes by he'll put Moses in a cleft in the rock and cover him with his hand until he's passed by, so as to protect Moses from seeing his face. And Elijah was now on that same mountain.

Then a powerful wind tore into the mountain and shattered the rocks, after the wind an earthquake hit the mountain, and after that a fire, and then the whisper of a voice. Elijah heard the voice and pulled his cloak over his face and stood at the mouth of the cave. Again the voice asked him, "What are you doing here, Elijah?"

Elijah gave the same answer as before and the Lord said to him, "Go back the way you came and go to the Desert of Damascus, and when you get there anoint Hazael king over Aram. Also anoint Jehu king over Israel, and anoint Elisha to succeed you as prophet. Jehu will put to death any who escape the sword of Hazael, and Elisha will put to death any who escape the sword of Jehu. Yet I reserve seven thousand in Israel who haven't bowed down to Baal and all who haven't kissed him."

Elijah left there and made the long journey back. He found Elisha who was ploughing with twelve yoke of oxen, and he was driving the twelfth pair. Elijah went up to him and threw his cloak around him. Elisha knew what this meant and he left his oxen and ran after Elijah. "Let me kiss my parents good-bye, and then I'll come with you," Elisha said.

"Go back, but remember what I've done to you." Elisha went back and slaughtered his oxen and burned the ploughing equipment to cook the meat and he gave it to the people to eat. Then he set out to follow Elijah and became his attendant.

Elisha had made a full and complete break with his former life. When Jesus was still selecting his disciples he saw a tax collector by the name of Levi sitting at his tax booth and he said to him, "Follow me," and Levi got up, left everything and followed him. Levi held a feast for Jesus at his house, and a large crowd of tax collectors and others were there eating. Also there were Pharisees and the teachers of the law who belonged to their sect. They were critical of who the disciples socialised with, "Why do you eat and drink with tax collectors and sinners?" they asked.

Jesus answered them, "It's not the healthy who need a doctor, but the sick. I've not come to call the righteous, but sinners to repentance."

When Ahab died his son Ahaziah became king of Israel, and he, like his parents, served and worshipped Baal.

Ahaziah fell through the lattice of his upper room in Samaria and injured himself, so he sent messengers to go and consult Baal-Zebub, the god of Ekron, to see if he would recover from his injury. Ekron was south-west of Samaria, in Philistia.

An angel of the Lord said to Elijah, "Go and meet the messengers of the king of Samaria and ask them, 'Is it because there is no God in Israel that you're going off to consult Baal-Zebub, the god of Ekron?' This is what the Lord says: 'You'll not leave the bed you're lying on because you'll certainly die!'" Elijah delivered that message and when the messengers went back to the king, he asked them, "Why have you come back?"

"A man came to meet us," and they went on to tell the king what this message was.

"What kind of man was it who met you and gave you this message?"

"He was a man dressed in hair and with a leather belt round his waist."

"That was Elijah!" the king said.

Fifty men under a captain were sent to arrest Elijah and bring him to the king. They found him sitting on top of a hill, "Man of God, the king says, 'come down!'"

"If I am a man of God," Elijah said to the captain, "may fire come down from heaven and consume you and your men." Then fire came out of the sky and destroyed the captain and his men.

Another captain and his men were sent by the king to Elijah. Exactly the same exchange of conversation occurred with the same devastation results. Now, a hundred charred bodies littered the hillside.

A third contingent of fifty men were sent out, but this time the captain went up and fell on his knees before Elijah, "Man of God," he pleaded, "please have respect for my life and the lives of these fifty men, your servants. We can see what's happened to the others that the king sent." The angel of the Lord spoke to Elijah, "Go down with him, and don't be afraid of him." So Elijah got up and went down with him to the king.

He said to the king what he had told the king's messengers and added, "Because you've done this, you'll never leave the bed you're lying on. You'll certainly die." So he died, according to the word of the Lord that Elijah had said.

The time was fast approaching for Elijah to be taken away and it was an open secret that he was to leave. "Stay here," Elijah said to Elisha, "the Lord has sent me to Bethel."

"As surely as the Lord and you live, I'll not leave you." So they both went down to Bethel. At Bethel, where there was a school for prophets, Elisha was asked, "Do you know that the Lord is going to take your master from you today?" "Yes, I know, but don't talk about it," Elisha answered.

"Stay here, Elisha, the Lord has sent me to Jericho."

"As surely as the Lord and you live, I'm not leaving you." So they both went to Jericho. At Jericho there was another school of prophets, and they too asked Elisha if he knew that Elijah was leaving that day, and Elisha gave the same reply as before; he didn't want to talk about it.

Elijah tried again, "Stay here, the Lord has sent me to the Jordan." And he got the same response, so they both went to the Jordan. Fifty of the prophets stood at a distance from where Elijah and Elisha were. Elijah took his cloak and rolled it up, and then he hit the water with it and the water divided apart allowing the two men to cross over on dry land.

Once they were across Elijah asked Elisha what he could do for him before he leaves. "Let me inherit a double portion of your spirit," Elisha replied.

"You've asked a difficult thing, "Elijah said, "but if you see me when I'm taken from you, it'll be yours, if you don't, it won't."

They talked as they walked together, and suddenly a chariot and horses of fire separated them, and Elijah was taken by a powerful wind up into the sky. Elisha cried out, "My father! My father! The chariots and horsemen of Israel!" And Elijah disappeared from Elisha's view and he tore his clothes apart.

He walked over to where Elijah's cloak had fallen and picked it up and went back to the riverbank and said, as he hit the water with it, "Where now is the Lord, the God of Elijah?" And the water divided, as before, and he crossed over. The prophets who saw all this said, "The spirit of Elijah is resting on Elisha," and when they reached him they bowed and said, "There's enough men with us, let them go and search for your master. Perhaps he's been set down on some mountain or in some valley."

"No, don't send them." Elisha replied. But as they kept on at him he finally gave his permission and the fifty men went out searching for three days, but didn't find him. When they returned to Elisha, who was staying in Jericho, he said to them, "I told you not to go."

Nobody knows where Elijah was taken; many believe he was taken up into heaven and never died, but three points from the biblical text should be considered before such an assumption is made. First, 'Man is destined to die once, and after that to face judgment' (Hebrews), everyone dies. Secondly, "No-one has ever gone into heaven except the one who came from heaven—the Son of Man" (Jesus speaking to Nicodemus), the dead aren't in heaven. Peter told the crowd on Pentecost that David didn't go to heaven. And lastly, Elijah later wrote a letter after his departure to Jehoram, king of Judah, which is recorded in the second book of Chronicles. The dead know nothing; they 'sleep' or 'rest' until the time comes for their resurrection; either the first, the 'better resurrection' or the second—to judgment and punishment. This 'sleep' is not to be confused with the term 'soul sleep' which is a non-biblical expression. Our soul is our life and isn't immortal as many are taught. It's our spirit that returns to God when we die.

Jesus taught that for those who suffer persecution as one of his disciples their reward in heaven is great and the majority of Christians have been led to believe that their reward will be given them when they go to heaven, yet Isaiah said twice that the Messiah will bring their reward with him when he comes, 'See, his reward is with him, and his recompense accompanies him'—'See, the Sovereign Lord comes with power, and his arm rules for him. See, his reward is with him.' This is consistent with what Jesus said; "For the Son of Man is going to come in his Father's glory with his angels and *then* he'll reward each person according to what he has done." Paul, writing to the Corinthians, said, 'For we must all appear before the judgment seat of Christ, that each one may receive what is due to him for the things done while in the body, whether good or bad.'

Paul wrote to the Colossians saying, 'When Christ who is your life appears *then* you also will appear with him in glory.' Yet so many teach that Christians are in glory and with the Lord the moment they die.

We've all been deceived and failed to challenge those who teach that the saved go to heaven when they die.

We're saved because of God's grace, not because of any good things we've done, yet our reward is according to how we've lived in the knowledge of the grace that we've been given. Some will be given more than others because of what they did with what they'd been given. One of Jesus' parables compares what we do with what we're given. 'After a long time the master of those servants returned and settled accounts with them. The man who had received the five talents brought a further five he'd gained; "Master, you entrusted me with five talents—see, I've gained five more."

"Well done, good and faithful servant," his master said to him. "You've been faithful with a few things; I'll put you in charge of many things. Come and share your master's happiness."

One who had received one talent and had hid it and not used it was told by Jesus that he should have at least put the money on deposit so that when he returned he would have received it back with the interest. Because of his negative response to what he'd been given that one talent he had was taken from him and given to the one had the ten talents, "For everyone who has (put his 'money' to work) will be given more, and he'll have an abundance. Whoever doesn't have, even what he has will be taken from him and throw that worthless servant outside into the darkness where there will be weeping and gnashing of teeth." This terrible anguish will not be eternal suffering but the response from those who clearly see what their choices in life have led them to—a fire that will consume them until they are ashes—instantly, from which there is no further resurrection.

The last king of Israel was Hoshea, who had been the king of Assyria's vassal, but he was discovered to be in negotiations with the Egyptian king to make a coalition against the Assyrians, and had also stopped paying his tribute taxes to Shalmaneser, king of Assyria. Hoshea was taken and imprisoned. The country was then was invaded. Samaria was laid siege to for three years and then, when Shalmaneser died, his successor Sargon II captured the city. The Assyrians deported 27,300 Israelites to Assyria and settled them in Halah, in Gozan on the Habor River and in the towns of the Medes. This was 721BC.

All this happened because the Israelites sinned against God, who had brought them out of Egypt. They worshipped other gods and followed the practices of the nations that God drove out before them, as well as the practices that the kings of Israel introduced. The Israelites secretly did things against God that were not right. From watchtower to fortified city they built high places in all their towns. They set up sacred stones and Asherah poles on every high hill and under every spreading tree. They wouldn't listen and were as stiff-necked as their fathers who didn't trust in the Lord their God. They imitated the nations around them even though the Lord had warned them through his prophets: "Turn from your evil ways and observe my commands and decrees, in line with the entire Law that I commanded your fathers to obey." But they wouldn't listen. They bowed down to the stars, and worshipped Baal, and sacrificed their children in the fire. They practiced divination and sorcery and sold themselves to do evil in the eyes of the Lord.

The king of Assyria repopulated the towns of Samaria with people from Babylon, Cuthah, Avva, Hamath and Sepharvaim. Each group made their own gods. Some even worshipped the Lord but also served their own gods in accordance with their own traditions which they brought with them.

In 445BC Jerusalem was separated from Samaria and the province of Judea was restored and in 332BC Alexander made Samaria a part of his empire. The Samaritans revolted against Alexander and when he returned from Egypt, he destroyed Samaria, killed the leaders, expelled its population and resettled it with Macedonians, which accounts for the

Hellenization of Samaria. Those who were expelled made Shechem their new capital, and built a temple on Mount Gerizim. In the time of Jesus there existed a deep prejudice between Samaritans and Jews (there was no association with each other; Peter told Cornelius that "it's against our law for a Jew to associate with a Gentile or visit him") which forms the background to a hot mid-day conversation between Jesus and a Samaritan woman.

Jesus was alone and sitting by a well near the Samaritan town of Sychar when a Samaritan woman came to draw water, Jesus asked her if she would give him a drink and she said to him, "You're a Jew and I'm a Samaritan woman. How can you ask me for a drink?"

"If you knew the gift of God and who it is that asks you for a drink, you would have asked him and he would have given you living water."

"Sir, you have nothing to draw with and the well is deep. Where can you get this living water? Are you greater than our father Jacob, who gave us this well and drank from it himself, as did his sons and his flocks and herds?"

"Everyone who drinks this water will be thirsty again, but whoever drinks the water I give him will never thirst. The water I give him will become in him a spring of water welling up to eternal life."

"Sir, give me this water so I won't get thirsty and have to keep coming here to draw water."

"Go, call your husband and come back."

"I have no husband."

"You're right when you say you have no husband. The fact is, you've had five husbands, and the man you're now with isn't your husband."

"Sir, I can see you're a prophet. Our fathers worshipped on this mountain, but you Jews claim that Jerusalem is the place where we should worship."

"Believe me a time is coming when you'll worship the Father neither on this mountain nor in Jerusalem. You Samaritans don't know what you worship, but we do know because salvation is from the Jews. Yet a time is coming and has now arrived when the true worshippers will worship the Father in spirit and truth, because they're the kind of worshippers the Father looks for. God is spirit, and his worshippers must worship in spirit and in truth."

"I know that the Messiah is coming, and when he comes he'll explain everything to us."

"That Messiah is me."

Many people rejected Jesus on the grounds of where he came from. Nazareth wasn't held in high regard even by people from that area. Nathanael was told by Philip that they've found the one Moses wrote about in the law and about whom the prophets also wrote and when he mentioned where Jesus came from Nathanael said, "Nazareth! Can anything good come from there?" But when he later met Jesus he was convinced that Philip was right.

Others rejected the claim that Jesus was the Messiah because the Scripture says that the Messiah will be a descendant of King David and be from Bethlehem, the town where David lived, so how can the Messiah come from Galilee? Nicodemus, a member of the Jewish Council asked the chief priests, "Does our law condemn a man without first hearing him to find out what he's doing?" The leaders of the Council replied, "Are you from Galilee too? Look into it, and you'll find that no prophet comes out of Galilee."

The Messiah was to be traced from the line of David and was to be born in Bethlehem, and Jesus was descended from that line and born in Bethlehem, but his move north as a youngster gave him his Galilean accent.

22

The Last Days of Judah

The last king of Judah was Zedekiah, who was twenty-one when he became king, and he reigned in Jerusalem for eleven years. He did evil just as his father did, although the prophet Jeremiah had repeatedly warned him to submit to the Babylonians and so save the city, and his life, but he wouldn't listen. He rebelled against king Nebuchadnezzar, who had given him the throne in Jerusalem and had made him take an oath of loyalty in God's name. He became stiff-necked and hardened his heart and wouldn't turn to the Lord, the God of Israel. All the leaders, both religious and political, became more and more unfaithful, following all the detestable practices of the nations and defiling the temple of the Lord, which he had consecrated in Jerusalem.

When Jesus approached Jerusalem and looked at the city, he wept over it, and said, "O Jerusalem, Jerusalem, you who kill the prophets and stone those sent to you, how often I have longed to gather your children together, as a hen gathers her chicks under her wings, but you were not willing. The days will come upon you when your enemies will build an embankment against you and you will be surrounded. They'll hurl you and your children to the ground and they'll not leave one stone on another, because you didn't recognise the time of God's coming to you."

In the ninth year of Zedekiah's rule, the Babylonian army under Nebuchadnezzar laid siege against Jerusalem and a year and a half later the city wall was broken through and the whole of Zedekiah's army fled at night through the gate between the two walls near the king's garden and headed towards the Jordan valley, but the Babylonians pursued and overtook them in the plains of Jericho. They captured the king after all his soldiers were separated from him and scattered. He was taken north to Riblah in the land of Hamath, where Nebuchadnezzar pronounced sentence on him. They killed Zedekiah's sons in front of him and then took his eyes out; they secured him with bronze shackles and took him to Babylon.

The Babylonians set the royal palace on fire as well as all the other notable buildings. They also broke down the city walls. The commander of the imperial guard Nebuzaradan took as prisoners Seraiah the chief priest, Zephaniah the priest next in rank and the three doorkeepers. Of those still in the city, he took the officer in charge of the fighting men, and seven royal advisers. He also took the secretary who was chief officer in charge of conscripting the people of the land and sixty of his men who were found in the city. He took them all to the king of Babylon at Riblah where they were executed.

He also carried into exile the remaining people, who were left in the city, but he left behind some of the poorest people who owned nothing and they were given vineyards and fields to take care of. He had been given orders concerning Jeremiah that he was to find him and take care of his needs. The commander said to Jeremiah, "The Lord your God decreed this disaster for this place, and now the Lord has done just what he said he would do. All this happened because you people sinned against the Lord and didn't obey him. But today I'm releasing you from the chains on your wrists. Come with me to Babylon, if you want to and I'll look after you, but if you don't want to, then don't come. Look, the whole country lies before you; go wherever you please." Before Jeremiah answered Nebuzaradan added, "The king of Babylon has appointed Gedaliah over the towns of Judah, go to him and live among the people, or go anywhere else you please."

Then the commander gave him provisions and a gift and let him go. Jeremiah went and stayed with Gedaliah at Mizpah among those who were left behind.

Gedaliah advised the people not to be afraid to serve the Babylonians, settle down in the land, serve the king of Babylon and it'll go well with you. He would stay in Mizpah to represent them before the Babylonians who would come to them, but they were to harvest the wine, summer fruit and oil, and put them in their storage jars, and live in the towns they've taken over.

Many of those who had left Judah came back when they heard that Gedaliah was the new governor and they harvested an abundance of wine and summer fruit.

Some army officers who were still in the open country came to Gedaliah and said to him that Baalis king of the Ammonites has sent Ishmael, one of Judah's army officers, to assassinate him, but Gedaliah didn't believe them. Privately, Johanan, one of the officers who had warned him, said, "Let me go and kill Ishmael and no-one will know it. Why should he take your life and cause all those around you to be scattered and die?"

"Don't do it!" Gedaliah said, "What you're saying about Ishmael isn't true."

Ishmael was of royal blood, and he and ten men came to see Gedaliah, and while they were eating together they killed him and the Jews who were with him as well as the Babylonian soldiers who were there.

The day after this assassination, and before the news of it got out, eighty men who had shaved off their beards, torn their clothes and cut themselves came from Samaria, bringing grain offerings and incense to the house of the Lord. Ishmael left Mizpah to meet them. Appearing tearful when he met them he asked them to come to meet with Gedaliah, and they all went into the city. They were then slaughtered and thrown down a cistern, except for ten of them who pleaded not to be killed because they had supplies hidden in a field, so they didn't kill them.

The rest of the people at Mizpah—including the king's daughters, were made Ishmael's captives, and they intended to cross over to the Ammonites. When Johanan and the other loyal officers heard of Ishmael's crimes they took all their men to fight Ishmael. They caught up with them near the great pool in Gibeon and when all the people who were held captive saw Johanan and those with him they were glad and relieved, and turned away from Ishmael, who with eight of his men escaped into the land of the Ammonites.

Under the leadership now of Johanan, the plan was to take all the survivors down to Egypt because of what the Babylonians would do once they learned of what happened to the appointed governor Gedaliah. But first they wanted to speak with Jeremiah, who was with them. They said to him, "Please hear our petition and pray to the Lord your God for all of us. We need to know where we should go and what we should do."

"I hear you," answered Jeremiah, "I'll certainly pray as you've requested and I'll tell you everything the Lord says and I'll keep nothing back from you." Then they said to Jeremiah, "May the Lord be a true and faithful witness against us if we don't comply with whatever the Lord tells you. We will obey."

Ten days later God spoke to Jeremiah, so he called together Johanan and all the army officers, and all the people, he said to them, "This is what the Lord God of Israel says, 'If you stay in this land, I'll build you up and not tear you down; I'll plant you and not uproot you, because I'm grieved over the disaster I've inflicted on you. Don't be afraid of the king of Babylon, who you now fear, don't be afraid of him, because I'm with you and I'll save you from his hands—I'll show compassion so that he'll have compassion on you and restore you to your land.'

"However, if you say, 'We'll not stay in the land,' and so disobey the Lord your God, and if you say, 'no, we'll go and live in Egypt, where we won't see any war or hear the trumpet or be hungry,' then listen to what the Lord God says to you, 'if you're determined to go to Egypt and settle there then the sword you fear will overtake you there and the famine you dread will follow you into Egypt and there you'll die.'"

When Jeremiah had come to the end of God's answer to the people's request, one of the men spoke up and said on behalf of the others, "You're lying! The Lord our God hasn't sent you to say we mustn't go to Egypt. Your secretary, Baruch is inciting you against us so we can be handed over to the Babylonians, and they'll kill us or take us into exile to Babylon."

Johanan and the rest of the army officers then led all the men, women and children, and the king's daughters into Egypt in disobedience to the Lord and went as far as Tahpanhes, near the coast of northern Egypt (called Lower Egypt).

While in Tahpanhes Jeremiah received a message from the Lord, "Make sure the Jews are watching and take some large stones and bury them in the brick pavement at the entrance to Pharaoh's palace, and then say to them, "The Lord Almighty, the God of Israel says, I will send for my servant Nebuchadnezzar king of Babylon, and I'll set his throne over these stones I've buried here; he'll spread his royal canopy above them. He'll come and attack Egypt, bringing death for those destined for death, captivity for those destined for captivity, and the sword for those destined for the sword. He'll set fire to the temples of the gods of Egypt and take their gods captive. There in the temple of the sun he'll demolish the sacred pillars and burn down the temples."

God, through Jeremiah said to them, "Again and again I sent my servants the prophets who said, 'Don't do this detestable thing that I hate!' but they didn't listen or pay attention; they continued to burn incense to other gods, so my fierce anger was poured out and Jerusalem became a ruin.

Therefore, you will all perish in Egypt, from the least to the greatest. None of those left from Judah will escape or survive to return to their homeland; none will return except for a few fugitives."

Then all the men who knew that their wives were burning incense to other gods, along with all the women who were present and all the people living in Lower and Upper Egypt said to Jeremiah, "We won't listen to your message, and we'll continue to do everything we said we would—we'll burn incense to the Queen of heaven and pour out drink offerings to her, just as we and our fathers, our kings and officials did in the towns of Judah and in the streets of Jerusalem. When we were doing that we had plenty of food and were well off, but ever since we stopped worshipping the Queen of heaven we've had nothing but the sword and famine."

Jeremiah said to all the people, "This is what the God of Israel says, 'you and your wives have shown by your actions what you promised when you said, 'We'll certainly carry out the vows we made to burn incense and pour out drink offerings to the Queen of heaven.'

"Go ahead then, do what you promised! Keep your vows! But hear the word of the Lord, all Jews living in Egypt; no-one from Judah living in Egypt shall ever again invoke my name or swear, "As surely as the Sovereign Lord lives," because I'm watching over them for harm, not for good. The Jews in Egypt will die by sword and famine until all are destroyed. Those who do escape and return to the land of Judah will be very few, then they'll know whose word stands—mine or theirs.

23

Baruch and Ebed-Melech

Before the fall of Judea by the Babylonians Jeremiah was seen as helping the enemy by his repeated calls to submit to the Babylonian king and rid themselves of all their pagan attachments which they persistently clung to, he had written, 'But you said, 'It's no use! I love foreign gods, and I must go after them,' and he lamented over the people's resistance to believe what God was saying through Jeremiah; 'to whom can I speak and give warning? Who will listen to me? Their ears are closed so that they cannot hear. The word of the Lord is offensive to them; they find no pleasure in it.'

Jesus found the same attitude in those who opposed him; "I know you're Abraham's descendants, yet you're ready to kill me because you've no room for my word."

But Jeremiah was not the only one claiming to speak on behalf of God to the people. Jeremiah wrote of what God said of these other prophets: "Don't listen to what the prophets are prophesying to you; they fill you with false hopes and speak visions from their own minds, not from God.

"They keep saying to those who despise me, 'The Lord says: You'll have peace.' And to all who follow the stubbornness of their hearts they say, 'No harm will come to you.' I didn't send these prophets, yet they've run with their message; I didn't speak to them, yet they've prophesied, but if they'd stood in my council they would have proclaimed my words to my people and would have turned them from their evil ways and their evil deeds."

Paul warned the Thessalonians about those who bring messages of false hope; 'Now brothers, about times and dates we don't need to write to you for you know very well that the day of the Lord will come like a thief in the night. While people are saying, "Peace and safety," destruction will come on them suddenly, as labour pains on a pregnant woman, and they'll not escape.'

Jeremiah grieved over his generation, and wrote that God understands how the people were thinking; "Have I been a desert to Israel or a land of great darkness? Why do my people say, 'We're free to roam; we won't come to you anymore.' Does a lady forget her jewellery or a bride her wedding ornaments? Yet my people have forgotten me, numberless days.

"How skilled you are at pursuing love! Even the worst of women can learn from you. On your clothes is found the blood of the innocent poor, even when there was no evidence against them. Yet in spite of your guilt you say, 'I'm innocent; God isn't angry with me.' But I'll pass judgment on you because you say, 'I've not sinned.'"

When Jeremiah wasn't able himself to speak publically he asked Baruch, who had been taking dictation from him, to take the scroll with God's message on it to the temple and there read it out aloud. It was read to everyone who was there, and one of the government officials heard it and Baruch was asked to bring the scroll to one of the government offices and sit down and read it to a group of men who were close to the king, who at that time was Jehoiakim.

When Baruch had finished reading it the men looked at each other in fear and said to him, "We must report all these words to the king; tell us, how did you come to write all this? Did Jeremiah dictate it?"

"Yes, he dictated all the words to me, and I wrote them in ink on the scroll."

"You and Jeremiah go and hide. Don't let anyone know where you are."

The officials went to the king and reported what had happened, and the king sent for the scroll, and while all the officials were standing close by, the scroll was read out to him. The king was sitting in the winter apartment, with a fire burning in the brazier in front of him. When he heard a section the king, using a scribe's knife, cut it off the scroll and threw it into the brazier, he did this until the entire scroll was turned to ash in the fire. The king and those close to him showed no fear or appeared moved by what they heard, although three of them urged the king not to burn the scroll, but he didn't listen to them, instead he ordered the arrest of Baruch the scribe and Jeremiah the prophet, but the Lord had hidden them.

Jeremiah received another message; "Take another scroll and write on it everything that was on the first scroll plus this message for the king, 'You burned the scroll with its message that the king of Babylon will come and destroy this land, as a consequence of what you've done none of your children will inherit the throne and you will be thrown out into the heat of day and the frost of night, and every disaster that I've pronounced will come on everyone living in Jerusalem and Judah because they've not listened.'"

Jeremiah gave another scroll to Baruch and dictated the same message that the king had burned in the fire and extra notes were added to it.

After that writing was finished Jeremiah said to Baruch, "This is what the Lord, the God of Israel, says to you, Baruch: You said, 'My life's terrible! The Lord has added sorrow to my pain; I'm worn out with groaning and have no rest.' I will overthrow what I've built and uproot what I've planted throughout the land. Should you then look for a great life? Don't look for that, because I'll bring disaster on everyone, but wherever you go I'll let you escape with your life."

The new king Zedekiah paid as much attention to what Jeremiah was saying as his predecessor Jehoiakim did. (There was the reign of Jehoiachin, but that only lasted three months and ten days, before he was carted off to Babylon in what is known as the second deportation—five years later God began to give messages to Ezekiel the priest for the Israelites in exile) But surprisingly, he sent two of his men to ask Jeremiah to "Please pray to the Lord our God for us." Jeremiah was at that point free to move around when he received a message for the king, "Pharaoh's army, which is on its way to support you, will return to Egypt. Then the Babylonians will return and attack this city and burn it down."

Jeremiah was later arrested for leaving the city on the charge that he was deserting to the Babylonians, although that was not true. He was beaten and imprisoned in the house of Jonathan the secretary, which was converted into a prison. He was placed in an underground cell and remained there for some time. The king sent for him and he was brought to the palace where he asked him privately, "Is there any word from the Lord?"

"Yes, you'll be handed over to the king of Babylon—what crime have I committed against you or your officials or this people that you've put me in prison? Where are those prophets of yours who said that the king of Babylon won't attack you or this land? But now, my king, please listen and let me speak to you because if you send me back to that prison I'll die there.

The king then gave orders for Jeremiah to be confined in the courtyard of the guard and given bread each day until there's no more bread left.

Four of the king's officials said to him, "This man should be put to death. He's discouraging the soldiers who are left in the city, as well as all the people, by the things he's saying to them. This man isn't seeking the good of these people but their ruin."

"He's in your hands," the king weakly answered, "I can't oppose you."

They took Jeremiah and lowered him by ropes into the thick mud of the cistern belonging to the king's son, Malkijah, and he sank down into the mud.

Ebed-Melech, an official in the royal court heard what they'd done to Jeremiah and quickly left the palace and went to the Benjamin Gate where the king was and said to him, "My Lord the king, these men have acted wickedly in what they've done to Jeremiah—they've thrown him into a cistern and if he stays there he'll starve to death when the bread runs out."

The king commanded Ebed-Melech, who was an Ethiopian, to take thirty men with him and get Jeremiah out of that cistern before he dies. Ebed-Melech took the men and went to a room under the treasury in the palace where he took some old rags and worn-out clothes from there and let them down with ropes to Jeremiah, "Put these old clothes and rags under your arms to pad the ropes," he told him, then they pulled him up out of the cistern. And Jeremiah stayed in the courtyard of the guard.

King Zedekiah sent for Jeremiah and said to him, "I'm going to ask you something, and don't hide anything from me." They were alone together.

"If I give you an answer, you're going to kill me, and if I did give you good advice, you wouldn't listen to me."

"As surely as the Lord lives, who gives us breath, I will neither kill you nor hand you over to those who want you dead."

Having the king's permission Jeremiah said to him, "This is what the Lord God Almighty says, 'If you surrender to the officers of the king of Babylon, your life will be spared and the city won't be burned down, and you and your family will live. But if you don't surrender the city will be burned down and you won't escape.'"

"I'm afraid of the Jews who have gone over to the Babylonians, because I may be handed over to them and I'll be badly treated."

"They'll not hand you over, obey the Lord by doing what I tell you, then it'll go well with you and your life will be spared, and this city will not be burned down; you and your family will live, but if you refuse to surrender all the women left in your palace will be brought out to the officials of the king of Babylon and they'll say to you, 'They misled you and took you in—those trusted friends of yours, and now you're up to your knees in mud and your friends have deserted you.'"

"All your wives and children will be brought out to the Babylonians and you'll not escape—you'll be captured and this city will be burned down."

"Don't let anyone know about this conversation, or you may die. If the officials hear that I talked to you, and they ask you what you said to me, and threaten you, then tell them that you were pleading not to be sent back to die in Jonathan's house."

The officials did come and question Jeremiah about what was said, but they accepted what he said, because no-one else was close enough to overhear what they were speaking about. Jeremiah remained in the courtyard of the guard until the day Jerusalem was captured. While he was confined there the word of the Lord came to him: "Go and tell Ebed-Melech the Ethiopian, 'I'm about to fulfil my words against this city through disaster, not prosperity. At that time you'll see it, but I'll rescue you on that day and you won't be handed over to those you fear. I will save you—you won't be killed—you'll escape with your life, because you trust in me.'"

Two very different men, one disappointed where his life had led him, feeling that it was now ruined, and the other, a palace official, most certainly appointed to die a dreadful death, perhaps impaled on a stake, or skinned alive at the hands of the Babylonians, but both were going to escape with their lives—they were being saved and rescued! This was because they believed and trusted God, and in their weakness and fear he saved them.

Solomon wrote, 'Have no fear of sudden disaster or the ruin that overtakes the wicked, for the Lord will be your confidence and will keep your foot from being snared.' He had earlier written, 'The fear of the Lord is the beginning of knowledge, but fools despise wisdom and discipline.' Peter was to write, 'Since you call on a Father who judges each person's work impartially, live your lives as strangers here in reverent fear.'

John wrote in Revelation, 'He said to me: "It is done. I am the Alpha and the Omega, the beginning and the End. To him who is thirsty I will give to drink without cost from the spring of the water of life. He who overcomes will inherit all this, and I will be his God and he will be my son. But the cowardly, the unbelieving, the vile, the murderers, the sexually immoral, those who practice magic arts, the idolaters and all liars—their place will be in the fiery lake of burning sulphur. This is the second death."'

(This punishment is called 'the second death' and there is no Scriptural indication that once they are thrown this future furnace they would somehow survive, even though many teach that special bodies would be provided so that they could remain alive in continual suffering there is nothing in Scripture to support this belief. It is the end of their lives not the beginning of an eternity of torture)

24

Saving the World

The brothers were terrified; years before they had conspired together to kill their brother because they hated him for saying that they all would bow down to him, Reuben tried to rescue him but they were persuaded by another of the brothers, Judah, to sell him into slavery instead. They were now standing before a man second only to Pharaoh who could easily order their execution. He had been a stranger to them and they had bowed down to him as governor of the land and now they remembered how he had pleaded with them for his life; this time their lives were in his hands.

He had been speaking to them through an interpreter but now he said to them in their own language, "I am Joseph! Is my father still living?" but they were too afraid to answer.

"Come close to me," Joseph said to his brothers, "I'm your brother Joseph, the one you sold into Egypt! And now don't be distressed and angry with yourselves for selling me here, because it was to save lives that God sent me ahead of you. For two years now there's been famine in the land and for the next five years there'll not be ploughing and reaping. But

God sent me ahead of you to preserve for you a remnant on earth and to save your lives by a great deliverance."

Jesus, in speaking of Zacchaeus to those who considered this wealthy chief tax collector as a sinner, said, "Today salvation has come to this house, because this man too is a son of Abraham, for the Son of Man came to seek and to save what was lost."

The Jews at the time of Jesus looked and hoped for the 'anointed one' the Messiah, to come and rid their nation of the Romans and restore the kingdom to Israel. Their prophets had spoken of God himself coming to his people and gathering them together, and healing the breach between Judah and Israel who fought against each other from the time the one nation was split in two. What they didn't like to be reminded of though, was the promises that the Gentiles would also be part of that new nation ruled by God. When Jesus spoke positively about them, those listening to him either didn't understand or they reacted with hostility.

The apostle Paul spoke in terms that went far beyond the people of Israel, which brought down on him much hostility from his own people. He wrote to the Galatians saying, 'You're all sons of God through faith in Christ (Messiah) Jesus, for all of you who were baptised into Christ have clothed yourselves with Christ. There is neither Jew nor Greek, slave nor free, male nor female, for you are all one in Christ Jesus. If you belong to Christ, then you are Abraham's seed and heirs according to the promise.'

The bad news is that, as Paul wrote earlier, 'the Scripture declares that the whole world is a prisoner of sin,' locked up without any possibility of release. John Stott in his commentary on Galatians sums up the human condition and our relationship to the law and God in this way: 'After God gave the promise to Abraham, he gave the law to Moses. Why? Simply because He had to make things worse before He could make them better. The law exposed sin, provoked sin, condemned sin. The purpose of the law was, as it were, to lift the lid off man's respectability and disclose what he is really like underneath—sinful, rebellious, guilty, under the judgment of God, and helpless to save himself.

'And the law must still be allowed to do its God-given duty today. One of the great faults of the contemporary church is the tendency to soft-pedal sin and judgment. Like false prophets we 'heal the wound of God's people lightly.' This is how Dietrich Bonhoeffer put it; 'It is only when one submits to the law that one can speak of grace . . . I don't think it is Christian to want to get to the New Testament too soon and too directly.' We must never bypass the law and come straight to the gospel. To do so is to contradict the plan of God in biblical history.

'Is this not why the gospel is unappreciated today? Some ignore it, others ridicule. So in our modern evangelism we cast our pearls (the costliest pearl being the gospel) before swine. People cannot see the beauty of the pearl, because they have no conception of the filth of the pigsty. No man has appreciated the gospel until the law has first revealed him to himself. It is only against the inky blackness of the night sky that the stars begin to appear, and it is only against the dark background of sin and judgment that the gospel shines forth.'

Paul wrote to the Romans, 'All who sin apart from the law will also perish apart from the law, and all who sin under the law will be judged by the law. For it's not those who hear the law who are righteous in God's sight, but it's those who obey the law who will be declared righteous.' Having written that that Jews and Gentiles alike are all under sin, he goes on to say, 'But now a righteousness from God, apart from the law, has been made known, to which the old testament testifies. This righteousness from God comes through faith in Jesus Christ to all who believe. There's no difference because everyone has sinned and fallen short of the glory of God and are justified freely by his grace through the redemption that came by the Messiah Jesus. God presented him as a sacrifice of atonement, through faith in his blood.'

When Jesus went to Nazareth, where he had been brought up, he went into the synagogue on the Sabbath day as was his custom, and he stood up to read. The scroll of the prophet Isaiah was handed to him. Unrolling it he found the place where it's written: "The Spirit of the Lord is on me, because he has anointed me to preach good news to the poor. He has sent me to proclaim freedom for the prisoners and recovery of sight for the blind, to release the oppressed, to proclaim the year of the Lord's favour." Then he rolled up the scroll, gave it back to the attendant and sat down. The eyes of everyone in the synagogue were fastened on him, "Today," he told them, "this scripture has now come true."

Jesus had come to release and free people; he was going to save them and enable them to escape a terrible fate. It involved their sin which had separated them from God, making them enemies of God and belonging to the evil one, who unseen, was and is ruling all the kingdoms of this world.

"He who belongs to God," Jesus told those who resisted him, "hears what God says. The reason you don't hear is that you don't belong to God."

God had rescued one nation from enslavement to Egypt, yet they, on the whole, remained rebellious and disobedient to God throughout their history. The prophets wrote of a new covenant, not because the first was at fault, but because the fault was with the people. This new covenant isn't written with ink but with the Spirit of the living God, not on stone but on the human heart. Human nature hasn't changed, and we're no different from the people we read of in Israel's history. For them it was being saved from slavery and it's the same today. Without realising it, we're in spiritual slavery and stand under the sentence of death unless, as John the Baptist and Jesus himself said, we repent of our rebellion and disobedience because God's kingdom is coming, and when it does come the door of this age will be closed and the door of the new age will be opened.

Paul wrote to the Thessalonians on what was reported to him, that they had 'turned to God from idols to serve the living and true God, and to wait for his Son from heaven, whom he raised from the dead—Jesus, who rescues us from the coming wrath.' 'Let no-one deceive you,' Paul urges the Ephesians, 'with empty words, for because of such things (a list is given) God's wrath comes on those who are disobedient.'

We need to remember and rely on the love of God but never forget his warnings of destruction to those who remain in their rebellious and stubborn attitude to God. 'The Lord isn't slow in keeping his promise, as some understand slowness. He's patient with you, not wanting anyone to perish, but everyone to come to repentance,' as Peter wrote in his second letter.

Quite rightly we focus on what Paul wrote of the kindness of God which leads us towards repentance but we would be unwise to forget what follows: 'but because of your stubbornness and unrepentant heart, you're storing up wrath against yourself for the day of God's wrath, when his righteous judgment will be revealed.'

Jesus was asked by someone, "Lord, are only a few people going to be saved?" and he answered, "Make every effort to enter through the narrow door, because many, I tell you, will try to enter and will not be able to. Once the owner of the house gets up and closes the door, you'll stand outside knocking and pleading, 'Sir, open the door for us.'

"But he'll answer, 'I don't know you or where you come from.'

"Then you will say, 'We ate and drank with you, and you taught in our streets.'

"But he'll reply, 'I don't know you or where you come from. Get away from me, all you evildoers!'

Jesus had said before, "Not everyone who says to me, 'Lord, Lord,' will enter the kingdom of Heaven (God), but only he who does the will of my Father who is in heaven. Many will say to me on that day, 'Lord, Lord, didn't we preach in your name, and in your name drive out demons and perform many miracles?' Then I'll tell them plainly, 'I never knew you. Get away from me, you evildoers!'

On the surface we may appear committed and devoted to the cause of Christ yet under his penetrating and discerning gaze we are exposed as still remaining a part of this divisive and violent world. God knows who are his and his condemnation in both testaments is for the false shepherds who lead their flocks astray.

Jesus had many confrontational contacts with those who saw themselves as guardians of their religion and these teachers were critical of the disciples of Jesus for not giving their hands a ceremonial washing before they ate. This tradition of theirs was very important to them.

Jesus responded to this accusation by saying, "Isaiah was right when he prophesied about you hypocrites; as it's written: 'These people honour me with their lips but their hearts are far from me. They worship me in vain; their teachings are but rules taught by men.' You've let go of the commands of God and are holding on to the tradition of men."

How you wash your hands isn't a problem today within the churches but there are 'traditions of men' that are still expected to be followed such as the days we observe and the way in which we keep them, so that frame of mind that the religious hypocrites who opposed Jesus on a matter of tradition is with us today.

In writing to the Galatians Paul wrote, 'Grace and peace to you from God our Father and the Lord Jesus Christ, who gave himself for our sins to rescue us from the present evil age.' There was a price to pay for our sins and it was paid in blood and this sacrifice of a perfect righteous life rescued us not only from our sentence of death but made us part of the age to come. We remain here on earth being tested and equipped in this hostile environment for a position of service in the world to come, not to leave the world but waiting for when the time comes to be a part of the solution the world needs but in this age rejects.

John wrote, 'Don't love the world or anything in the world. If anyone loves the world, the love of the Father isn't in him because everything in the world—the cravings of sinful man, the lust of his eyes and the boasting of what he has and does—comes not from the Father but from the world.' James adds to this by writing, 'anyone who chooses to be a friend of the world becomes an enemy of God.'

The Israelites had God to rule over them, but they rejected that rule for the rule of a man, and all that led to—high taxation, exploitation, corruption and Baal worship. At the heart of the human problem is our heart, or, to be more precise, our mind, which is our spirit. In contrast to God's Spirit, which is his mind, we're by nature sinful, Jeremiah wrote, 'The heart is deceitful above all things and beyond cure. Who can understand it? "I the Lord search the heart and examine the mind, to reward a man according to his conduct, according to what his deeds deserve."' And Jesus said, "Which of you, if his son asks for bread, will give him a stone? Or if he asks for a fish, will give him a snake? If you then, though you're evil, know how to give good gifts to your children, how much more will your Father in heaven give the Holy Spirit (God's mind and nature) to those who ask him."

A young man ran up to Jesus and falling on his knees asked him, "Good teacher, what must I do to inherit eternal life?"

"Why do you call me good?" Jesus answered, "No-one is good—except God alone." God's holy law doesn't make us righteous, it's powerless to do that, rather it shows us how sinful we are and how far short we fall of God's standard. Paul wrote to the Galatians, 'All who rely on observing the law are under a curse . . . clearly no-one is justified before God by the law.' 'Through the law,' as Paul told the Romans, 'we become conscious of sin,' and we're only set free from slavery to sin by faith in Christ, and becoming slaves to righteousness. The wages of sin is death (not ever-lasting torture in fire) but the gift of God is eternal life (it's a gift that we don't have naturally, even though millions believe that we have an immortal soul—a teaching taken from Greek philosophy and adopted by the early church fathers) in Christ Jesus our Lord.

The good news that Jesus brought and the prophets wrote of centred on the soon coming kingdom of God and its establishment here on earth. He spoke about it more than any other subject, and sent his disciples out to preach it. He never said anything about going to heaven; the emphasis was always his return and the beginning of the new age. At the start of his ministry he spoke of the kingdom and before his ascension he spoke about the kingdom of God. The last words in the book of Acts are, 'Boldly and without hindrance he (Paul) preached the kingdom of God and taught about the Lord Jesus Christ.' The Christian message isn't centred on love, mercy and forgiveness as many are taught but on the priority of the kingdom of God arriving with the return of Christ, and our need to repent of our spiritual lawlessness.

We have demonstrated that we are unable to govern ourselves, and even when God's word is close and familiar to us we are disqualified from ruling the world because of our sinful nature, and no effort of man will bring about that kingdom. Even the best of evangelical work by dedicated Christians will not bring it, or will the work of the church change this world even though some teach that the church can change the world. The miracles done in the time of Moses didn't change the hearts of the people, no more than the miracle on Mount Carmel turned the nation from Baal worship, except for those seven thousand who hadn't bowed down to Baal.

Many Christians are urged to pray for revival and are busy with humanitarian projects, but that won't bring the kingdom, rather, Christians are being led to neglecting their primary purpose of sharing the good news of the kingdom of God which is what the world needs to hear, even though it won't be believed or accepted. It should be delivered as a witness against this world, just as the prophets didn't pull back from giving the stark warning of what would happen if God's warning were ignored and rejected. There were blessings to be reaped through belief and obedience and curses for disbelief and disobedience.

Jeremiah wasn't listened to even though he faithfully passed on God's warning against resisting the Babylonians which would save them and their city. Christians today should warn their people that a far greater power than the Babylonians is coming and we must become its subjects now so that we can be saved the devastation that will be brought on earth because of its stubborn resistance to the one living God. To the world this is working against them just as Jeremiah was thought of as working for the enemy but he was actually working for their salvation not their destruction. Christians must be willing to become strangers in this world rather than being a part of it.

The blessings and curses Moses commanded to be spoken from Mount Gerizim and Mount Ebal were focused on the quality of their lives and while the new covenant has blessings and curses they are not dependent on our physical state or the quality of our lives, but on our attitudes and motives. The old covenant didn't ignore the matter of the heart and mind in fact, it lay at the core of its teaching. Jeremiah wrote, 'Circumcise yourselves to the Lord, circumcise your hearts,' which is in line with Moses' command to 'Circumcise your hearts, therefore, and don't be stiff-necked any longer.' This change of heart and mind isn't accomplished by human effort but by God himself; 'The Lord your God will circumcise your hearts and the hearts of your descendants, so that you may love him with all of your heart and with all your soul, and live.'

When that circumcision is done what was written by Isaiah no longer applies: 'You have neither heard nor understood; from of old your ear has not been open.' Paul explained this new condition to the Romans, 'A man is not a Jew if he is only one outwardly, nor is circumcision merely outward and physical. No, a man is a Jew if he is one inwardly; and circumcision is circumcision of the heart, by the Spirit, not by the written code. Such a man's praise isn't from men, but from God.' We all need to be spiritually circumcised, and when this happens we can say as Job said, "My ears have heard of you but now my eyes have seen you. Therefore I despise myself and repent in dust and ashes."

The last prophet in the Old Testament, Malachi, has as his last words, "See, I'll send you the prophet Elijah before that great and dreadful day of the Lord comes. He'll turn the hearts of the fathers to their children, and the hearts of the children to their fathers; or else I'll come and strike the land with a curse."

John the Baptist fulfilled that role of calling people to repentance for the forgiveness of their sins, but there was no 'great and dreadful day of the Lord,' as they expected; that is still in the future, which calls for yet another Elijah to proclaim his coming as a voice preparing the way for the Lord. That Elijah will lift up its voice without fear and say, "Here is your God! Look, the Sovereign Lord comes with power and his arm rules for him. Look, his reward is with him." That Elijah isn't one man in the desert, as it was then, but Christians in the spiritual wilderness of this world, called Babylon, proclaiming that same unchanging message.

God has his people in every century, no matter what is happening in history. They come from all denominations and none, but they belong to him because he called them and made them his. Christians are divided by different teachings but in God's eyes they are one body. God wants, and teaches us, to pray for his kingdom to come—there is no other solution to the world's problems and its divisions but all too many Christians are believing they're going to heaven and are living a life of dedicated service to others but have not considered or been taught that their purpose is preparing for God's government here on earth, not to abandon it to be destroyed as many believe but enabling others to see that the evil in this world will not always be here. The dragon's days are numbered.

That preparation is to become like Jesus. 'The grace of God,' Paul wrote to Titus, 'teaches us to say "No" to ungodliness and worldly passions and to live self-controlled, upright and godly lives in this present age, while we wait for the blessed hope—the glorious appearing of our great God and our Saviour Jesus Christ who gave himself for us to redeem us from all wickedness and to purify for himself a people that are his very own, eager to do what is good.'

Even at the last supper there was a dispute among the disciples as to which one of them was considered as the greatest, but Jesus said to them, "The kings of the Gentiles lord it over them; and those who exercise authority over them call themselves 'benefactors,' but you're not to be like them, instead, the 'greatest' among you must become the junior and the one who has authority as the servant. I'm among you as one who serves and you are those who have stood by me in my trials and as my Father has conferred a kingdom on me so I confer a kingdom on you where you'll eat and drink at my table and sit on thrones judging the twelve tribes of Israel." That is to be their responsibility in the kingdom but there are many other positions to be filled, "In my Father's house are many rooms; if it were not so, I would have told you, I'm going there to prepare a place for you (judging the twelve tribes of Israel). And if I go and prepare a place for you, I'll come back and take you to be with me that you also may be where I am (he's coming back! And his people will be with him here on earth).

The dragon has deceived all of us and has succeeded in splitting us into many competing factions, but in God's eyes we remain one people, no matter what our church leaders may teach against other denominations, and their claim to be more faithful to Scripture than the other fellowships. 'The Lord knows those who are his,' because his people all share the same heart and mind which comes from God—the Spirit of God.

Jesus told his disciples that some who were standing there would see the kingdom before they died. Almost a week later Jesus took Peter, James and John to a high mountain where he was changed and his clothes became dazzlingly white, and there talking to him were Elijah and Moses about his departure (his exodus) that was soon to happen. The disciples were naturally frightened and didn't know what to say and Peter began to make a suggestion when a bright cloud came over them and a voice said, "This is my Son, whom I love; with him I'm delighted—listen to him! When they heard that voice they were terrified and fell to the ground. Then Jesus came and reassured them "Get up—don't be afraid. After everything went back to normal Jesus ordered them not to tell anyone what they had seen until the Son of Man had risen from the dead. They kept the matter to themselves, discussing what 'rising from the dead' meant.

What they experienced was a trailer, a preview and a vision of what was to come. Elijah and Moses were still dead and would wait, like every other child of God for the resurrection, but what the disciples saw was a glimpse into the future after Christ returns and with all the saints he begins to govern the earth. We do not go to heaven, but wait until that mighty call, that unique voice that wakes us from our sleep, just as Lazarus was woken from his sleep of death.

This dark and evil age will then give way to the kingdom of light and be liberated from the horrors that have gone on since the beginning and all of its bondage to decay will be brought into the glorious freedom of the children of God. We are now, as Peter calls us, 'strangers in the world,' but one day Jesus will say, "Well done, good and faithful servant. You've been faithful with a few things; I'll put you in charge of many things. Come and share your master's happiness." This isn't a call to rest but to divine action in the new age.

"You are worthy to take the scroll and open the seals, because you were slain, and with your blood you purchased men for God from every tribe and language and people and nation. You have made them to be a kingdom and priests to serve our God, and they will reign on the earth."

Christians will reign on earth yet millions are taught that we leave earth behind. Satan does not want his position to be taken away from him so he has deceived people into believing that instead of him leaving earth, we do. He has led the whole world to think that our future is away from the earth rather than a healed, restored and saved earth which Christ will begin to do at his return.

Not all that is promised happens at the same time—the first man Adam was a natural human being—the last Adam, Christ, a life giving spirit. First there is the physical and mortal and last the spiritual and immortal. Christ came the first time to offer himself as the perfect atonement for the sins of the world. He returns as King to rule the world. Peter writes, 'the day of the Lord will come like a thief. The heavens will disappear with a roar; the elements will be destroyed by fire, and the earth and everything in it will be laid bare.' This total change and destruction of the earth is in the context of, as Peter goes on to say, 'looking forward to a new heaven and a new earth, the home of righteousness.'

When Christ returns nations, no longer being led by Satan, will be taught the way of peace and 'the earth will be full of the knowledge of the Lord as the waters cover the sea.' If everything and everyone except for the saints are destroyed in this world engulfing fire who would be left to teach the knowledge of God and to put an end to all wars?

That destruction by fire comes after the reign of Christ has completed all that needs to be done; many believe as scripture says, that it'll be a 1,000 year reign and when that is fulfilled then the human race itself will have become spirit and that then the new heaven and new earth will come through fire; what happens after that hasn't been revealed but what has been revealed is our need to repent and put our trust in Jesus before his return. Peter goes on to write, 'So then, dear friends, since you're looking forward to this, make every effort to be found spotless, blameless and at peace with him, bearing in mind that our Lord's patience means salvation.'

Fire destroys. The Bible gives us examples of God using fire to destroy his enemies and to demonstrate who he is working through. People who claim it is Christian to call fire down for 'special anointing' are practicing a counterfeit form of worship that has deceived millions and opens the door to the powers of spiritual darkness.

In Paul's first letter to Timothy he wrote, 'God our Saviour wants all people saved and come to a knowledge of the truth, for there is one God and one mediator between God and humans, the man Christ Jesus, who gave himself as a ransom for all.' That knowledge is that God doesn't want anyone to perish but all to come to repentance. So Jesus knowing that there was no-one righteous came to call all to repentance and to give them immortality through faith in him—that is God's message today to this world, but the churches have greatly distorted that message from the announcement of his soon coming kingdom to one of teaching that we all have an immortal soul and that God lives in us and loves us. 'We live forever' is the claim of many but we need to remember that Satan tried to undermine what God told the first humans regarding the tree of the knowledge of good and evil by saying, "You won't really die," and he deceived the woman into thinking that she could become like God—this was Satan's aim and his pride was his downfall. We are mortal and as Paul said, 'at the resurrection we will be clothed with immortality.' and if there were no resurrection we would stay dead—totally dead.

25

Reconciliation

Paul spoke of his ministry as one of reconciliation; this is because our sins separated us from God and we became his enemies bringing his anger against us. Because of our rebellion and disobedience towards him we were under the sentence of death, and there was nothing we could do or achieve that would remove that sentence that hung over us.

The answer to this unsolvable dilemma wasn't trying harder or living a better life because that death sentence had already been passed. Paul wrote to the Romans; 'Once I was alive apart from law; but when the commandment came, sin sprang to life and I died. I found that the very commandment that was intended to bring life actually brought death.' Yet God takes no pleasure in the death of the wicked and his love is so great that he gave of himself so that we could be saved from him. Jesus was handed over to those who wanted him dead according to God's set purpose and foreknowledge. He was nailed to a cross by men, but it was God's decision that it should happen. That was the extent of his love.

Peter wrote that, 'He committed no sin, and no deceit was found in his mouth' (quoting Isaiah). 'When they hurled their insults at him, he didn't retaliate; when he suffered, he made no threats. Instead, he entrusted himself to him who judges justly. He himself bore our sins in his body on the tree, so that we might die to sins and live for righteousness; by his wounds you've been healed. We were like sheep going astray, but now you've returned to the shepherd and Overseer of our lives.' Peter addressed his letter 'to God's elect, strangers in the world, scattered throughout . . .'

Christians are described as strangers in the world but so many Christians are being led to identify themselves with the world and its needs and in so doing gain the worlds' respect rather than be considered as 'the scum of the earth, the refuse of the world.' As Paul told the Corinthians. Christ was rejected by the world yet we desire the worlds' admiration and recognition for our good works, and of course to improve the quality of the lives of those with difficulties and hardships to live with is a good thing, but If we truly identify with Christ and his message we will be rejected and hated by the world, yet if we belong to the world and focus on what the world considers important it will recognise and respect you as one that belongs to it. It's not showing love to the world if we don't speak of guilt, righteousness and judgment. The ruler of this world—Satan, would prefer we avoid those subjects and whispers, 'People won't listen to your message if you're a Jeremiah, speak of God's grace and don't be confrontational.'

The only way humanity can be reconciled with God is for God himself, the Lord God Almighty of Israel, to come and take our place in judgment, and die the death we were due to pay—the righteous for the unrighteous—the innocent for the guilty; that is what brought us to God. 'All this,' as Paul wrote in his second letter to the Corinthians, 'is from God, who reconciled us to himself through Christ and gave us the ministry of reconciliation: that God was reconciling the world to himself in Christ, not counting men's sins against them. And he has committed to us the message of reconciliation. Because of this we're

Christ's ambassadors, as though God were making his appeal through us. We implore you on Christ's behalf: Be reconciled to God. God made him who had no sin to be sin for us, so that in him we might become the righteousness of God.'

In the first of John's letters he writes, 'My dear children, I write this to you so that you'll not sin, but if anyone does sin, we have one who speaks to the Father in our defence—Jesus Christ, the Righteous One. He's the atoning sacrifice for our sins, and not only for ours but also for the sins of the whole world.'

In writing to the Romans Paul said, 'since we've been justified by his blood, how much more shall we be saved from God's wrath through him! For if, when we were God's enemies, we were reconciled to him through the death of his Son, how much more, having been reconciled, shall we be saved through his life!' Reconciliation is here referring to individuals being justified before God; in the future it will encompass the whole world because Christ will be here in person and 'the shroud,' as Isaiah writes, 'that enfolds all people—the sheet that covers all nations will be destroyed.'

In the first letter of Peter he writes that 'since you call on a Father who judges each person's work impartially, live your lives as strangers here in reverent fear,' later he wrote, 'Dear friends, I urge you, as aliens and strangers in the world . . .' which is how the people of faith were described in the letter to the Hebrews, 'All these people were still living by faith when they died. They didn't receive the things promised; they only saw and welcomed them from a distance, and they admitted that they were aliens and strangers on earth. People who say such things show that they're looking for a country of their own . . . they were looking for a better country—a heavenly one, so God isn't ashamed to be called their God, because he's prepared a city for them.'

That city of the living God is God's people—the church of the firstborn; it's a spiritual house built with living stones and has become a holy nation, a people belonging to God—the 'Israel of God' as Paul called it in his letter to the Galatians. When Paul wrote of the reconciliation between Gentiles and Jews through faith in Christ, he said to those who were at Ephesus, 'consequentially, you're no longer foreigners and aliens, but fellow-citizens with God's people and members of God's household, built on the foundation of the apostles and prophets, with Christ Jesus himself as the chief cornerstone. In him the whole building is joined together and rises to become a holy temple in the Lord. And in him you too are being built together to become a dwelling in which God lives by his Spirit.'

Paul taught the Ephesians those who belong to God are 'to be made new in the attitude of your minds; and to put on the new self, created to be like God in true righteousness and holiness.' God gives of his mind and nature so that we can be like him.

If someone was to ask what is the purpose and aim of this building of people into a nation that is not accepted or recognised by this world, we would come to the answer of what the destiny of this world is, and what connection there is between earth and heaven. This is perhaps the greatest question we can ask. 'Where is it all leading?' This mystery is answered by Paul in that same letter to the Ephesians:

'He has made know to us the mystery of his will according to his good pleasure, which he purposed in Christ, to be put into effect when the times will have reached their fulfilment—to bring all things in heaven and on earth together under one head, even Christ.'

Heaven and earth together! There'll be a time in the future when there'll be no difference between heaven and earth. Heaven will be on earth and God himself will live here. This is what Jesus asked his disciples to pray for, "your kingdom come, your will be done on earth as it is in heaven.' No contrast or conflict between earth and heaven. Each day brings that event closer and this earth has a glorious future, however, the earth at this time is enemy held territory, and God's people live in an environment that is hostile towards them, but at the same time they are citizens of a future world government that will never end, as Daniel saw in a vision while he lived and served in the government of Babylon, 'He was given authority, glory and sovereign power; all peoples, nations and men of every language worshipped him. His dominion is an everlasting dominion that will not pass away, and his kingdom is one that will never be destroyed.'

Many Christians and others have been led to believe that the Kingdom of God is already here on earth. The new age has begun and it's for the church to expand that kingdom—that is a great misunderstanding that presents the church as the kingdom and the conversion of the world its mission. The restoring and healing of the earth will not even begin until Christ returns, that is why we urgently pray for Christ to return and also pray for his people as they participate in the sufferings of Christ: we inwardly rejoice as we wait for his glorious appearing. Paul wrote to Timothy, 'I've fought the good fight, I've finished the race, I've kept the faith. Now there is in store for me the crown of righteousness, which the Lord, the righteous judge, will award to me on that day—and not only to me, but also to all who have longed for his appearing.'

In speaking to a crowd of astonished people at the healing of a man crippled from birth Peter told them of their own guilt in the death of Jesus, "you disowned the Holy and Righteous One and asked that a murderer be released to you. You killed the author of life, but God raised him from the dead—we're witnesses of this. By faith in the name of Jesus, this man who you know was made strong. It's Jesus' name and the faith that comes from him that has given this complete healing to him, as you can all see.

"Now, brothers, I know that you acted in ignorance, as did your leaders, but this is how God fulfilled what he has previously said through the prophets, saying that his Messiah would suffer. So repent and turn to God so that your sins may be wiped out—that times of refreshing may come from the Lord, and that he send the Messiah, who has been appointed for you—even Jesus. He must remain in heaven *until the time comes for God to restore everything*, as he promised long ago through his holy prophets."

Before the dragon, that old serpent the devil, became an enemy of God and mankind he oversaw this earth with angels under him but he became filled with pride on account of his wisdom and splendour and made an attempt to overthrow God and in that time of spiritual rebellion this earth that was created billions of years ago was destroyed along with the other planets in our solar system. Six thousand years ago when the earth was desolate and darkness covered everything God renewed the earth and told our first parents to replenish and take care of it. But they too rebelled against their Creator as we've all done since and the history of mankind has been written in blood and suffering while we all without exception have been affected and influenced by the spirit of this world.

The Roman Christians, and we, are able to read that 'just as the result of one trespass was condemnation for all men, so also the result of one act of righteousness was justification that brings life for all men.'

Satan, the prince of this world, as Jesus called him, has deceived all of us (If Penn & Tellar, Derren Brown and David Blaine can reduce us to speechlessness by their amazing performances then how much more can an intelligent spirit being who has been here since before the creation of humans), by convincing us that our political, religious or humanist viewpoint is the right one and that all the others are wrong. The various governmental systems, from the democratic to the communist, and the world's faiths and philosophies are not from God; they're based on lies and haven't brought peace to the world because the spirit that has inspired them comes from another source other than God. That dark spiritual power which Paul called the god of this age or the spirit of this world has blinded the minds of unbelievers so that they cannot see the light of the good news of the glory of Christ who is the image of God. As God said "Let light shine out of darkness;" he has made his divine light enlighten our minds so that we can know Christ.

It is clear from the degree of division within Christianity that the dragon has done his main work of deception amongst God's own people in convincing each denomination that all the others are mistaken in their teachings. This deep divide is a part of the greater division of this world and will only be corrected (in spite of many reforms) by the return of Christ and the 'seizing of the dragon, that ancient serpent, who is the devil, or Satan, and binding him for a thousand years. He (the angel) threw him into the Abyss, and locked and sealed it over him, to keep him from deceiving the nations any more until the thousand years were ended. After that, he must be set free for a short time.'

A person who is deceived can't recognise that they're deceived but can see clearly how others are. That is why each evangelist and those working in evangelism, on the street and from door to door (as I have done as a part of an evangelical fellowship) is convinced that they need to protect those not in a church from others who may call at their door and present themselves as the true representatives of Christ little realising that none of us have been immune to the distortions that came into the official teachings of the church in the early centuries after Christ, and the later distortions from the 19ᵗʰ century which have misdirected us all from the good news of the coming Kingdom of God.

That divine government under Christ will rule over the nations and will end all cruelty and injustice. In that age lies and deception will not succeed in convincing people of what is untrue, but in this age all claim to be sharing the truth and even Satan masquerades as an angel of light. He knows what he's doing but we teach in all sincerity what we believe is true, yet have unknowingly carried the theological distortions from door to door. None of us have been exceptions to this, so cleverly has the enemy done his work. But as long as we saw the errors of others there was no need to check our own teachings. We've seen the speck in the other's eye but have missed the plank in our own.

Salvation is a rescue operation. It rescues people from a world of hate and division and leaves them in that world as ambassadors of a future world. Our rescue hasn't taken us from the world but made us lights in the world. "I have given them your word," Jesus prayed, "and the world has hated them, for they are not of the world any more than I am of the world. My prayer is not that you take them out of the world but that you protect them from the evil one. They are not of the world, even as I am not of it. Set them apart by the truth; your word is truth. As you sent me into the world, I have sent them into the world."

Some of God's people achieved notable success as the writer of Hebrews wrote, 'but others were tortured and refused to be released, so that they might gain a better resurrection. Some faced jeers and flogging, while still others were chained and put in prison. They were stoned; they were sawn in two; they were put to death by the sword. They went about in sheepskins and goatskins, destitute, persecuted and ill-treated—the world was not worthy of them. They wandered in deserts and mountains, and in caves and holes in the ground.

'These were all commended for their faith, yet none of them received what had been promised. God has planned something better for us that only together with us would they be made perfect.'

This strongly suggests that what happens to the saints, both those who have died and those who remain alive will happen at the same time. It isn't that some have gone to heaven and are waiting for the others to arrive but that at Christ's return the dead will be resurrected and those belonging to Christ who are alive will be 'changed—in a flash, in the twinkling of an eye, at the last trumpet. For the trumpet will sound and the dead will be raised imperishable and we'll be changed. For the perishable must clothe itself with the imperishable and the mortal with immortality' as Paul wrote to the Corinthians.

Christ was the first to be resurrected; when he returns all those who belong to him will be resurrected; 'then he will reign until he has put all his enemies under his feet. The last enemy to be destroyed is death. When he has done this, then the Son himself will be made subject to him who put everything under him, so that God may be all in all.' That is the sequence—death followed by the resurrection; then the reign of Christ and then, when death is abolished, everything will be made new.

"For the Son of Man is going to come in his Father's glory with his angels. And *then* he will reward each person according to what he has done." That is the day Paul was looking forward to. That is the day we'll see Christ.

As the suffering of this world continues coupled with worldwide deception and wars and rumours of wars God's people have an announcement to make: 'The good news of that coming kingdom will be preached in the whole world as a witness to all nations, and then the end will come,' as Matthew wrote. Not the end of the world but the end of this evil age or as Paul called it, 'the dominion of darkness.' Satan will be made inactive and the world for the first time will experience peace from all that is hurtful.

No work of man, or any church or combination of churches will bring that kingdom to earth. Even the message of that coming kingdom will be rejected as it's given as a witness against this unbelieving world and it will come only when He returns as King, 'then all the nations will be gathered before him, and he'll separate the people one from another as a shepherd separates the sheep from the goats.'

Then as the prophet Micah wrote, 'He will judge between many peoples and will settle disputes for strong nations far and wide. They will beat their swords into ploughshares and their spears into pruning hooks. Nation will not take up sword against nation, nor will they train for war anymore.'

'Endure hardship as discipline; God is treating you as sons, the writer of Hebrews tells us, 'God disciplines us for our good that we may share in his holiness.' Isaiah wrote of God's heart towards Israel, "in a surge of anger I hid my face from you for a moment, but with everlasting kindness I will have compassion on you. Though the mountains be shaken and the hills be removed, yet my unfailing love for you will not be shaken nor my covenant of peace be removed."

And so Peter reminds those who are suffering 'not to be surprised at the painful trial you are suffering, as though something strange were happening to you, but rejoice that you participate in the sufferings of Christ, so that you may be overjoyed when his glory is revealed . . . for it is time for judgment to begin with the family of God; and if it begins with us, what will the outcome be for those who do not obey the gospel of God . . . humble yourselves under God's mighty hand, that he may lift you up in due time and cast all your anxiety on him because he cares for you.'

26

A light in the World

The three naked and condemned men had been hanging for about three hours in pain and extreme discomfort while their agony was witnessed by thousands of people. Those who were passing that busy road junction which was just outside the city gates and couldn't avoid this dreadful spectacle of these men nailed to trees, and those who would always turn up at a public execution to satisfy their evil desire to see men die a slow death.

The condemned man between the two others was being ridiculed and insulted for claiming he was the Messiah, yet while he was being mocked he continued to ask for forgiveness for those who were putting him to death and for the others who were perversely enjoying this cruel punishment.

He had told the people that he was the light of the world and that whoever follows him would never walk in darkness but would have the light of life. John the Baptist said that this person, who was now suffering a death that by law no Roman citizen would suffer, was that true light that gives light to everyone.

It was noon and darkness came over the whole land and that darkness lasted till about mid-afternoon. The prophet Amos had written, 'I will make the sun go down at noon and darken the earth in broad daylight.' The day of the Lord will be a day of darkness with no light—it will be a day of judgment on the whole world, but not that day, that day God's anger fell on just one man as he hung on a tree close to death as if he were carrying the sins of the whole world.

The light that came into the world was about to go out. Jesus had told his disciples, "You're going to have the light just a little while longer. Walk while you have the light, before darkness overtakes you. Those who walk in the dark don't know where they're going. Put your trust in the light while you have it so that you may become children of light."

It was now about three in the afternoon and darkness covered everything. Jesus called out with a loud voice, "Father, into your hands I commit my spirit." He then died. Those who knew him, including the women who had followed him from Galilee, stood at a distance watching what had happened. Matthew records that at that moment there was an earthquake and the centurion in charge of the execution squad along with his men were terrified and exclaimed, "Surely he was the son of God!" At the same time the heavy curtain that separated the Holy of Holies from the inner court of the temple was torn in two from top to bottom. Tombs also were broken open and some of those who died were raised to life after Jesus' resurrection. Later it would be written, 'we have confidence to enter the Most Holy Place by the blood of Jesus by a new and living way opened for us through the curtain, that is, his body.'

I picked up a Christmas card that had a beautiful painting of a baby with stars in the background. Three elegantly drawn words proclaimed its message; 'Peace on earth.' The sadness of these words is that there was no peace then and there is no peace on earth now, yet many assume that was why Jesus came—to bring peace, and as others would justifiably say that if that's why he came then he failed, but Jesus himself said that we are not to think that he came to bring peace but rather division between people, and he taught that world conditions wouldn't change for the better because of his birth. The Christmas story, as well as not being presented accurately, which many church leaders knowing better acquiesce to, omits to say that peace will only come with his return and then only by force. A baby will not speak, no more than a dead man hanging on a cross can speak but the world celebrates these two images, perhaps because in both Jesus is silent; a stranger to us.

On that autumn night when shepherds stayed with their flocks overnight they saw an angel and the glory of God lit everything around them and they were terrified. "Don't be afraid," the messenger from God said, "I'm bringing you great news for the people of Israel that today in the town of David, a Saviour has been born; he's the Messiah, the anointed one, the Lord. You'll find the baby wrapped in cloths and lying in an animal's feeding trough in a stable. Suddenly an vast army of angelic beings appeared and the shepherds heard their voices saying, "Glory to God in the highest, and on earth peace to those on whom his favour rests."

Who are those whom God's favour rests? Not everyone, but those who Mary spoke of in her prayer, "His mercy extends to those who fear him . . . he has scattered those who are proud in their inmost thoughts. He has brought down rulers from their thrones but has lifted up the humble." Those who fear God and are humble are those whom his favour rests.

Luke tells us that the parents of John the Baptist were upright in the sight of God, observing all the Lord's commandments and regulations blamelessly, as were the parents of Jesus. And so on the eighth day he was circumcised and 33 days later came the purification ceremony as Moses commanded the Israelites, 'A woman who becomes pregnant and gives birth to a son will be ceremonially unclean for seven days, just as she is unclean during her monthly period. On the eighth day the boy is to be circumcised then she must wait 33 days to be purified from her bleeding.'

So it was that when that purification period was completed Joseph and Mary took the baby to the temple in Jerusalem to present him to the Lord as the Lord had said to Moses, "Consecrate to me every firstborn male. The first offspring of every womb among the Israelites belongs to me, whether man or animal.

"When the days of her purification for a son or daughter are over she is to bring to the priest at the entrance to the Tent of Meeting a year-old lamb for a burnt offering and a young pigeon or a dove for a sin offering, if she cannot afford a lamb, she is to bring two doves or two young pigeons, one for a burnt offering and the other for a sin offering. In this way the priest will make atonement for her, and she will be clean."

Joseph and Mary offered the sacrifice of the two birds, not being able to afford the lamb. At that moment a man approached them and put out his hands to take the baby and Mary placed the baby in his arms. His name was Simeon, who was a righteous and devout man who looked forward to the coming of the Messiah and the end of all rulers like Herod. He praised God saying, "Sovereign Lord, as you've promised I can now die peacefully because I've seen your liberator which you've prepared in plain view—a light for revelation to the gentiles and for glory to your people Israel." Zechariah, John's father, had prayed of the "tender mercy of our God by which the rising sun will come to us from heaven to shine on those living in darkness and in the shadow of death, to guide our feet into the path of peace."

As the baby's parents marvelled at what was said about him Simeon blessed them and directed his words to Mary; "This child is destined to cause the falling and rising of many in Israel and to be a sign that will be spoken against, so that the inner thinking of many will be exposed, and you will be hurt deeply too."

There was at that same time in the temple an old woman named Anna, a very devout woman of the tribe of Asher, one of the tribes that were deported by the Assyrians. Asher was born to Zilpah, Leah's servant, when she found that she wasn't conceiving anymore—there was a rivalry between Leah and Rachel over providing Jacob with children! When Leah's servant bore Jacob a second son, the first was Gad, she was thrilled, that's why she named him Asher meaning *happy*.

Anna came to Joseph and Mary and gave thanks to God and spoke about the child to all who were looking forward the saving of Jerusalem.

Thirty years later Jesus began teaching and thirty-seven years after that Jerusalem was destroyed by Titus, son of the new emperor Vespasian.

Jesus had said, "When you see Jerusalem being surrounded by armies you will know that its desolation is near. Then let those who are in Judea run to the mountains and those in the city get out and don't return. Because this is the time of punishment in fulfilment of all that has been written. How dreadful it will be in those days for pregnant women and nursing mothers! There will be great distress in the land and great anger against this people. They'll fall by the sword and will be taken as prisoners to all the nations. Jerusalem will be trampled on by the Gentiles until their time is completed."

Looking beyond the fall of Jerusalem to an even greater conflict he said, "There will be signs in the sun, moon and stars. On the earth, nations will be in anguish and perplexity at the roaring and tossing of the sea. Men will faint from terror, apprehensive of what is coming on the world, for the heavenly bodies will be shaken. At that time they will see the Son of Man coming in a cloud with power and great glory. When these things begin to take place, stand up and lift up your heads because your liberation is near.

"Be careful, or you'll be weighed down with sinful pursuits and the anxieties of life, and that day will close on you unexpectedly like a trap. Because it'll come on all those who live on earth, so be always on the watch, and pray that you may be able to escape all that is about to happen, and that you may be able to stand before the Son of Man."

Several times Paul wrote that he didn't want his readers to be ignorant of the reality of what happened in the past, because they serve as examples for us today; written as warnings so that we wouldn't do as they did. He wrote that 'everything that was written in the past was written to teach us, so that through endurance and the encouragement of the Scriptures we might have hope.'

Throughout the centuries of human cruelty, disobedience and rebellion against God there has always been a voice calling people to remember and repent, and the book of books which has often been held back from the people by princes and bishops and distorted by those with authority to teach, and yet sections of the Bible have always been close to us as familiar stories, words and sayings. For many the Bible has been presented in a language that is four hundred years old and its relevance to us today has not been made clear. For others the traditions established by law under the emperor Constantine's direction and enforced by regional bishops who often violently disagreed with each other has shaped what we believe as biblical truth yet the creeds that were made mandatory on all believers were a radical distortion of the simple and plain message that had been consistently preached from the beginning.

Some may see the Council of Nicaea (325) as settling the fundamental biblical truths once and for all but this isn't what happened. The big question for Christian leaders in the 4th century became a political issue that remained unresolved for the next several hundred years.

Bishop Gregory of Nyssa described the situation in Constantinople in 378: "In this city if you ask anyone for change, he will discuss with you whether the Son is begotten or unbegotten. If you ask about the quality of bread, you will receive the answer that 'the Father is greater, the Son is less.'" The Council of Constantinople in 381 was destined to set the course for Christian orthodoxy down to modern times.

That question was 'are the Father and the Son "identical" or only "similar?" There were at least four theological positions; first there is the Arians whose watchword was 'dissimilar' (*anomois*) and their belief was that the Father and the Son are dissimilar in essence. The supporters of Arius were a powerful group of Eastern bishops, including Constantine's advisor, Eusebius of Nicomedia, all of whom were opposed to the Nicaean doctrine of identical substance because, in their view, it obliterated the distinction between the Father and the Son.

Arianism flourished in the East until Theodosius 1 presided over its demise at the Council of Constantinople in 381. By that time it had been transmitted to the Goths north of the Danube by their first bishop, Wulfila, an Arian. Goths later brought Arianism to the West, where it remained an obstacle to religious unity for the next 400 years.

Then there were the Semi-Arians whose watchword was 'similar' (*homoios*). They believed that the Son is similar to the Father but not in all things. He is not a 'creature' of God in the way that angels and mankind are defined as 'creatures.' The word *homoousios* (of identical substance) used by the Nicaeans is wrong because it is not in the Bible. The word *homoios* (similar) is in the Bible and therefore acceptable. In support of this position were Emperor Constantius (reigned 353-361) and several prominent bishops led by Basil of Ancyra.

The Nicaean's watchword was 'of identical substance' (*homoousious*). They believed the Father and Son are of identical substance with each other. The Son must have full divinity in order to vanquish evil and save sinners.

In support of this were Athanasius of Alexandria (who wasn't against some physical coercion to get his way, later Augustine of Hippo was to argue that punishment and fear might move people to repentance in ways that love and patience do not. His stance served ever after as an example to which some of the European churches darker tacticians might appeal, and in the medieval, Reformation, and Counter-Reformation periods, legitimacy would be sought for more than a few programs of brutal repression by citing Augustine's moves against the Donatists. 'A Public Faith' volume two, Ivor J. Davidson, p177), Hilary, bishop of Poitiers, and others, especially in the West. Constantine endorsed the Nicaean side during the Council of Nicaea and for a while afterward but seems to have spent his later years endeavouring to accommodate and reconcile all sides.

The Nicaean party was vindicated at Constantinople in 381, thanks in part to the backing of Theodosius 1, and then again in 451 at the Council of Chalcedon. Eastern and Western churches remained divided on some issues, but the Nicene Creed, as put forth by the Nicaeans and their allies, the Cappadocians, has remained a basic article of faith for Christians East and West ever since.

The watchword of the Cappadocians was 'of like substance' (*homoiousios*), and like the Nicaeans, the Cappadocians belived that the Father and the Son were of identical substance; but they also emphasised that the Father and the Son were distinct, though equally divine—hence their term *homoiousios*, 'of like substance.

The advocates for this were Bishop Basil of Caesarea, Bishop Gregory of Nyssa, and Bishop Gregory of Nazianzus, who were all from the province of Cappadocia (in present-day turkey).

Cappadocians joined forces with Nicaeans in 381 and were instrumental in winning over enough Eastern bishops to condemn Arian and semi-Arian hold-outs. This dispute has come to be known as the battle over an i: Homoousios or Homoiousios? (From the Reader's Digest book 'After Jesus' page 222)

This bitter engagement over philosophical speculations (many do not realise how strongly influenced these ecclesiastic leaders were by Platonism) has to be considered in the light of what the apostle Paul said concerning how much in this life we can really understand. He wrote in his first letter to the Corinthians that 'Now we see but a poor reflection as in a mirror (not the sort of mirrors we have today!), then we shall see face to face. Now I know in part; then I shall know fully, even as I am fully known.' The ordinary Christians were made to accept whatever was decided at the various Councils and would be considered as heretics if they didn't, and then they would face severe punishments.

People are still taught today that the way to learn and memorise the fundamental truths and the essential beliefs that cannot be compromised is to know the Creeds. We are told that like fences they protect us from heresy and are a defence of the faith. This means that Scripture alone isn't sufficient and it needs to be supplemented by decisions made hundreds of years after the Bible was finished. The just charge that the Mormons and Jehovah Witnesses have added to Scripture by their own distinctive teachings can also be levelled at all the churches that claim that what is central to our faith is contained in the Creeds.

Peter quoted Moses saying, "The Lord your God will raise up for you a prophet like me from among your own people; you must listen to everything he tells you. Anyone who doesn't listen to him will be completely cut off from among his people." It is to his voice we must return and not to those who came later and enforced their authority on those they ruled over.

"Indeed, all the prophets from Samuel on, as many as have spoken, have foretold these days, and you are heirs of the prophets and of the covenant that God made with your fathers. He said to Abraham, 'Through your offspring all peoples on earth will be blessed.' When God raised up his servant, he sent him first to you to bless you by turning each of you from your wicked ways."

Abraham listened and acted on what God told him, so did all of God's servants even in the face of great opposition and anger. God says to each one of us to listen to what his Son says and put it into practice. Traditions and misinformation regarding what Jesus did say have effectively distorted his message leaving millions ignorant of fully understanding what the good news is and so the darkness of this world continues and will remain until his return when, as Isaiah writes, 'Men will flee to caves in the rocks and to holes in the ground from the dread of the Lord and the splendour of his majesty when he rises to shake the earth'

'In that day men will throw away to the rodents and bats their idols of silver and gold which they've made to worship. They'll flee to caverns in the rocks and to the overhanging crags from dread of the Lord and the splendour of his majesty when he rises to shake the earth. Stop trusting in man who has but a breath in his nostrils. Of what account is he?'

Paul had written to Timothy saying, 'For the time will come when men will not put up with sound doctrine. Instead, to suit their own desires, they will gather around them a great number of teachers to say what their itching ears want to hear. They will turn their ears away from the truth and turn aside to myths.' Earlier he had warned the church leadership that very soon 'savage wolves will come in among you and will not spare the flock. Even from your own number men will arise and distort the truth in order to draw away disciples after them. So be on your guard! Remember that for three years I never stopped warning each of you night and day with tears.'

It's always easier for somebody else to do the reading for us, 'Just give us the bullet points, we're pretty sure we know what it's about anyway, even if we haven't read it!' For some they prefer a condensed, abridged and shortened version of a book that they don't have the time or the desire to read for themselves. Perhaps the mini-series 'The Bible' will cover the main points but that inadequate adaptation with its samurai sword-wielding angels is as inaccurate as Mel Gibson's film 'The Passion' and the great sadness of that film wasn't Mel Gibson's theology as much as was the vast numbers of Christians who endorsed and recommended it.

And so the misunderstandings, misrepresentations and ignorance of what the Bible really teaches and what happened in the history of Israel and why it happened remains to a large extent reduced to a series of unrelated Sunday-school stories that has led many to be ignorant of the main biblical theme of liberating mankind from this kingdom of darkness. Paul wrote to the Christians at Ephesus, 'For you were once darkness, but now you are light in the Lord. Live as children of light.'

The writer of Hebrews, addressing Christians from an Israelite background writes 'In the past God spoke to our forefathers through the prophets at many times and in various ways, but in these last days he has spoken to us by his Son, whom he appointed heir of all things, and through whom he made the universe.

'The Son is the radiance of God's glory and the exact representation of his being, sustaining all things by his powerful word. After he had provided purification for sins, he sat down at the right hand of the Majesty in heaven. So he became as much superior to the angels as the name he has inherited is superior to theirs.

'We must pay more careful attention to what we've heard, so that we don't drift away. Because if the message spoken by angels (at Sinai) was binding, and every violation and disobedience received its just punishment, how shall we escape if we ignore such a great salvation? This salvation, which was first announced by the Lord, was confirmed to us by those who heard him. God also testified to it by signs, wonders and various miracles, and gifts of the Holy Spirit distributed according to his will.

'It's not to angels that he has subjected the world to come, about which we're speaking. But there is a place where someone has written:

"What is man that you are mindful of him, and care for him? You've made him a little lower than the angels, and crowned him with glory and honour and put everything under his feet."

'In putting everything under him, God left nothing that is not subject to him, yet at present we don't see everything subject to him, but we see

Jesus, who was made a little lower than the angels, now crowned with glory and honour because he suffered death, so that by the grace of God he might taste death for everyone.

'In bringing many sons to glory, it was fitting that God, for whom and through whom everything exists, should make the author of their salvation perfect through suffering. The one who makes men holy and those who are made holy are of the same family, so Jesus isn't ashamed to call them brothers.

'Since we are flesh and blood, he too shared in our humanity so that by his death he might destroy him who holds the power of death—that is, the devil—and free those who all their lives were held in slavery by their fear of death. It's not angels he helps, but Abraham's descendants (all those with faith, whatever their ethnicity). For this reason he had to be made like his brothers in every way, in order that he might become a merciful and faithful high priest in service to God, and that he might make atonement for the sins of the people (and in doing so turn aside God's wrath, from them to himself). Because he himself suffered when he was tempted, he is able to help those who are being tempted.

'Because of this, holy children of God who share in the heavenly calling, fix your thoughts on Jesus, the apostle and high priest who we believe in. He was faithful to the one who appointed him, just as Moses was faithful in all God's house. Jesus has been found worthy of greater honour than Moses, just as the builder of a house has greater honour than the house itself. Every house is built by someone, but God is the builder of everything.

'Moses was faithful as a servant in all God's house, witnessing to what would be said in the future. But Christ is faithful as a son over God's house, and we are his house, if we hold on to our courage and the hope we confidently speak off.'

In this age Christians are subject to Christ and strangers in the world yet they are his body here on earth; they've been liberated and freed from the spiritual slavery of this world and as individual members that make up that one body of Christ are united even though they're unaware of each other. In the age to come the whole world will be liberated and freed, and the dominion, power and authority that Christ now has will extend throughout the world and over all nations, never to end.

Paul writes, 'I consider that our present sufferings are not worth comparing with the glory that will be revealed in us. The creation waits in eager expectation for the sons of God to be revealed. For the creation was subjected to frustration, not by its own choice, but by the will of the one who subjected it in hope that the creation itself will be liberated from its bondage to decay and brought into the glorious freedom of the children of God.

'We know that the whole creation has been groaning as in the pains of childbirth right up to the present time. Not the creation only, but we ourselves, who have the firstfruits of the Spirit, groan inwardly as we wait eagerly for our adoption as sons, the redemption of our bodies. For in this hope we're saved, but hope that's seen is no hope at all. Who hopes for what he already has? But if we hope for what we don't yet have, we wait for it patiently.' And in the meantime, as Paul wrote to the Philippians, 'Do everything without complaining or arguing, so that you may become blameless and pure, children of God without fault in a crooked and depraved generation, in which you shine like stars in the universe.'

Daniel, who was known as Belteshazzar to the Babylonians, was told by an angelical messenger that "there will come a time of distress greater than anything since the beginning of nations until then, but at that time your people, everyone whose name is found written in the book, will be delivered. Multitudes who sleep in the dust of the earth will awake: some to everlasting life, others to shame and everlasting contempt. But those who are wise will shine like the brightness of the heavens, and those who lead many to righteousness, like the stars for ever and ever. But you, Daniel, close up and seal the words of the scroll until the time of the end. Many will go here and there to increase knowledge."

Daniel wanted to understand what these and other messages meant but he was told, "Go your way, Daniel, because the words are closed up and sealed until the time of the end. Many will be purified, made spotless and refined, but the wicked will continue to be wicked and none of the wicked will understand, but those who are wise will understand . . . As for you, go your way till the end. You'll rest and then at the end of the days (referring to a specific numerical prophecy given to Daniel) you'll rise to receive your allotted inheritance."

The writer of Hebrews wrote right at the beginning of the letter that the last days began in the days that Jesus taught, and will continue to be the last days until his return.

The dead will sleep in death until the time comes to awake. Those who are strangers now will then be united with all those whose names are written in God's book. Their denominational differences will not matter then as God has united them all through his own mind and nature to be like his Son and to accept rejection and suffering as following in his footsteps.

The Lord told Moses to instruct his brother Aaron in the form of words he was to use in blessing the Israelites and as God's people now are the true 'Israel of God' they inherit as a chosen people these same words:

"The Lord bless you and keep you;
The Lord make his face shine upon you and be gracious to you; the Lord turn his face towards you and give you peace."

Acknowledgements

I am indebted to a number of sources in writing this book, among which is: The Macmillan Bible Atlas. (Yohanah Aharoni and Michael Avi-yonah), Cruden's Complete Concordance to the Old and New Testaments, Lutterworth Dictionary of the Bible, The Oxford Companion to the Bible, The Bible Chronicle (Derek Williams), plus various commentaries and other books that are mentioned in the text, but primarily to the Holy Bible, New International Version © 1973, 1978, 1984 by the International Bible Society, which I have attempted in many places to modernise. However inadequately I have been in presenting this account my hope and prayer is that the reader will see past my failings to the uniqueness of Holy Scripture and its power to comfort, encourage and strengthen those who put their trust in its divine author.

About the Author

Phil Hinsley is the author of The Dragon the World and the Christian, a controversial book that exposes the four most commonly held beliefs of most Christians as myths.

He was born in Barry, South Wales and now lives in Watford with his wife Anne and works for the site team in the Girls Grammar School, alas they only have one Gerbil now.

Lightning Source UK Ltd.
Milton Keynes UK
UKOW03f1352240114

225205UK00002B/160/P